Fear of Landing

Also by David Waltner-Toews

Short Stories

One Foot in Heaven

Poetry

That Inescapable Animal

The Earth Is One Body

Good Housekeeping

Endangered Species

The Impossible Uprooting

The Fat Lady Struck Dumb

The Complete Tante Tina: Mennonite Blues and Recipes

Non-Fiction

One Animal Among Many

Food, Sex & Salmonella

Good for Your Animals, Good for You

Ecosystem Sustainability and Health

The Chickens Fight Back

Fear of Landing

David Waltner-Toews

Poisoned Pen Press

First Edition 2007

10 9 8 7 6 5 4 3 2 1

Library of Congress Catalog Card Number: 2006940848

ISBN: 978-1-59058-349-4 Hardcover

Poisoned Pen Press
6962 E. First Ave., Ste. 103
Scottsdale, AZ 85251
www.poisonedpenpress.com
info@poisonedpenpress.com

Printed in the United States of America

This book is dedicated to Dan Unruh,
who solved the mystery of the pre-Eid al-Fitr epidemic
in buffaloes, and devoted his life to working with
the poor farmers of Indonesia.

Although there have been large milk production development projects in the central Javanese district of Boyolali, and some of the places mentioned in this book are real, there are no places, as far as I know, called Gandringan or Perusahaan Susu Senang. All events and characters in this book are fictional.

Chapter One

There is something warm and comforting about doing an autopsy on a cow. It's real. You don't have to worry that they don't speak English or Flat German. You don't have to speak Indonesian or Javanese. You forget about your addiction to chewing sunflower seeds. All you need is a sharp knife and all your senses on heightened alert: touch, sight, smell, even sound. You lightly brush your hand over the coarse hair along the belly, feeling the stiff hairs flip back against your palm, ruminating on the life of this beast, one of those infinitely curious bovines, dwelling in her ever-present years with a kind of dim-witted patience that sometimes passes for wisdom. Perhaps, in a devious and fast world, this is, indeed, a kind of wisdom. But where did this one's nose lead her? What salt did she lick from whose hand?

For a minute, while he mentally blocked out the crowd of villagers gathering around him, Abner Dueck stood over the cow and scanned the body for any obvious bleeding. With anthrax, you would see blood oozing from the orifices. There were, he knew, cows dying of anthrax down at Perusahaan Susu Senang, directly translated from Bahasa Indonesia as "The Happy Dairy Farm," some Ottawa development officer's fantasy name, which sounded to Ab perilously close to a kind of retreat for disturbed or mentally challenged bovines. It was usually just called Susu Senang, or "Happy Milk," for short. It was the main farm for a large dairy development project from which all the imported cattle like this one were distributed to smallholder farmers in the area.

Seeing no obvious bleeding, he probed his fingers into the wide, maternal nostrils, pushed his fingers into the mouth, between the sharp bottom incisors and the toothless pad at the roof of the oral cavity, and the heavy grinders top and bottom at the back, a combination so perfect for cutting the grass and cud-chewing. He pulled out her thick, muscular tongue, checked for little parasite cysts, lifted her eyelids and observed the sclera, raised her tail and palpated around the anus.

Every orifice tells a story.

Squatting next to the carcass, with the Javanese sun already singeing the treetops, Ab sliced into the pits between the legs and the body and pushed the legs back and out of the way. He slit through the layers of the belly wall to expose the glistening, yellow, under-skin fat. He loved the part where he was inside the body, running his bare hand over the big fleshy expanse of the rumen, that big swamp of a stomach every cow carries around inside her. He dug in, up to his elbows in the slippery offal, running the soft, splotchy sausages of the intestines through his hands. On a good day, he felt an irrational urge to just dive right in. He knew that this work was dangerous, that he should be wearing gloves, like a condom, putting his hand where no hands were meant to go. Protection against all the little bugs he could pick up.

Once he'd checked all the surfaces, he stabbed into the rumen and leaned into the scent. He relished the rich sour scent of fermented grass wafting up into his face, the pungent breath of life, still here, in death. Those bacteria produced over three hundred gallons of gas a day, and kept right on chugging well after the cow was dead. A cow in the sun could blow up like a fat balloon and then quickly putrefy. He leaned again into the scent. There was something off, more bitter than usual.

He dug his hand down through the swampy fluids, into the muscular second stomach, the reticulum. This was where nails, wire, and metal farmyard junk of various sorts usually got caught. Sometimes the stomach would clench it and a cow would stab herself as the piece of wire pierced through into the heart. His hand brushed against something cool, and hard. He closed his fingers around it and withdrew his hand. With his other hand, he brushed away the bits of half-digested grass and straw. Just fitting comfortably across his palm lay a silvery, capsule-shaped chunk of metal. He moved his hand up and down, feeling its weight. It was smooth and heavy. In North America, farmers sometimes forced cattle to swallow these large silvery magnets. The magnet dropped through the rumen into the reticulum and, so the theory went, kept the nails and bits of wire from wandering.

Here, in Indonesia, this was not a common practice, but all the cows at Susu Senang were given one of these. He wiped it clean again. There was a length of string taped to it, and, on the other end of the two-inch string, a piece of plastic bag with holes poked in it. Some white crystals were stuck to the inside of the plastic. He stuck the magnet and plastic into the pocket of his coveralls. He reached in again and his hand brought out a second magnet, but with no bag attached.

Ab looked around, resting his hand still in the warm flesh, thinking. He tried to ignore his sore back and cranky knees, and, looking over his shoulder, the audience: the Lura; a distraught farmer; the usual crowd of little kids; and another man, looking upset and angry. Who was that, and why was he so upset? He wished Soesanto were here to translate from the Javanese. He scanned the body and fondled the second magnet as if it were a small religious artefact. He always hoped to make these occasions into learning opportunities for Soesanto, his Indonesian counterpart from the Gadjah Mada veterinary college in Yogyakarta. The farmer's tragedy could at the very least be salvaged as an object lesson. One man's shit, another man's bread and butter, as the old saying went. But this had been a two-day trip. The first day he and Soesanto had driven an hour out to Susu Senang to check on some sick cattle; it looked like anthrax, and they'd had to set up vaccination and treatment protocols. Ab stayed overnight at the main farm, just to have a night of fresh air, away from the heavy mix of diesel and garbage that the city offered; Soesanto had gone back to his home in Yogyakarta. Indonesian veterinarians often held down several jobs, just to make ends meet, and Soesanto couldn't always get away for extended periods. In fact, as far as Ab could see, he often disappeared to his *other* jobs for extended periods, without saying where he was going.

This morning, in part to clear his head in the slightly cooler, cleaner air of the green country-side, and in part because there had been reports of cattle deaths up in this area, Ab had decided to come up here to this village just to look around.

The village leader, the *Pak* Lura, or, less formally, the Lura, said he'd called Soesanto already, but if he'd called this morning, Soesanto wouldn't be here until late morning. For a post mortem, that would be too late. By now, Ab felt the sharp fingers of the tropical sun already frisking the top of his head, and was glad for the baseball cap with the shade turned back shielding his neck. He had been thrilled to have been presented with such a fresh carcass. As his pathology professor back in Saskatchewan would have said, it enabled him to better *appreciate* the lesions. Here in Java, a freshly dead body was a rarity. Usually the body would already be bloated with the legs stretching like a post-prandial yawn into the blue sky, so if you poked the rumen there would be a big putrid sigh of relief. Then, if you had the guts to cut it open, the inside was a gelatinous mass, not dust to dust, just muck to muck and slime to slime.

This fresh post mortem exam had almost not happened. An hour earlier, just after dawn, Ab had driven his sporty little Suzuki Jimny 4X4 into the tiny village of Gandringan, just outside the central Javanese city of Boyolali, capital of the district of Boyolali. He was happily chewing a mouthful of southern Manitoba sunflower seeds. The Lura came out in his traditional, tight-fitting black jacket, traditional dark blue-and-black batik sarong, and the little black Muslim hat atop his head. Ab smiled despite himself, despite almost two years of seeing those hats everywhere. His mind unexpectedly flipped back twenty-five years to 1957, to the Mennonite World Conference in Ontario, when his parents had taken him and his two sisters on a side trip to Niagara Falls.

The Falls thundering like a steaming avalanche terrify me, stir up in me a deep urge to fly over the flimsy railing, to soar into the mist. What a stupid primal urge, the urge to fly. Like a good Canadian, I re-direct my primal desires into shopping. I drag my parents—two older sisters trailing, scoffing and complaining of sissy brothers—back away from the platform behind and under the Falls. I want to be away from there, where the mist hisses and sprays and the thunderous grey waters make it seem as if the whole world is crumbling down around me. Back up through the slippery, claustrophobic tunnels we climb, up the stairs, into the safety of the souvenir shop. Souvenir shops in such places thrive on re-directed anxiety. They know we are coming. They have been waiting for us. My father, hesitating in a moment of weakness and love—or inspired by the thrill of seeing fear in my eyes—buys me a black Shriners-type cap with a picture of the Canadian Falls painted on its side in lurid fluorescent paint.

The hat the Lura was wearing was almost exactly like the one purchased by his father, but without the picture. This was the first time that a memory of his father had ever made Ab smile. The Lura returned his smile, and Ab wondered suddenly what was behind it. Was he smiling at Ab's smile? Had he opened the door into a forgotten room in his own labyrinth of memories? Was so-called cross-cultural communication really just a way of opening doors into each person's own experience, and therefore not really communication at all? The thought was disorienting and distancing. He could barely understand his own culture. What made him think he could do any better here?

Ab had stood outside for a moment, drawing the cool, slightly steamy green air of this rural village, or *kampung*, so close yet so far from the tarmac roads below, deeply into his lungs. The rich air grounded him. His body was suffused with the scent of palm trees, composting earth, spilling-over-itself-abundant, over-ripe vegetation, the friendly smell of buffalo belch gas, the homey comfort of cow dung. He emptied his mouthful of sunflower seed shells into the bushes beside the door. Doing this discreetly was the kind of skill you learn by practising with wads of gum in church in Winnipeg on hot Sunday mornings, the way other people stubbed out cigarette butts, those worms of half-burnt leaves covered with spittle.

He followed the Lura into the spacious front room to sign the guest book: name, address, purpose of visit, religion. Carefully, he wrote *Abner Dueck*, and stared at it for a minute. Someday, he would have to change that and go back to a name unmodified by ignorant immigration officials. Abraham Van Dyck or Van Dijk or something like that. He sighed. *Address:* Gadjah Mada University. *Purpose of visit:* disease investigation. *Religion.* He paused again. In earlier centuries, the Bugis, the sailors and pirates of South Sulawesi, had made themselves feared and respected throughout the archipelago, the South-East Asian version of the European Bogeymen, malicious Viking spirits with which to frighten children. But for President Suharto, who had come to power in Indonesia in 1966 in a C.I.A.-inspired bloody massacre, the real Bugi-men were what the government called latent communists. Now, everyone in Indonesia was required by law to have a religion. Available options were: Muslim, Buddhist, Hindu, Christian, Catholic, and Traditional. Ab wrote *Mennonite.* He had been tempted to write Russian-Canadian Mennonite Brethren in order to differentiate himself clearly from the black-hatted horse-and-buggy Mennonites, but writing Russian into an Indonesian guest book would be really pushing your luck. He was asked to be seated on a very hard, cane-backed chair.

Within moments, a grey-haired, somewhat chubby lady brought in a tray of coffee and cassava sweets and set it on the table before him. The Lura motioned for him to eat. He took a sweet and motioned for the Lura to also help himself. The Lura declined, and seemed content to simply watch Ab eat for a few moments, as if the sight of a foreigner eating local food were pleasure enough to pass a slow morning.

◇◇◇

After a few moments of watching, the Lura had said, "It is Ramadan. I cannot eat or drink until sunset." He had paused, as if wondering whether he should let the next sentence out. "We have a dead cow. I mean, one that has just died."

Ab had set his cup down, surprised. He stood up. "Well, then we should go have a look at it." The Lura had waved him back down. Ab remained standing.

"The dead cow will wait. I have called for Dr. Soesanto to come."

Ab had stayed standing. He knew better. He knew about the urgent need for the dead to flee whence they had come, back into the primordial soup, resurrected in flies and fertilizer for food crops. "But perhaps it will then be too late."

The Lura had laughed at the absurdity of this, or perhaps at the delightful thought that Ab had so quickly understood the nature of things. Ab stared into his coffee. Why did the country that gave the world Java coffee serve the worst sludge at home, coarse dregs mixed with equal parts sugar in lukewarm water? Soesanto's answer would be that Indonesia's elites needed foreign exchange, so that they sold their best products overseas. Ab tipped the cup back and felt the swamp crud accumulate in his teeth as some of the liquid trickled through. Was this the cost of being part of some global trading system?

The Lura did not elaborate on his laugh. No one ever elaborated on things in this country. If people misunderstood each other, well, what else was new with the world? At best, a long explanation just filled the air with unwelcome noise. If you communicate clearly, then people will not only hear what you say, but they will understand. He wondered if that was the point. They didn't want you to understand. Obtuse communication was a way of guarding privacy on a crowded island ruled by a dictator, where your every step could be watched, and where you never knew who was listening. Ab had set down his cup, but did not sit. The Lura, a tall, very thin man with eyes that appeared to be perpetually smiling, either in mockery or simple happiness, remained where he was. Finally, when he had realized that Ab wasn't about to sit down again, he had risen and had motioned for Ab to go outside and to a nearby farmstead. On the way, Ab stopped at his car and pulled out a pair of coveralls, which he pulled over his plain cotton pants and batik shirt.

Now, with the post mortem finished, Ab stood up and stretched his legs and pushed a hand into the small of his back. He could hear the whining of a vehicle coming up the track from the main road. In a moment, a Toyota Land Cruiser entered the small clearing behind them, with Soesanto at the wheel. American development projects had to buy Jeeps to support American business. British projects usually bought British Land Rovers. Everybody else, Canadians included, bought whatever would handle rough back roads, was cheapest and most easily serviced, in this case the Japanese Land Cruiser. Like many of the expatriates, Ab had bought a hardy little Suzuki for personal use, but used it mostly for work. He was never sure when the project vehicle might be available. It always seemed to be commandeered by bureaucrats for their own personal reasons.

Soesanto had made good time from Yogyakarta. Must have been driving recklessly fast. Well, good. There was still time to review with him the highlights of the autopsy. Then they would need to interview the farmer in some detail about exactly when and how this death had occurred.

At that same moment, a frantic, dishevelled teenager rushed past the arriving car, brandishing in the air a wavy-edged knife, shouting in Javanese. The Lura rose immediately from the wooden chair on which he had been perched while watching the autopsy. He called to the teenager in a serious but calm voice. The boy shouted something in response and then turned to run back down the lane whence he had come. The Lura followed him, oblivious now to Ab and to Soesanto, who was watching this through the open car window.

Ab walked over to the Land Cruiser and looked past Soesanto into the empty passenger seat.

"No driver?" Each project car was assigned a driver, who was supposed to chauffeur the *real* project workers anywhere and everywhere. This was a way of spreading development money around, and freeing up the professionals to think about more important things than traffic. Ab also suspected that there were liability issues involved. The rules of road accidents were that the bigger vehicle was always at fault, no matter what, but a wealthy person or a foreigner trumped everything. They had to pay no matter what happened. It was a kind of insurance for development projects to hire experienced, and lower class, drivers. Soesanto looked at the seat next to him, almost as if expecting to see someone materialise.

"I found the car parked at the university, but the driver doesn't seem to be here, does he?"

Sometimes—often on this project it seemed—drivers went AWOL, or were commandeered by senior bureaucrats for their own uses.

"With that leg, I didn't know you could drive."

Soesanto pushed open the door and lowered himself out of the car with a wooden cane. Soesanto had a gimpy leg from a bout of polio as a child. He looked down at his bad left leg, then back up at Ab. "Have you ever seen a dog with three legs? Or even two. I once saw a dog in the village hopping around on two legs." He snorted. "We have our ways of getting by."

"How did you get here so soon? You must have really been screaming down that highway."

"I was going to ask how it is you are here at all."

"I asked first."

"Actually, the Lura phoned the vet college yesterday afternoon and left a message. He just wanted to talk about some unspecified problems. I left pretty early, which is why I got here so soon. I stopped by Susu Senang but you'd already left, nobody knew for where, so I decided to come on my own." He paused. "I would have been here even earlier, but there was military roadblock on the road. I guess someone tried to blow up part of the Hindu temple at Prambanan."

"Blow it up?"

"They managed to destroy a minor deity."

Ab shook his head. "Last week it was Buddha losing his head at Borobudur. This week it's Shiva under attack. What's happening?"

Soesanto looked around, as if checking the weather, then switched from Bahasa Indonesia to English, which is what he did when he didn't want to be overheard. "Borobudur I can understand. It is being re-built with all that outside money, IBM and all that. Besides, the president's oldest son was visiting, just to make sure that the work is on schedule. So one can understand," he smiled very slightly before continuing, "even if one does not approve. But Prambanan." He looked around again. "The usual idiots trying to make history by destroying history I suppose."

"So, after sixteen years, Suharto still isn't in control?"

"Still too much in control," Soesanto muttered, then, more loudly, in Bahasa, "So, and you, what brought you up here? You also must have left home before the cow died. Must be that superior Western scientific knowledge."

"Ah, no such thing, I'm afraid. I stayed at the guesthouse on the main farm at Susu Senang last night. Just wanted to get out of the city and breathe some fresh air. George also said there were cows dying up in this area, although he didn't think the causes were the same as on the main farm. So I came up first thing this morning just to check in and arrived just in time to do a post mortem on a freshly dead cow."

Soesanto rubbed his bad leg and poked with his cane at a rut. "Freshly dead. A miracle then. And, was it anthrax?"

Ab's mind reviewed the post mortem he had just completed.

"The animal had thin, white, watery fat. There was no major bleeding either externally or internally. The spleen looked normal. There were tiny red, measle-like speckles all through the flesh. The rumen gas smelled off. More bitter than normal I'd say."

Soesanto grinned. "A test! Given the lack of major bleeding, it wasn't anthrax and not likely hemorrhagic septicemia. The watery fat means that the cow lived mostly on fresh green air, some roadside grass and a lot of rice straw. That's not unusual for a poor Javanese farmer. The petechial hemorrhages are a sign of acute distress. This one did not die quietly or slowly."

Ab drew the magnets out of his pocket and held out his hand.

Soesanto picked up each of the magnets in turn, and then set them back into Ab's palm. "Magnets for hardware. Been years since I've seen one, and that was back in the States. I assume that George and his co-workers administer these at the main farm before they distribute the cows to the villages. But why two magnets?" He tugged at the string and rubbed the plastic bag between his thumb and forefingers. "And what's this?"

"Good questions. I would guess that somebody really wanted that cow to swallow whatever was in the bag, and wanted her to keep it there, not regurgitate it and ruminate." Ab stuck the magnets back into his pocket and gestured after the shouting teenager with the knife. "What was all that about?"

Soesanto shrugged.

"Well, we might as well follow. We won't get our interview with the farmer until this is sorted out."

They walked down the village path in the direction in which the teenager and the Lura had disappeared. They were joined as they walked by an assortment of children from the village, who seemed almost as interested in Ab as anything else. Ab filled his lungs again with the thick country scents of foliage and dung. It was *such* a pleasant change from the sour odours of diesel and open sewage in the city. They arrived shortly at the gate leading to a house from which shouts and cries emanated. After about ten minutes of this shouting and hysterical crying from inside the house, a man emerged, head down, and stormed past the onlookers at the gate. Ab recognized him as the upset man who had been leaning over his shoulder during the post mortem. He was followed a few seconds later by the teenager, *sans* knife, and finally, a thin, dark man, who mounted a motorbike and snarled out of the village. Ab stared after him; there was something vaguely familiar about him. Finally, the Lura came out, smiling. Soesanto talked with him in Javanese as they walked back to the cars.

It still annoyed Ab to have learned Bahasa Indonesia, the national language, and to be able to speak it in all his daily conversations, only to have the nationals fall back to Javanese whenever they spoke of anything of substance. How easily language could shift from being a means of communication to being a veil separating people from each other. How easily a few words in the wrong language could cut a person off from the shared complexity of physical and social reality.

At the supper table. I am thirteen years old and can speak God's mother-tongue, high German, but not Flat German, the Mennonite tongue of everyday life, of jokes, the one in which God isn't supposed to be listening. Suddenly my father, in mid-sentence, switches to Flat German. This is the language they use to keep secrets from me. I know he is talking to my mother about me, probably about whether I will be allowed to go to play with George Grobowski, the Greek Orthodox kid from across the street. I strain to understand that rough, guttural cousin to Yiddish, with its resonance of barn gutters and cow manure. It is the language that makes many Mennonites feel at home. I understand only that they are talking about me and that it must be important. I look over at my oldest sister. She is ahead of the game and understands what they are saying. She is smiling. Later, if I want to know what they said, it will cost me something. A chore, like washing dishes. Home: I can't wait to take off, to get out of there.

Within a year, his father would be dead, and not that many years later, Ab would get his wish. He was out of there. But where had it got him?

Soesanto dropped back to talk with Ab, the children still crowding around, tugging at Ab's coveralls. He brushed them away.

"So what really happened?"

Soesanto sighed. "Even I am not so sure. I think it was like this. There was a fight between the butcher and his, um, cousin."

"The teenager?"

"No. The butcher was the upset older man who came out first. The teenager was the butcher's son. He had come for help from the Lura to break up the fight. The man on the motorbike is the cousin. Did you recognize him?"

"I think I have seen him somewhere before."

"Waluyo. The new farm manager at Perusahaan Susu Senang. This is his home village."

"Oh yeah. George said something about a new manager. Okay, so what was the fight about?"

Soesanto paused, as if carefully weighing each word. "Money, I suppose you would say. But it is more than that. The butcher and his wife have had a difficult time making a living here in the kampung and Waluyo has been helping them out. In a traditional Javanese kampung, everyone has an obligation to help everyone else. The quarrel seemed to be over the kind of help Waluyo has been giving, and something about what he was expecting in return. I think that had something to do with the *kris*, that knife the boy was waving. Living in a kampung is like being part of a family, only more so. If you lived in a kampung, for instance, you, as a veterinarian, would have to share your skills for free."

"Have to?"

"Have to. In your country, you take your rights seriously. Here, our obligations are what matters." Soesanto paused a moment. "It is a common story in the countryside, that people are forced by economics to leave, torn from their obligations." And then, more quietly, "At least now, since Suharto's American friends have come."

They were now back at the Lura's yard. "And now can we go back to the farmer and ask him more about the cow?" Ab suggested hopefully.

Soesanto motioned to the Lura's house. "I must go in and sign the book and have something to eat first."

"This is Ramadan. I thought you were Muslim."

Soesanto turned to him and Ab thought he caught a hint of a smile. "I am traditional."

"Which is exactly what, I've often wondered?"

"Which is what you are when you are hungry." Now there was a real smile.

Ab pulled off his dirty coveralls, and tossed them into his car, but not before he had transferred the two magnets to his trouser-pockets. Back at the Lura's, drinking tea, Soesanto turned to Ab. "The Lura now wants to know your impressions."

Ab set down his tea. "Impressions of what?"

"Him. His village."

He looked over at the Lura, sitting behind a desk, watching his guests drink tea and eat sweets, smiling broadly. Several of his front teeth were missing. "I think you have a very nice village," Ab said in Bahasa Indonesia. "Only I think it would be nicer with snow. Next time I go home to Canada, I will send you back a jar of snow."

Everyone laughed uproariously. It was an old line based on a stale joke, going all the way back to Voltaire, who had called Canada a few acres of snow. Ab was depressed and felt reduced to those few acres, dissociated both from his past and from his present surroundings. He was also getting anxious about interviewing the farmer, and wondered if they would ever get around to it. Apart from the extra magnet with the bag attached, there had been nothing outstanding in the post mortem. She had died suddenly. The straw in the stomach meant the farmer was poor, and the cow had been very hungry, but she hadn't died of starvation. She still had some body fat. That wasn't much to go on. He would need a good clinical history to start to figure out what had happened.

Tea was followed by dinner in another room: heaping plates of rice, quail eggs in a very hot, spicy sauce, a kind of vegetable stew, and, for the Canadian, a heaping plate of boiled potatoes. Ab took a plate of rice, some eggs, stew, and, to be polite, a couple of pieces of potato.

"Oh, already eating rice?" The Lura seemed amused at this.

"Yes, already." It was a way of saying you were now at home here. Fat chance. Fat chance that he would be at home anywhere these days.

"Take more potatoes. They are for you," said Soesanto.

"In Canada, when we eat rice, we usually don't eat potatoes as well. We eat one or the other." Soesanto stared at Ab. Ab took several more potatoes.

The Lura and Soesanto watched Ab eat. When he was almost done, Soesanto dug into his non-Muslim repast as well, but the others kept their eyes trained on Ab. Soesanto cleaned off two platefuls, as a man who had known hunger, or who might not know where his next meal was coming from.

After the meal, they finally returned to the home of Pak Machmud, the farmer whose cow had died. The carcass was no longer there, nor was the butcher. Machmud, a thin, middle-aged man, sat in shorts on a stiff bamboo chair next to his doorway. His ragged shirt hung open in the limp heat, and he slowly bounced a bare-bottomed baby in a T-shirt on his knee. His wife, looking half his age, wrapped in a faded sarong, leaned in the doorway. Machmud spoke Javanese, with Soesanto translating into Bahasa. He had been awakened early this morning by the sound of his animal bellowing and thrashing around in the barn. Quickly he had fired up his lantern, but by the time he arrived at the barn, the animal was quivering on the ground, gasping out its last breaths. Soesanto listened to the next few sentences, then turned to Ab. "You are going to have to buy the cow."

"I'm...*what*?" He looked around. "Where is it anyway?"

Soesanto put his arm around Ab's shoulders and guided him to the side before speaking quietly, in English. "Actually, he says that the cow was not quite dead when you arrived. The butcher was going to do a halal kill and give him a decent fee. When you arrived unexpectedly, they were not sure what to do, and the cow died before the farmer and the butcher could agree on a price."

Soesanto looked questioningly at Ab, then turned to ask the farmer a few more questions. "Just a few thousand rupiahs." Ab stared at him, recalling the distraction of the butcher's "cousin." Soesanto stared back. Ab dug into his pocket. He wished he were back with his hands in the carcass. "Well it looked pretty dead to me. Anyway, where is the animal?"

Soesanto waved his hand into the air. "Something to do with the feast of Eid al-Fitr. It seems the butcher might be able to use the meat after all, maybe as a donation to the poor, even though it is not worth paying for. The cost of the meat covered the cost of carcass disposal. Consider your payment as a donation to the poor." Ab pulled the magnet with the plastic out of his pocket.

"I'll give him some money in a minute. But first, does the farmer know anything about this?" He handed the magnet with the bag attached to Soesanto, who handed it to the farmer and said something. Machmud shook his head.

After Ab had handed over the money, they went to the barn and Machmud showed them the place where the cow had thrashed a hollow in the straw. Ab brushed the chickens aside, picked up some of the straw and sniffed it. Normal, fresh, musty manure odour. No sour diarrhea smell. He turned to the Lura. "Have there been any other animals like this?"

"Many. Here, there." He pointed in various directions, naming people, counting on his hand. "Ten, twelve."

Ab tugged at his beard, badly wanting sunflower seeds to help him think, but instead lifted his baseball cap and scratched the top of his head. And were the signs always the same?

"The animal is very stiff, and seems to be lame, and then they fall down and will not stand up. After this, we know they will die."

"And these animals, are they all in Gandringan? Or the next kampung? The animals that die, have they had any contact with each other?"

"They are mostly in Gandringan," answered the Lura, "but just one here, one there. Never in a group or on the next farm. Only a few in other kampungs. All in Boyolali District." He was silent a moment. "So, what is this disease?"

Ab combed his fingers through his beard. He recalled the scent of the gas from the rumen. He had an idea, but the idea contained an accusation, not something lightly made in this country. He said: "Don't know. I don't know any diseases that act like this."

Soesanto, who had until that point been content to merely interpret and translate, suddenly said, "Do any buffaloes die?"

The farmer shook his head. "No, only cows."

"And these cows that die, are they all foreign animals?"

The Lura thought a moment, then broke in. "Most of them. Yes. Perhaps all."

Ab looked at Soesanto. "You think these foreign animals are more susceptible to tropical diseases? After all, they haven't been exposed before to most of the bacteria and parasites you have here."

Soesanto smiled. "Maybe."

Before leaving, Ab handed the Lura a business card, with both his home and the university number on it. "I know you called Dr. Soesanto very quickly this morning. That was very helpful. It would help us if you did that next time as well. You have Dr. Soesanto's number at work. You can also call me at home, and we will come. Maybe if we can see one of them *before* it dies we can tell what it is."

The Lura looked at the card in his hand and seemed bemused. "Even as Lura, I do not always know beforehand when animals will die." He paused. "But I will keep your number, just in case."

A short time later, as Ab got into his Suzuki, Soesanto came over and leaned on the door. "Maybe it is not the particular disease we should look at; maybe they are just dying of whatever is convenient," he said, quietly, in English, through the window. "Maybe the cows just do not like it here, these American dairy cows. Too hot, wrong kind of people."

Ab rested his hand on the key for a moment before starting the engine. "Will I see you at the office tomorrow?"

Soesanto nodded, then stepped away and leaned on his cane as Ab started the engine. Too hot. Wrong kind of people. As he drove away from Gandringan, Ab considered his first diagnosis: deliberate poisoning. He would have to talk about this later with Soesanto. Who were the wrong kinds of people? What was the point of killing dairy cows?

Chapter Two

The deeply rutted narrow mud track plunged down from the village to the highway through damp, cool shade, flanked by bamboo fences and rows of cassava, coconut, and papaya trees. Everywhere in this island, where there weren't fields of rice or cane, where even two or three shaggy-headed trees gathered, shaking weary heads in the slow breeze, there in the brown and green shade, hidden as sunken galleons in murky reefs, would be houses, compounds, people, hundreds and thousands of people, and their animals. This was not the outskirts of Winnipeg at dusk, with, as far as the eye could see, the indulgence, the luxury of space, the illusion of individual freedom.

He spun onto the road and laid rubber careening down the main highway that would take him first eastward toward Surakarta, called Solo by the locals, and then southwest toward Klaten and Yogyakarta. Technically, one drove on the left, but in reality, you drove wherever there was room. This morning, he had come cross-country from near Klaten. The Perusahaan Susu Senang farm was located just off the stretch of road between Klaten and the T-intersection where you could head to Solo or the city of Boyolali. The road from the farm near Klaten to Boyolali cross-country was rough, even by Indonesian standards, and he wasn't sure how much more abuse his little Suzuki could take.

Even this main road, a one-lane, pot-holed blacktop, left a few things to be desired. Veering instinctively from one available road space to the next, he drove down the brown and green canyon of mahogany trees. The trees, neatly planted along the roadsides, were a legacy from the Dutch colonials. They kept the roadsides green-cool in the mid-day heat. A few months from now, in the monsoons, they would be less useful. During a heavy downpour, this road could be transformed in less than an hour into a torrent of water. *Kretek* booths and chickens and bicycles and pedestrians would be washed away in the sloshing wake of buses, Land Cruisers, and a variety of other Japanese cars. Now in the dry heat, it was like a video arcade game, dodging buses and trucks. It seemed a good metaphor for life here in general, at least for a middle-aged white foreigner. Surprises seemed to jump into his line of vision and then disappear without warning. Sweat pooled at his neck and spilled down his spine. His lungs balked at sucking in hot diesel fumes. He rolled up his window and turned on the air conditioning. The hair on the back of his neck prickled as the sweat evaporated. He thought that if he were an American dairy cow in this place he might just drop dead, poison or no poison.

A week ago Ab had taken a trip to Bali, his first vacation after almost a year here. It seemed to him, with the normal half-days of work on Fridays and Saturdays, and the fact that cattle diseases never took holidays, that he had been working every day since he arrived. The days of the week were a blur.

He had not relished the flight, but it seemed somehow unconscionable to be so close to that proverbial paradise and not visit at least once. His queasiness about flying had less to do with the perils of taking off than with an exaggerated fear of landing. He was usually fine on take-off, although even that required a stiff drink these days. He was amazed and exhilarated that a chunk of growling, screeching metal, more improbable even than a bumble bee, could snap the stretching bands of gravity and spring free, leaping over mountains. The flight itself, high above green jungles, volcanoes, and wisps of clouds, was sufficiently unreal to require simply a suspension of belief. Landing was another matter entirely. How did the pilot know just the right moment, the one exact second, when that easing down to the runway was possible, was necessary to avoid somersaulting steel over scream into death at the end of the runway? It was a question, a dream, from his childhood, one that had followed him, plagued him, and had taken on new layers of meaning. He knew deep down that this fear was not about flying at all; it had something to do with his life, the fleeing from the religious traps of his childhood, the fear of landing somewhere and finding himself ensnared in some deathly, prefabricated, unquestioning mental and physical routine. Not being able to clearly articulate the question, he was no longer sure he would recognize the answer even if it stalked him, caught him with claws and teeth, wounded him.

It was a short, one-hour flight from Yogyakarta to the airport in Denpasar, the capital of Bali. He stayed at the paradisiacal white Poppies Cottages, set in a pleasant green garden with splashing streams, ponds and winding paths, surrounded by walls over which cascaded bougainvillea. He slept late, feasted under tall palms at an open-air restaurant on jaffles, specially toasted and sealed sandwiches with cheese or bananas and peanut butter, sat in the sunken tub, sprawled on the bed and watched the overhead fan circling until he dozed off. Later he walked down the sandy path to the beach, and across the foot-stinging, achingly hot white sand of Kuta Beach. Too late, he realized that this paradise was a fantasy created not by hedonistic noble savages, but by self-absorbed white folks quarrelling with their mortality. He felt old there, amid the bared, perky twenty-year-old tits, the smooth legs, and beach-surfer-boy bodies. The fluffy clouds garlanded the blue sky, singing lines from Yeats, the young in one another's arms, no country for old men. It wasn't so much his thirty-five years, which wasn't, he thought, so very old. It was more the *weight* of his life, growing up in the midst of the 1960s culture of free love and happiness, but unable to break out of a Mennonite upbringing which defined love as bondage to Jesus and duty to community. It made a person *feel* old. Sitting on the sand, he looked over at the German girl with the green eyes and the tiny multi-coloured braids all over her head, trying to be lackadaisical, making conversation. Trying to be careless, like her, but his Mennonite eyes, like terriers, never having been taught exactly how to look at a bare-breasted woman, kept escaping him, nipping down for a quick check. She finally picked up her towel and wandered off to another spot on the beach, far away from him.

Ab spent the rest of that first day drinking Bir Bintang on the beach, getting sunburned. The next day he rented a car and drove up the narrow road through a village of professional stone sculptors, guarded by a giant stone Ganesh, special price for you today, and another whole village of painters, the dazzling greens and reds and yellows running amok across the canvases, rice paddies and people and mountains and amazing birds. At the rim of the quiet volcano, he looked out through the blue haze to the east. The next island over was Lombok, where local residents tied goats and chickens to trees so that tourists get a closer look at Komodo dragons, the last of the big lizards, beasts of myth and fear reduced to family entertainment. Between Bali and Lombok was the invisible Wallace's line; on the Balinese side Alfred Russel Wallace had identified Asian parrots and other birds that resembled those of Java and Westward. Beyond Lombok, the string of idyllic Spice Islands strung out like a green jade necklace to Timor, where the Indonesian army was quietly killing the Catholic Timorians. The animals in those islands resembled those of New Guinea and Australia. Out there, stranger animals than Europeans had ever imagined lingered in lost forests. It was a watershed line in evolution and ecology, and told a story that, perhaps, contained clues to the meaning of our own troubled and brilliant human story.

Ab felt dizzy, as if he were in a Balinese painting, where there is no perspective either of space or time, where everything is in a profusion of *now*. And yet, beneath all the unchanging green utopian villages, the volcanic magma circled for a way to reach the surface, the Komodo dragons pondered the blond children from Holland even as they tore at the goat flesh, the rebels in the hills of Timor polished their guns, and, deep inside his own restless heart, something had stirred, raised its head, and then disappeared.

The flight back to Yogyakarta was awful. A fog, unusual for Bali at this time of year, set in around the airport the morning that Ab left. Abruptly, halfway down the runway at the Denpasar airport, the engines died and the lights went out. He tightened his grip on the edge of the seat. The passengers grumbled, but there was no word, in the half-dark plane, from either the cockpit or the stewardesses. In a moment, the mist let out a snarl and two men on a 65 cc Honda motorbike materialized beside the plane, propped the cycle on a kick-stand, and disappeared under the body of the plane. There was a loud, metallic banging and then the airplane engines kicked in and the lights came back on. Without further ado or explanation, the plane returned to the head of the runway and made a full take-off. Ab recalled what Peter Findlay, an Australian intelligence officer, whatever that meant, had said. Australia wouldn't allow Indonesian planes landing rights because they had mostly been bought second hand from industrialized countries and hadn't been properly maintained. It spoke well neither for the sellers nor the buyers. Nor did it inspire confidence in those passengers who knew this. Ab had not stopped deep-breathing until they were at cruising altitude.

He examined his face in the window: the bristles of brown hair over his somewhat large head, recently cut short by a street barber, the somewhat ragged beard, the boyishly round face looking somehow gaunt and weathered, the weary-seeming blue eyes. Was that just the start of wrinkles at the corners? Then he pulled out the bottle of gin from his carry-on, sipped, and stared out the window into the blurred vision of green mountains and white clouds. He recalled again what Peter Findlay, or maybe this time it had been the Brit Harold Wilkinson, had explained to him. The Yogyakarta runway was particularly short to accommodate a river cutting across the end of the valley. For landing, the surrounding mountains made it necessary to drop fast in order to hit the runway with enough room left over to come to a stop. My body is like a rickety, single-engine plane circling, circling, running out of fuel, he had thought, staring out the window at the tops of the volcanoes pushing up through the clouds, tipping back his bottle. But there is nowhere I really want to land.

Bali now seemed like another country, another age. He felt cold, suddenly. He turned off the AC and opened the window.

He swerved to miss one of those ubiquitous mini-buses which had just careened past him, the driver's helper hanging out the door, condescending to pat the hood of Ab's Suzuki, as if to quiet an impatient dog. Everyone called them Colts, because many of the old originals were Mitsubishi Colts, but Ab, having seen the wobbly running of newborn horses, brought other images to mind. No sooner had the Colt swerved through the breech than it screeched to a halt directly in front of him. He cut sharply to the right and around it. A wrinkled, mouse-like grandmother under a gigantic sack of carrots was unceremoniously dumped from the Colt into the grime and dust beside the road. That was how fresh produce from the mountains reached valley markets: resilient grandmothers. In the same authoritative sweep of his arm, as a buffalo's tongue might encircle and pull up a clump of elephant grass, the helper pulled in a neatly pressed student, trim in his white shirt and blue pants. It was not entirely clear that the student was waiting for a bus, but those kinds of details could always be worked out later. In this country, if you weren't for a moment paying attention, you could be pulled into things pretty quickly. Ab always paid attention, except when it involved women, where he paid attention to the wrong things. Four hundred years of Mennonite history couldn't, after all, be overcome in a lifetime.

He passed the cluster of sheds that served as a bus stop, a kretek shop, and local hobnobbing place for the underemployed millions. A smoky whiff of cloves fanned his face. Damn, those kretek cigarettes smelled good. This was followed by the ubiquitous fried chicken and the sweet rot of old bananas and papaya. All was inextricably mixed with the blast of American country music from a kiosk selling pirated tapes. He breathed it all in, filling his head with the overwhelming celebration of scents, so far from the austere prairie air of his childhood.

Ab mulled over his situation. He was here on contract with a Canadian government project to import North American dairy cows into Java. He was the veterinarian who was supposed to keep them healthy, and train a counterpart, Soesanto, to take his place over the period of a couple of years. Ab's childhood friend George Grobowski was the animal scientist who was overall project manager. The idea was to make Indonesia self-sufficient in milk production, rather than relying on imported powdered milk from New Zealand. Susu Senang was the first stop, after quarantine, for all the cows on this project. From there, after a period of acculturation to the tropical heat, vaccination and treatment for parasites and infections, cows were distributed to small-holder farms throughout central Java in a kind of pyramid scheme. The farmers got one or two cows, but were then required to buy extra feed and to sell their milk back to a cooperative run by the main farm. Given the cheap price of imported powder and the crowded landscape of Java, Ab thought the idea was hare-brained, but not the worst development project he had ever seen. Besides, like many expatriates in these kinds of jobs, he had motives besides altruism for taking the job.

Ab and George had grown up as neighbours and best childhood buddies in Winnipeg. They had met Sarah when they were all in their teens. She was from the village of Plumstein, Alberta, but her widowed father had sent her to a Mennonite summer camp on Lake Winnipeg. Two years older than Ab and George, she had then attended the same Mennonite high school in Winnipeg as Ab as a boarding student. George, whose mother was absent and whose father was, at least to him, unknown, lived across the street from Ab with his grandparents. George was aggressively gregarious, and seemed, to Ab, to be lacking a certain sense of belonging, of home, both physically and spiritually. It was the kind of friendship that created distance even as it begged proximity. George seemed to find Mennonites, particularly some Mennonite girls, aggravatingly interesting. The three of them remained buddies all through their teenaged years. Ab had had it in his mind that he would someday marry Sarah. He had always, somehow, known that. He thought of it as God's will. They were after all both Mennonites, and George was officially Eastern Orthodox, although he seemed to have, in his search for belonging, espoused a New Age mix of any and all religions.

Sarah was the only one who seemed to have career plans. She had always talked about being a veterinarian, and her enthusiasm was infectious. Without any clear direction, and wanting to spend time together, George and Ab had also signed up for animal science and biology classes. Then, in 1967, when they had completed their second year of university and Sarah had completed her undergraduate degree, a bombshell: George proposed to Sarah. They were married the following year. Ab left to go to veterinary college in Saskatoon, then to a job in northern Alberta, and then on to study tropical veterinary medicine in Edinburgh. Sarah completed a master's degree in biology, and, while George worked on his own master's, worked for a few years as a research assistant at the university. They were both working in 1974, paying off debts, and Sarah was talking again about veterinary school, when Frieda was born. By that time, George was moving up in the feed co-op where he worked. And then Nettie came along, and Sarah's career seemed to go on hold.

Then, just over a year ago, out of the blue, this opportunity had come up for the old friends to reunite. George had applied for, and gotten, the job as project manager for a dairy development scheme. Surplus dairy cows were being "given" to Indonesia by a large American dairy company. In truth, it was a way of dumping surplus cows as farmers in the American Midwest were consolidated into larger farms or went out of business. Canadians were providing the management expertise for the project. What they needed was a veterinarian to help the faculty at the local veterinary college recognize the diseases that imported cattle might suffer from, and to provide the best veterinary care possible. Was Ab interested? Ab, with recently acquired credentials in tropical veterinary medicine, thought: Why not? It was a chance to work in an interesting place with old friends. He arrived just a few months after George and Sarah. Now that he was here, he realized something else: why he had gone to work so far away from Winnipeg, but closer to Sarah's home of Plumstein, why he had never settled into a steady relationship with anyone. He was still, deep down, not over Sarah.

His wandering mind jerked into the panic-mode present, a hood-mounted foghorn blasting into his back window. The Colt was off again, snorting at his back bumper. The driver's helper hung out the side door and waved an annoyed hand at the little Suzuki. Ab wiped the soot-filled sweat from his forehead and reached into the bag of sunflower seeds on the passenger seat next to him. He was tempted to ease out further into the middle of the road. Who would defer, the Colt, or the on-coming full-sized Mercedes bus from Yogya? From the wrecks of both Colts and buses that littered the roadside, Ab knew that he wasn't the only one who occasionally tempted fate. The Colt blasted its horn again, nosing around him. Without thinking, he pulled to the right, toward the middle of the road. The Colt pulled back. He was starting to feel good again.

He was now in the wake of a big Mercedes diesel bus, World War Two vintage. A great black cloud of particulates swam through the shimmering heat, billowing into his face. This was the scent of the modern tropics, progress with an industrial face: partly combusted ashes and diesel fuel. He rolled up his window, wiped the profuse sweat from his forehead again, pulled at his beard, brushed a few sunflower seed shells from his shirt front, took two deep breaths and shifted down. His sweaty hands slipped on the wheel. The Colt behind him blasted its foghorn furiously. The two magnets in his pocket were pressing against his leg and he lifted his hip to pull them out of his pocket and drop them on top of the dirty coveralls crumpled up on the seat beside him, just as he had to swerve to miss a man on a bicycle carrying two large rolls of palm-leaf matting. Just past him, he dodged a horse cart before the bus in front of him slammed to a full stop. He swung the Jimny around the bus, but the Colt behind him was double passing. Suddenly, around the edge of the Colt, a motorcyclist was triple passing, almost into the face of an oncoming truck.

A beggarly looking chicken made a frantic dive for an imaginary grain of corn on the road just in front of him, leaving fluffs of feathers hovering in the air. These were the closest living relatives of the majestic Javanese Jungle Fowl, progenitor of all the world's races of chicken. Reduced to ragged beggars in their own paradise, they were marginalised, reduced to scavengers by fat white imported birds fed imported feed in imported houses on the outskirts of the big cities. Welcome to the future. In his rear-view mirror, Ab could see that the chicken had made it back to the safety of the roadside. A girl on a bicycle, also swerving to miss it, was not so lucky. She had plunged off the road into the hot, slick, sun-glaring surface of a newly planted rice paddy. She stood up, dripping and laughing.

Ab looked beyond the road at the paddy fields in various stages of planting, sheets of black water or blinding mirrors where the sun hit them or bright green or slightly yellowing. Separating the paddies, like fence-rows, stood thin cassava trees or newer leguminous plants brought in by development workers to squeeze even more out of this little bit of land. Ahead of him, the man on the motorcycle had already disappeared into the haze.

Waluyo, that was name of the guy on the motorbike at Gandringan. Was he connected to the cow poisonings? Morose little devil. Used to hang around the veterinary school. Now, according to Soesanto, Waluyo was the new farm manager at Perusahaan Susu Senang. He would have had access to the magnets. The cows were distributed from there one and two at a time to smallholder farmers in the area: a master-serf relationship, since the farmers were then in hock for life to the owner of the big mother. This was called, by some at least, development.

Ab took a deep breath. If Waluyo was killing cows, what was in it for him? And then he thought, if I am driving dangerously around a tropical island trying to change a complex culture I don't understand, what is in it for me?

Chapter Three

Along with millions of Javanese, Ab usually ate his breakfast from one of the small street-side cafes, or *warungs.* Most Javanese ate out because they couldn't afford the cost of kerosene to run cooking stoves, this in an OPEC country of all things. Ab ate out at least one meal a day on principle, to be with the people. He sometimes cooked for himself, but refused to hire a cook. A night watchman he could justify, and someone to wash the dishes and clean the house, just to keep the ants at bay. But a cook? A man who couldn't cook was only half a man, always dependent on others to stay alive. Once, shortly after he had arrived, Sarah had told him that she understood his Mennonite neuroses, but argued that hiring as many servants as he could was a way of ploughing some of his exorbitant salary back into the local economy. Even as she argued this, she was working in the kitchen beside their cook. When Ab pointed this out, she nearly throttled him. That was before he knew that the Indonesian government refused to issue her a work permit, and that she was seriously demoralized by this.

He looked over the menu. A plate of fried rice was the usual for Javanese, but too greasy first thing in the morning for Ab. Nor could he stomach the thought of chicken-intestine soup. A bowl of real chicken and rice stew, *soto ayam*, hit the spot. He sat on the splintery wooden bench against the linoleum-covered counter, barely wide enough for his bowl of soto. The shop was often packed at this time of day, but with Ramadan on, all the Muslims were fasting, so he could spread his elbows a bit.

He stared at the poster directly in front of his nose, his mind, at first, drifting, trying to rise above the rich scent of rotting papayas, pineapple, bananas, and durian wafting up from the open sewer just outside the door. Durian: was that in season already? Durian was the fruit with the hard spiky outside and the mucoid inside, so smelly that it was illegal to carry on buses and planes in Indonesia. It was an acquired taste, like eating ice ream in an outhouse, George had said. George, who was afraid of nothing, tried everything, in religion, in life, and actually *liked* durian. The smells increased with the heat of the day. It would be worse later. The poster in front of him came suddenly into focus: the turquoise blue of Lake Louise, Alberta, surrounded by the snow-capped Rocky Mountains. What struck him first was not the cultural displacement of seeing a poster of a Canadian scene in Java, but, for a brief, sharp moment, an intense desire for snow, for a biting wind in his face and big flakes melting on his eyelashes and on his beard. He wished for a few moments of quiet respite in one of the snow forts he and George used to dig and build every year in the great heaps of hardened snow along the side of the driveway. He would sit there alone after school in the cool silence. What actually came to him was a memory from his time of working in Beaver Lodge.

The left flank of the cow is puckered wide open where I have just pulled the calf out, her body heat steaming around my arms. I take my time up to my elbows inside her, sewing up the uterus, and hold my hands inside so they thaw sufficiently for me to sew up the flank muscles, quickly, flaking the ice off my surgical instruments. She is tethered to a pole in a three-sided pole barn. I am up to my knees in a drift of shifting, sandy-dry snow. My feet are numb in rubber boots. When I finally get to sewing up the last layers of skin, the cow's internal body temperature must have dropped a couple of degrees. She survives.

He pulled himself out of his memory like a shirt from the wash. That was about all the snow he needed for now: one picture and a few clear remembrances. That's what home was for, wasn't it? To provide comfort and strength in places far away? One wouldn't want to live there.

Ab stood up and made his way into the already stifling heat on the street. He flagged down a *becak*. He loved these over-decorated, streamered, hot-rod bicycle rickshaws that filled the streets of Yogyakarta and other Indonesian cities, and which the government was trying to make illegal. How could a big oil-exporting country tolerate bicycle transportation? It was un-Indonesian. They had thrown thousands of them into the Jakarta harbour. Ab bargained half-heartedly with the cheery stud in the torn University of Florida T-shirt, another farm boy out of work. He eased himself into the seat in front of the cyclist, closed his eyes, and felt the bump of the wheels rolling under him. Why would anyone in his right mind want to travel any other way?

When he got into the office, he picked up the English-language Indonesian newspaper lying on the table just inside the door. "Press asked to curb crime reports," said a headline. The government was concerned that too much crime reporting might give readers, both Indonesians and foreigners, the wrong idea about their country. "All meetings banned close to election," read another headline. And "People spend too much time in the toilet and partying, and not enough demanding political rights," says Foreign Minister. And, in small print, on the second page, a brief mention of a disturbance at Borobudur and about a man who had been taken prisoner for political terrorism in 1966. Only now, 16 years later, had he been sentenced to be shot.

"Well Dr. Ab, are you reading about the Sukabumi lass who turns into a monkey at the full moon, or the protest by the transvestites that they have been insulted by the Vice President?" Soesanto had come in, the quiet thump and swish of his cane and dragged leg across the floor. He was looking over Ab's shoulder.

Ab folded the newspaper into squares, with the article about the shooting of the prisoner on top. "I was reading about the execution of Budiharto. Seems a bit after the fact, doesn't it? To execute a man so long after he commits a crime? Or do they really think he master-minded the explosions at Borobudur and Prambanan?"

Soesanto took the paper and stared at the article, his face struggling, it seemed, with what could or could not be said. "Those kinds of statutes of limitations only apply to simple crimes like murder and theft. If once you have had the wrong political ideas, you are at risk for the rest of your life." He set down the paper, his face a cipher.

Ab turned toward the computer. "And what about the President. If he has the wrong ideas, is he also at risk?"

Soesanto leaned on his cane, and over Ab's shoulder, too close for Ab to turn around and look at the Indonesian's expression. The voice over his shoulder said quietly, "We were going to check some computer files this morning, weren't we?"

"Yes. Some records from all the villages in Boyolali District, including Gandringan. I wanted to see if that cow we saw yesterday was part of a pattern of some sort." The computer had been purchased by Ab as part of his program to improve diagnostic record keeping. Although pirated computers were already becoming readily available in Indonesia, their use for a project like this was novel. It required both good data and a willingness to make it openly available to others. Ab had started with the illusion that technical information might be politically neutral, but he was rapidly learning that this was not necessarily so. Getting someone who lived in a dictatorship to design data systems that were transparent and open to questioning was an uphill battle.

He had been working in particular on setting up computerized records for Susu Senang: records on the destination of the new animals, and any disease information they had on them after they got to the village were supposed to be included. How many sick or dead ones, for instance, had there been in the last few weeks? What had the clinical symptoms been? Were the death rates in imported cattle really higher than in the local ones? Ab had written a special health-reporting program for the veterinary college and hoped the technician had been using it. Now, he tried to call up the disease reports file, but the computer program responded with: *No such file exists. No files have been created.* "Shit," he mumbled.

Soesanto leaned even closer. "Is anything the matter?"

Ab put his forehead down on to the keyboard. "Nothing. Except that our disease data seem to have disappeared."

Soesanto sat down at the desk next to him. "Yes, I had meant to tell you we have been having some problems. Power ups and downs. Tri was working on it and then suddenly all the files disappeared. But there are paper records." He waved at a great stack of papers in the corner of the room. "If you can fix the program, we'll just get Tri to type it in again. That's her job." It occurred to Ab that, after he left the country, all records of this and other possibly embarrassing epidemics could well disappear. He looked over at Tri, her tiny, supple frame, her slender arms at the keyboard, her mascara-accentuated eyes with the permanently dilated pupils, her gentle smile. He took a deep breath.

"Yeah, I guess so. I just wanted to see if we could sort out any patterns in Boyolali. Is it all in Gandringan? Is it really an epidemic, or just random deaths we happen to notice because they are imported cattle which are monitored? For all we know, that cow yesterday at Gandringan was an anomaly. Going back through the paper records is time-consuming. By the time we get it back into the computer and analyse it, the outbreak could be long over." He wondered if this was exactly what someone wanted to happen, or if he was just being paranoid.

"An interesting concept, consuming time. Life consumes time. Is the consumption of time important?"

Ab tried to read the slight smile on his face. "In the face of an epidemic it is. I suppose we'll need to go up there and do a more thorough investigation."

The telephone rang. Soesanto picked up the old black phone. "*Yah? Kenapa? Berapa? Yah, bisa.*"

He hung up and turned to Ab. "That was your friend George. A new shipment of cows has arrived in port at Cilacap. He wants the animals checked before they get trucked up to the farm. If we want to do health checks on them we should go…" He looked at his watch. "It is about a six-hour drive. We can still get there tonight."

Within an hour they had packed bags and equipment—needles, drugs, papers, pencils, labels—and were on their way. They took Ab's Suzuki, since a local government functionary, whose connection to the project was unclear, and whom Ab had never met, was using the project Land Cruiser and driver for unspecified project business.

Ab tried to take his mind off the road by talking with Soesanto. Here in the car, away from anyone else who might understand English, he seemed willing to talk, his tongue loosened like a knife from its sheath. Soesanto pulled out a package of kretek, lit one, and watched the end crackle as he sucked in.

"That is bad for you and bad for me, you know." Ab looked at the sunflower seeds in his palm, which he was about to pop into his mouth. "My habits are messy but at least people don't die from eating seeds. And I'm getting as much smoke as you are." Even as he said this, Ab drew the sweet clove scent from Soesanto's kretek into his lungs.

Soesanto took the kretek out of his mouth, looked at it sideways, pulled a strand of tobacco from the corner of his lip. "Worse even than you imagine, Dr. Ab. We used to have a surplus of cloves, so the government invented these clove-cigarettes to use up the crop and make some money on the side. Of course we Indonesians being a patriotic bunch took up the cause, helping the economy. Now we are hooked and have to import cloves to make the damned things." He paused to take a deep draw. "On the other hand the invisible hand directing the market economy is making tons of money, and it's population control, you know, after the fact, all that untreatable cancer, so it's not all bad. And what's the story on your sunflower seeds?"

"In southern Manitoba, the province where I grew up, it is the equivalent to smoking. At least for the religious group I belong to." He waved in an off-hand way, as if it didn't matter. "We were not allowed to smoke. So we were encouraged in our seed addiction. Now, when I'm anxious, I chew to relax."

Soesanto eyed him through a haze. "And does it relax you?"

Ab rubbed his beard. "No." He considered this a moment. I could quit, he thought to himself, if I could find a good reason. Isn't that what all addicts said?

Soesanto dropped his kretek, ground it into the rubber mat with his foot, and looked out the window. "We don't study the toxic side effects of things like kretek here. Anymore." He became thoughtful. "We had a great toxicologist at the veterinary school once. Lost his job in 1966."

"Were there many?"

"Half the faculty. Two-thirds of the student body."

"And what happened to them?"

Soesanto looked at Ab as if trying to plumb the depths of his ignorance. He shrugged his shoulders. "Gone."

"Gone? Left the university?"

Ab could feel Soesanto's whole body tense up beside him and felt the intensity of his gaze into the side of his head. "Permanently, physically, gone. Deleted. Killed. Like a million or more people all over the country. In 1965, Indonesia had the third largest communist party in the world. We had three million members, twenty million supporters. Indonesians had two big choices: the nationalist party drew all those who cared only about Greater Indonesia. The Communist Party attracted anyone who had a social conscience and thought we should take an active role in reshaping the Cold War world. We were neither Soviet Stalinism nor American capitalism. We helped create a third way, the non-aligned movement, and became a world leader. In 1955 our President, Sukharno, brought this Third World together in Bandung, just up the highway from here.

"That was how it was in 1965. But I think neither the Americans nor the Soviets liked independent-minded people.

It was either for us or against us. By a couple of years later, seven generals were dead, Sukharno was under house arrest, and Suharto was in power. The one general left standing. It was a bloodbath. In some places the slaughter was a settling of old scores, religious, political, or otherwise. In other places it was a simple butchering of all Communist Party members, or Chinese-looking people."

"Why Chinese?"

Soesanto folded his hands in his lap. "There were rumours that the Chinese were communist infiltrators. They had money. They were Christians and friends of Christians. They were different." He pulled out another kretek. "We went from having the third largest Communist Party in the world to have no party at all. Where I worked there was an ad hoc committee to decide who should be killed, and who should be spared. There were people who sold official nationalist party membership certificates so that you could prove you weren't a Communist."

"And your toxicologist?"

"According to the reports, he moved back to his family farm near Klaten." He raised his kretek and exhaled a cloud of blue. "The farm which is now the base for your project."

"And then?"

"He was not happy about the expropriation of his land for the public good. He hung around and worked on the farm, first as a farm hand, and then was hired as manager for the project. Some foreigner thought he seemed to have the right experience. Then he, too, disappeared. Recently, actually. Just a few weeks ago."

Ab let this sink in slowly. "And you?"

"Why am I alive?" He leaned down to rub his bad leg. "Good question. Suharto was America's civilized answer to Pol Pot. He only killed half as many people as Pot. Makes a person want to flock to the American side." He straightened back up, thinking, turning over rocks in his mind that he must have visited a thousand times before. "For one thing, I am not Chinese. And why would they shoot a guy with a gimpy leg? What harm can I do? Harmless and non-Chinese." He grimaced, looked over at Ab, looked out the window. "I was in the Soviet Union in

1965, studying virology. Actually I was in Europe at a conference when the killing started, and a Russian colleague at the conference managed to get me a graduate position in the U.S., in Michigan. I worked on the effects of cold stress on the immune system of calves." He smiled through the clove-tobacco haze. "Wonderfully appropriate, don't you think?"

"Why come back?"

He drew hard on his kretek and thought a minute. He waved his hand for Ab to look out the window. They were slowly making their way through a seemingly endless stream of children on bicycles and on foot, all in their maroon and white or blue and white uniforms.

"Children coming home from school," said Soesanto. "Millions. Maybe without hope. Or maybe some hope for a future. Some small measure of justice. All that sentimental gut-wrenching stuff people die for." He paused. "Or live for. I would have had nothing to live for in the U.S. Here, my life still means something."

"You feel safe now? Gimpy leg and all? After all these years?"

Soesanto fell silent, leaned forward and rubbed his bad leg again. "You want to hear another irony? That Russian colleague of mine was actually working for the KGB, and came to the U.S. with me in '66. But he didn't want graduate studies. He was after money. Said he could use his KGB skills selling cigarettes as a symbol of freedom. You convince people to smoke because it's a symbol of freedom. You get them hooked. A kind of slavery to large capitalist enterprises, not much different from Stalin's state businesses. A lot more money than selling Brezhnev as a symbol of justice, but not all that much different." He chuckled quietly. "And a lot of the best customers are the same people who fled the Soviet terror. They've become slaves by nature, and refuse to see it."

"And you?"

Soesanto regarded his kretek as if it were some strange archeological artefact he'd just picked up. "Small comforts. It's all some of us have left. If I live long enough to get cancer, I will have had a good long life."

Ab pulled himself away from the mental and emotional confusion he felt arising within him. "So your colleague is living his capitalist dream, and you, now you have democracy."

"We can vote now, for the government party."

"Only for the government party?"

"Everyone who works for the government must vote for the government party."

"But how do they know? It's secret ballot, isn't it?"

Soesanto snorted. He looked down at his shirt, a government issue batik from Suharto family factories, tugged at the lapel.

"And if you don't vote for them?"

"You lose your shirt." He smiled at his own joke. "With you in it."

They were driving past rice paddies now. Everywhere rice at practically all stages of harvest, all made possible by an intricate irrigation system, itself dependent on a complex arrangement of mutual social obligations. And separating the rice fields, rows of orange trees, or cassava, or bananas. Nothing wasted. How much further could you push this system before it reached a limit? Was it a delicate house of cards? Was it at the limit now? Was there any way of knowing?

They arrived at Cilacap after dark to discover that the cattle had already, at least so they were told, been checked over by local government livestock officials. "I guess we can give them a quick check over the fence tomorrow. Maybe take a few temperatures. Listen to a few rumen movements." Ab looked at an opened package of the drug the quarantine station workers had given the animals as a preventive treatment, then handed it to Soesanto.

"Why would they use this? You and I both know it doesn't work."

Soesanto handed the package back and smiled. "Ah, you and I, yes, we know that."

"You don't think the quarantine station director knows that?"

"The quarantine station director just takes orders from Jakarta. Maybe someone in Jakarta got a good price on this. Maybe from a factory owned by Sani Sentosa, a friend of the

President, the money behind the project." Soesanto spat on the ground beside him and paused. "And a good friend of your expatriate colleagues the Wilkinsons, by the way."

They sat outside their guest house in wicker chairs. Ab leaned back and wondered what to do with that last bit of information. He stared at the porch ceiling, covered with tiny lizards. He watched as a *cecak* approached a fly near the bare overhead bulb. Bang. Fly gone. Or maybe somebody wants to see these cattle dead, was the thought that crossed Ab's mind. Drinking milk was a habit introduced from Europe and northern Asiatic cultures, so this dairy production project fit neither the culture nor the climate. Still, there were enough socially mobile people in this country who wished to emulate western ways that somebody could make a fast buck bringing dairy cattle into Java as part of an aid program. Every step of the way—shipping, quarantine station, trucking, the distribution farm, villages— someone was making money. You could bet it wasn't the farmers.

"Do you think there's someone who really wants these cattle dead?" Ab said, abruptly.

Soesanto drew long on his kretek. "They are a special gift from the President to the people. Why would anyone want them to die? Probably all just Third World inefficiency, don't you think?"

There was a long silence. Soesanto narrowed his eyes as the smoke came back into his face. He stubbed out his kretek and set it down carefully beside him, staring into the darkness. "Think, Dr. Ab. How did that farmer say his cow died?"

"Well, they get stiff and then..."

"Think again, Dr. Ab. Remember what he said."

A long pause. A couple of neurons connected in Ab's brain. "They *will* die...unless they are killed for salvage."

"We might want to find out if they all die that way."

"But why?"

"Think, Dr. Ab, think. What is coming up in a few days?"

"Coming up? What do you mean, coming up? Oh." He felt stupid. "Eid al-Fitr."

"The feast of. When there's a big market for meat. We might want to find out how the cattle are butchered, and which butchers are involved, if there's more than one. They'll want halal meat, which means there *must* be at least one proper butcher involved. I would start with the fellow we saw in Gandringan."

"Salvage butchering...brilliant, brilliant. Could get it cheap that way, and sell dear." Ab laughed through his nose. "Okay, so let's say it is deliberate poisoning. Say with strychnine, which is what I suspect. I've never seen strychnine poisoning in a cow. It's a dog poison. I don't think it's in the textbooks. You'd need bags of it. Where would you get it?"

"Dr. Ab, you're the foreign expert. I can't do all your work for you."

"By the time I get the lab work done to prove it, track down where it came from, prove the butcher did it, the feast of Eid al-Fitr will be over, as will the epidemic."

"Which will be noticed after you leave, so you can take the credit."

"The old epidemiologist's trick. Start your investigation after the epidemic peaks. You will always look good." He paused. "But there's still something missing. It seems too easy. I think this has to do with more than just cheap meat. After all, it's just the American cows dying. And what about the anthrax at Susu Senang? Those are non-salvageable. Is there a connection? What was Waluyo so worked up about up in Gandringan?"

Soesanto was drawing deeply on another kretek, massaging his bad leg. He wasn't about to say any more.

They stared out into the darkness, Soesanto smoking, Ab chewing and spitting seeds, filling the night air with cross-cultural debris.

Chapter Four

Two days after he and Soesanto had returned from Cilacap, there was a big party of expatriates. Ab usually avoided these parties, or sat in the corner thinking about high school days and morosely watching everyone else, imagining they were having fun. But this evening he wanted to talk to George. There was something screwy going on with the imported cattle, something more than just a few poisoned cows in a village, but he couldn't put his finger on it.

He knew Sarah wouldn't be there. He had run into her at Galael's Grocery Store the previous evening, where she had pushed an *International Herald Tribune* into his face. "See this?" she had hissed. "See this?" The paper fell open to the second page, where the large part of an article was covered with a black, tarry substance, with a blank piece of paper stuck to it. "What are we doing here Ab? What kind of a place are we working in? This isn't crokinole on Sunday afternoon. These are people's lives. But all those other expatriates treat it like some kind of elaborate parlour game. "

"Even George?"

"Even George." Suddenly she was almost pleading. "He's gotten mixed up in something. Talk to him. He's *your* friend."

"He's *your* husband," Ab had retorted. At which she had turned and walked to the checkout without looking back.

Ab pulled in ahead of George's truck; George and Sarah owned both a mini-van, which she used for carting the kids around, and this pick-up truck, which George used for work. Ab manoeuvred his own little Jimny snugly against the cement wall with the glass shards crowning it, and killed the motor. The same people, always. World citizens, misfits and screw-ups everywhere. Citizens, really, nowhere. He could feel the heavy beat of rock and roll thumping the night air, shaking the rutted road under his shoes, as if a desperate giant were trapped inside a barrel, beating his fists against the metal, frantic in his claustrophobic darkness. The sad thing was, he didn't even feel at home here, among the misfits.

The guard at the gate bowed and grinned repeatedly. "Yes, Agus. Me again. Couldn't stay away." He touched the guard's hand and then his own chest. For a moment he stood at the open gate and took a deep breath, his hand still resting over his heart. The Wilkinsons' white-pillared mansion was deceptively large, with its air of colonialism, the fake Greek columns and the swimming pool. But there was no yard, he had complained to them shortly after he had first arrived in the country. You could have all the house you wanted, he'd complained to Marie Wilkinson, but if you didn't have a rolling lawn and some maples and elms, you still lived in poverty. Marie Wilkinson had patted Ab on the arm and, in her infuriatingly sweet way, warbled, "How very Canadian of you to think that. Such a dinosaur attitude."

Ab felt stupid and embarrassed, even now, in retrospect. There were some ninety million people on this little island. Who had room for a yard? For a rolling lawn? Who was he kidding? And on top of it, this was clearly the future, as much as Canada, full of wide open spaces and still fighting stupid proxy wars for the British and French imperialists, the endless post-colonial quarrels parading as new nationalisms, was the past.

He adjusted his broad-rimmed black hat and brushed his beard and the front of his shirt with the back of his hand. Anyone from North America would recognize the black jacket and trousers as an Old Order Mennonite uniform from Waterloo County, Ontario, or Lancaster County, Pennsylvania. But even Canadians wouldn't know that sunflower seeds were a southern

Manitoba Russian Mennonite habit. And half-way around the world who knew or cared? In Canada, who knew or cared about differences of people from Timor and Java and Aceh and China? Who knew that in some parts of the world these things meant the difference between life and death?

As he approached the door, he thought: this is a mistake, both the outfit and coming to the party. All this masquerading again. It would be such a relief to go back to North America and just be...whatever. But when he'd said this once at the dinner table, Marie, in her motherly way, had patted him on the arm. "My dear, dear, dear. We expatriates see each other almost every day. At least every week. We eat together, swim together," she leaned close to Ab's ear and slipped her hand under the dinner table to squeeze his leg, "sleep together." He took her hand off his leg and held it for a moment before letting it go. Marie was pushing seventy, with overseas experience dating well back into the British Colonial Service. Ab was surprised at how worn and wrinkled and yet how sensual her hand felt. He was surprised and shocked at himself for wondering how her wrinkled body would feel next to his. She continued more loudly, although no one else at the crowded table seemed to be listening,

"We cling together. It would be unbearable *without* the masquerade. We already know each other too well. The nakedness! The unbearable nakedness! We're like a family, all grown up and still living together. If we didn't have our little games, we'd all end up in the madhouse." He thought he'd almost detected a lament, tinged with weariness and perhaps fear, in the tone of her voice, but she had quickly recovered and went on to speak of other things.

Ab stepped into the small reception area at the front of the house. He paused in the half-dark behind the carved teak room divider separating him from the main body of the house. In the shadowed corners around him, on teak tables and marble pedestals, stood various Balinese statues and painted *wayang goleck* puppets, like small clusters of conspirators whispering. There were three versions of the Ramayana tales performed in Java:

wayang orang, which involved real people on a stage, or once a year, outdoors, when there was a three-day performance at the Hindu temple complex at Prambanan; *wayang goleck*, a puppet show using these wooden puppets; and *wayang kulit*, which used flat figures intricately cut from buffalo hide to throw shadows against a screen. Yogyakarta was famous for wayang kulit, but the painted wooden puppets made more impressive souvenirs. On one wall, there was a rectangular glass-faced cabinet in which a row of traditional Javanese knives, kris, were displayed. Marie and Harold had always made much of their collection of what they considered to be important cultural artefacts. Ab noted that one of the knives was missing, like a missing front tooth in an open smile.

He looked past the room divider into the long room, the full length of the house, with a terrazzo floor, which could be used for weddings, funerals, or, in the case of expatriates, adapted for parties. We're like family. What did that mean? Having evolved from small groups to tribes to nations, were we now copping out, cowards, going back to family values? This *is* a madhouse, he thought. Like family. Indeed.

Who really knew one's father and one's mother and sisters? And did they ever know him? Would his mother see in his slightly reddish nose the signs of a fallen-away Mennonite, seduced by booze and the wicked world? Would she see in his eyes the sadness, the knowledge that he had fallen not quite far enough to enjoy the world, but only to be in it? Or would she see only her boy, the one who tugged at her skirt for fresh, home-made brown sugar platz, fresh from the oven. Would she see the boy who rushed outside with it, to share with George in the snow fort dug into the heaps of ice and snow beside the driveway? Ab recalled once, at a Bible-verse-reciting competition at Wednesday night church Young Peoples', how he had jumped up to yell, "Luke 14:26: If anyone comes to me and does not hate his father and mother, his wife and children, his brothers and sisters—yes, even his own life—he cannot be my disciple." And how, then, everyone was deadly silent. Was that really in the Bible?

◇◇◇

He sighed and stepped into the crashing sea of noise and a fog of clove-scented cigarette smoke, and wafts of various after-shaves, deodorants, and sweet, heavy tropical scents worn by expats to cover the fact that they, unlike the Indonesians, sweated. Profusely. The music went from Credence Clearwater Revival to The Rolling Stones.

"Abner Duck! Oh I am sorry! Don't look at me like that. Doo-eck. Abner Doo-eck. Welcome back! And dressed like a black Leprechaun! What a wonderful idea!"

Marie Wilkinson lifted her beaming face for a kiss on each cheek.

He leaned close. "Fiji."

She smiled conspiratorially. "My perfume, yes. An island of tropical delights. That's me." Her cheeks were rouged, and she wore a tight, shiny black halter top and what appeared to Ab to be black lacy tights with no skirt. She looked down at herself. "I'm a Black Madonna, could you tell?"

Ab ladled himself a tumbler of punch from the huge crystal bowl, gulped it back and winced. It burned all the way down. He eyed the white-haired lady in the teenage tights, slowly, up and down the length of her wiry little body, knowing she was watching and that this was what she expected him to do. "You do remind me of the icons and rosaries George and I used to go look at in the stores in St. Boniface, although somewhat more degenerate."

She laughed, leaning tipsily on his arm. "More mysterious. Our Lady of Montserrat and all that. We used to winter in Spain when I was a little girl."

Ab was surveying the crowd. "A bit of an extravaganza for a Thursday night, don't you think? The parties seem to be creeping back earlier into the week all the time."

She leaned up to kiss him on the cheek. "Call it an early Eid al-Fitr party. A kind of Muslim Mardi Gras, but on Thursday instead of Tuesday." She sighed extravagantly. "If you really want to know, it's the only day when everybody could come. Some folks are going away on holiday this weekend, and then it's the Yogya-Semarang Hash party, and I didn't want to be competing with that."

"No, I don't suppose you would." The hash. The Hash House Harriers, as the organization was officially called, was dedicated to jogging, seeing the countryside, and drinking beer, probably in reverse order. In fact, some said it was "a drinking club with a running problem." It had been organized initially in many of the ex-British colonies, but was now world-wide. About once a month, the expatriates in a particular city gathered at a pre-arranged spot to run a pre-arranged trail through a particular section of countryside. The expatriates were often joined in their run and fun by local people. In the case of the Yogyakarta hash about a third were Indonesians, usually from middle class or upper class backgrounds. At each hash event two people, called hares, laid a trail of their own choosing with bits of tissue paper. At the end of the one-hour run, a truck with beer and soft drinks would be waiting, songs would be sung, and beer poured over people's heads. A joint Yogyakarta-Semarang hash would really be a big drunken bash with people from both cities meeting at some central location.

A sudden stop in the music brought Ab's mind back to the room. "I see you've lost one of your kris out there. Security problem?" She pulled away and laughed. "Oh that. Been out of the case for months." She hung on his arm. "You really must come over more often. Harold loaned it out to a friend at work. When you've got the genuine article, you want people to handle it, yes?" Her hand was straying down the front of his shirt and he turned toward the room, away from her.

"Where *is* Harold?"

She waved towards a wicker couch where her husband was decked out in full papal regalia. In real life, Harold was a British advisor of some sort to the Indonesian army. "On non-military matters, really," Marie would say, explaining what her husband would rather leave unsaid. "Britain," she might add with a whisper, "wouldn't give a country like this military advice, you know, with all the secret killings in Timor and everywhere." *Ah,* thought

Ab, *the bullshit we tell ourselves to make money.* Harold himself was the perfect "advisor"; tall, rectangular-faced, moustachioed, straight-backed, he actually looked the part. More importantly, he also, always, kept his own counsel and no one else's. Unlike many of the others here this evening, he never spoke of his work, Indonesian politics, or even politics in general. This, in a sense, made him more like most Javanese of the economic and political ruling class, and, unusually for a foreigner, allowed him to make some friends among them.

This evening, Harold was giving advice to Gladys White, his nose almost into the cleavage of the buxom blond Australian anthropologist, wife of Peter Findlay. She was wearing a pith helmet and a low-cut white robe, as if she were a missionary for a California sex cult or explorer in the jungles of eroticism. Ab considered that this might not be too far off her actual avocation. He reflected, again, on the fact that he wasn't interested in her, and why that was. He looked back at Harold. "Black Madonna, eh?" He moved away from Marie into the crowd. "I should have known. The white abstinent Pope and his dark alter ego, the black Madonna. Quite logical, all that Catholic stuff, in an illogical sort of way."

He was halfway across the room when he realized that his glass was empty, that he didn't know where he was going in any case, just wanting to get away. He returned to the punch table. Marie had left. He re-filled his glass and looked again at Gladys and Harold. Gladys, the self-styled Sheila from the Outback, was telling stories about crocodiles and Aborigines. Harold was watching her bosom, taking it all in. Gladys had her eye on someone else. Ab followed her gaze: George, burly city boy playing farm boy, his curls poking out from under a cowboy hat, grinning ear to ear. He was making his way between the dancers in Ab's direction. Ab's eyes flew momentarily past George to the small, short-haired, olive-skinned lady with whom he had just been dancing. Claudia Hernandez was wearing a white eye-mask, white Stetson hat, very short white skirt, and high-heeled white boots. She sensed Ab's stare and waved and winked at him.

"Ab, good to see you could make it!" George threw his arms around Ab in a bear hug, pushing his hat back off his head. "Boy, things are so bad we gotta meet at parties, eh? Could be worse I guess. Things are so hectic on the project. How was Boyolali? Got it figured out?" He set two glasses down on the table. "The road to Solo is bad. Did you ever wonder why they call Surakarta 'Solo'? I think it's because there's no other place where driving sinks to so low a level of basic survival skills. You take your life in your hands every time you drive there. Still, I'm not sure that back country road from Klaten is much of an improvement. No trucks or buses, but hardly a road in places." He started filling the glasses, talking as he poured. "Anything new?"

Ab told him about the magnet and the plastic bag. George finished filling the glasses, then topped up Ab's glass as well and leaned back against the table. He took a sip and then said, almost to the air, "We had a few boxes of those magnets go missing at Susu Senang. That must have been six weeks ago, a few weeks before that Susilo fellow disappeared." He puffed out his cheeks and blew a long breath. "Irresponsible, they said. Just ran away. I don't know. Seemed steady enough to me." He seemed to come back from somewhere else. "Two, eh? We usually just put one in, and we don't attach little bags." He surveyed the crowd. Like checking a herd of cattle, thought Ab. George turned to him. "So what's the diagnosis?"

"Soesanto and I think that local butchers are poisoning the cattle to make them sick, and then offering salvage slaughter to the farmers…cheap meat for Eid al-Fitr. As for what's in the bag…" His voice trailed off and he shrugged. "I threw it into the fridge. My best guess is strychnine, but you'd need a huge dose. There was a kind of bitter scent and the clinical signs seem right, but we never see it in cattle. Unless you send it to the abomasums, where it doesn't get diluted in that big rumen. I'll see if the lab over at the hospital can test for it. If not, we'll have to send it to the central lab in Bandung, and that will take a while."

George lifted up the full glasses and turned to face him. "It sounds like you can explain everything except: why the imported cattle?" And, he took a deep breath. "And we're still seeing anthrax at Susu Senang."

Ab returned the stare. "You are doing everything we said? No post mortems. Everybody wears gloves and masks around the dead ones. Lots of washing. Bury the dead. Cover them with lime. Treat all the cattle with penicillin. Vaccinate."

"We've done all that. Well, I did a lot of the treatment and vaccination. Waluyo was doing the rest. He is the new farm manager." He set down one glass, raised his hand, pointed at the ceiling, and pronounced in a deep voice, "Chosen from above, no questions asked."

George played with the drink in his right hand, tried to look through it at the room. "Off the record. Rumour has it that Suharto was supposed to visit the farm next week. This is after all his home region, and it's a pet project. But with the explosions at Borobudur and Prambanan, the cows dying in the villages, and anthrax on the mother farm, rumour is he'll send a replacement. That would probably be General Witono. But Suharto is wily. He may still come himself. " He looked down at the floor and moved his cowboy boot in a circle.

"So you think this is all political—a way to somehow get at the President?"

George shrugged and looked around. "I was going to tell you this later, but when I was digging a pit yesterday to bury and lime the cattle bodies, we dug up some human remains. Recent ones." He glanced sideways at Ab. "I think it might be the former manager, Susilo, but nobody wants to talk about it at the farm. The rumors are all over the place. That's what happens in a dictatorship I guess." He looked nervously around. "I also found something else at the farm I'd like you to have checked out. Later."

George touched Ab on the arm, picked up the second drink, and then moved back into the crowd. "Come on. Claudia has someone she wants you to meet." He turned back just a second. "I do want to talk more later." Ab drank half his glass and refilled it.

Claudia. That stuff again. At least, when Ab thought about her, he forgot about Sarah. God, there were days he wished

George were dead he wanted her so badly. Still, dammit, after all these years. He shouldn't have come here, to Indonesia, but how could he have known? He had thought it was over. He followed George and, without thinking, blurted out, "Have you ever been in love with a married woman?"

George turned slightly without hesitating. "Hell yes, been married to one for, um, fourteen years." He paused a minute and lowered his voice. "She stayed at home tonight to read. She's into Wallace's *Malay Archipelago* now. Says Wallace, who was tramping around in the Spice Islands, apparently discovered evolution before Darwin, but Darwin got all the credit. Says if I want to understand Indonesia I should read more." He turned suddenly, so that Ab bumped into him. "Hell, if you can just *read* about places to understand them, why *go* anywhere?"

Ab looked around. "Is this helping us understand Indonesia?"

George guffawed. "Got a point there!"

They returned to manoeuvring their way between Queen Elizabeth, Gandhi, Davy Crockett and Tinkerbell to the far side of the room.

Claudia was talking with a lithe, very beautiful Chinese woman. She seemed almost too beautiful to be real, her black hair catching and reflecting the lights as it flowed down either side of her perfectly proportioned face. She moved with slow, sinewy grace, like some rare jungle cat. Briefly, the thought slipped through Ab's slightly inebriated brain that, like a jungle cat, she could kill, with one quick stroke of her hand. Then the pedestrian commander of his Mennonite brain took over and wondered if she were another opportunist looking for a man to marry and take her out of the country. There were a lot of young women in this oppressively beautiful country looking for a ticket out, usually a white male professional ticket. If she *was* an opportunist, he considered, she was also a gorgeous opportunity for a man rapidly slipping past his prime. Maybe a bit young, though. He approached Claudia from behind and laid a hand on her bare back. She leaned back into his hand, turned and smiled warmly. George was at her other side, putting a drink into her hand. As he did so, his hand slipped along her arm and fell lightly along her body, as if by accident. Claudia took Ab's arm, leaned up to kiss him on the mouth. He held his tongue back, barely. "Paloma Picasso," he said as their lips parted.

"Ab, mi amore, mucho gusto, you have such a wonderful, romantic nose. And I have just the lady for you. Nancy Martono, dressed as..." She looked her up and down. "An Indonesian? Meet Ab Dick, Canadian veterinarian, unattached, congenial. Dressed up as a..." She looked him up and down. "Some kind of Mennonite. We have those in Mexico too. Thought I wouldn't recognize it, didn't you?" She turned to the woman. "What more could you ask for?"

Nancy held a glass up to her eyes and looked at him through it. "What kind of a name is Ab Dick?" she said in perfect English.

"Same as Nancy Martono, if I know Indonesia. A mispronounced name of convenience."

"Convenience. So you're a criminal hiding from the law?" She smiled and brought her glass down to chest level, as if to focus his eyes at her cleavage. He resisted the temptation and looked over her shoulder. Claudia was slipping away. He wanted to ask her to dance. Nancy's answer startled him and his eyes jumped back to hers.

"Does that mean you are?"

She shrugged. "Then what convenience?"

He stared at her for a moment, trying to gather his thoughts. "Well, not to make too fine a point, in Canada, in the 1950s, a lot of people from non-English countries changed their names to get jobs. Or to fit in, because the English thought the names sounded ridiculous. See what you've done? Got me started. Our family name was something between 'Duck' and 'Dick' which neither the French nor the English Canadians can pronounce. We did everything and then still didn't feel at home." He looked down into his drink.

"So my father thought Dick was easier to pronounce than D U-with-an-umlaut K or even Doo-eck. He didn't realize it was also a bad joke. He could have gone back to the pre-German

Flemish origins. Anthony Van Dyck was a famous student of Rubens. At least the middle name puts the "fun" back into the name. God, I'm whining and getting pedantic. Too much to drink. I grew up in a Mennonite city with Harry Dicks and Peter Dicks and Peter Peters. Misguided attempts to belong in a culture that just laughed us off."

Nancy was grinning.

Ab chugged back the rest of his drink, looked for somewhere to set the glass down, and, seeing nothing, looked at Nancy again. "See, even you fall into that trap. I would have thought a Chinese person in Indonesia would know better. I have heard that many of you changed your names after the mass slaughter of '66. I know. My stuff is petty beside the Chinese question here. At least with us it was just getting laughed at and shut out of jobs, not having our throats slit."

"The Chinese question?" She flicked her hair away from her eyes with her free hand and looked at him expectantly.

"Jews of Asia and all that," he mumbled, feeling incredibly self-conscious and stupid.

She laughed. "And here I thought Jews were the Chinese of Europe. Damn, I'll never get my history right."

She wrapped one arm lightly around his neck, the other resting on his shoulder with her half-full glass of punch. "Let's dance." It was a slow dance. Vintage 1960s. He could not resist. His arms slipped around her waist, and immediately began inching up. "Since you were so good at Claudia's perfume," she whispered into his ear, "what's mine?"

He put his nose close to her neck. *Pure sex.* "Unlike us plebes from the crude West, you Indonesians don't sweat. You have your own, sweet, individual scent."

◇◇◇

Claudia was dancing with George, leaning into him. Across the room John Schechter, her American husband, the tall, bleach-blond volcanologist, was fondling Gladys' back, but his steely blue eyes were fixed on George and Claudia. John spent his days, and not a few nights, climbing in and out of the crater of

Merapi, the active volcano on whose flank Yogyakarta was built. Ab would not have been surprised to learn that John's blondness was from working near fire, a pure, ashen heat. He seemed like a smouldering, heaving, lava dome, on the verge of rupture. He had married Claudia while exploring volcanoes in Mexico.

"You don't really want to dance with Claudia," Nancy whispered into his ear. "It's not safe." She laid her head on his shoulder. At that moment, Peter Findlay cut deftly in on George. Findlay, the slim Australian, worked in "intelligence." It seemed an open secret, although no one knew, really, what he did. Talk to the underground opposition, they supposed. He let the rumours circulate, and gave no pretences. Ab noted that John relaxed visibly and turned to face Gladys.

Nancy raised her head abruptly from his shoulder and turned to look across the room.

Ab looked at her. "What's up?"

"I should be asking you. You're the one who went from wound-up tight to floor cushion relaxed."

"I did?" He dug his fingers into his trouser pocket and fiddled with a handful of sunflower seeds, let go.

He looked into her eyes, dark deep pools, throwing up shimmers of inquiry, lightness layered over deep sadness. A shiver went down his spine. She laid her head back down. "You did." Lust, that was it, that was the shiver down his spine, right down through his scrotal sac and on down to the adductor muscles, which were supposed to keep his legs extended.

He looked away over her shoulder at Harold Wilkinson and then Peter Findlay. "Don't you think it's odd that British intelligence and Australian intelligence are working here, but not the Americans? I mean, don't you think they would be here, after all their involvement in the 1966 coup?"

She put her head back and looked into his eyes. "How can such a smart man say such stupid things? Just think of somebody who goes to all the parties and works odd hours in dangerous places." She settled her head back down into the crook of his neck.

"Well, that really narrows it down, doesn't it?"

Marie was at the tape player. She faded out the slow song and popped in another tape: rock and roll. She grabbed her husband by the hand and began to leap about. "She's so smooth. She does it as if it were her music. Her music was...I don't even know. Long before that stuff." The music drowned out his words. He let go of Nancy, dancing without thinking, without a partner, though Nancy continued to move close to him.

"This music reminds me of 1967," Ab suddenly blurted out. "I hate it."

Nancy stopped abruptly and dropped her glass on the floor. It shattered and sparkled across the terrazzo as the other dancers, some of them in bare feet, skipped away. The music continued to blare and the dancers made a wide circle away from the shards. The Indonesian housekeeper, a grandmotherly woman, appeared with a broom and dustpan, and began sweeping up, oblivious to the commotion around her. Nancy and Ab stood motionless. He shrugged. "I guess the late 1960s weren't very good for a lot of people. Let's go for a walk."

He turned and walked to the main door. He stood there, his ears ringing from the noise, until he could feel her presence behind him. She laid her hands on the back of his shoulders and pushed him ahead of her out through the gate. In the laneway, she pressed her head into his back. "I'm sorry, that was stupid. How does anybody know what these things mean anyway?"

He turned and slipped his arms around her. "They listen to each other." They stood still and listened. From the house came the continuous thumping of the trapped expatriates. From down the lane came what sounded like a sermon blaring over a loudspeaker.

"I used to know a guy who sounded like that when he preached. I think he saved me once."

"Saved you?" She stood back from him.

"Yeah, saved. It's what happens when a preacher makes you cry and then you ask God to come into your life and then God promises not to torture you forever. Bill Janzen told us about saving the poor people in Asia, and then he sang a duet with his wife. And after church we came home to a house overheated from the oven being on all morning, and we ate a big beef roast, with mounds of mashed potatoes and boiled peas and carrots. Then Dad had a nap and Mom and my sisters did the dishes."

"And you?"

"Sat in my room. Bored. Story of my life. Like I'm boring you now. Let's go see that preacher."

"Yes, let's. The preacher." She seemed delighted at the thought.

They walked through this typical urban neighbourhood, past another white, walled-in house similar to the Wilkinsons', and then a small knick-knack store barely big enough to turn around in. They passed a ramshackle bamboo hut set back in an overgrown field, with two black and white cows grazing in front. Then they turned down another lane, some white-washed mud-walled houses, a palatial mansion, a bamboo hut. The lane opened out into a soccer field. The field was full of people, wandering about with their kerosene lanterns, like the grey and brown lost souls of purgatory. *George and me, sitting in the snow fort in our front yard, fantasizing that Jael Freed from school might join us, hopefully with her blouse half-unbuttoned. It is after supper, in the semi-darkness, recounting the scariest stories we know. Why do they always have to do with sex or religion?*

At one end of the field, a large movie screen was set up and just below that, a one-ton truck was parked. They followed the general push of the crowd toward the screen. Nancy leaned against his side and took his hand. He did not resist. The back of the truck was built up like a camper, but with side doors that were swung open to reveal several shelves of colourful boxes and bottles. Off to either side of the truck were sales booths. The trucks and booths were lit up with many-coloured lights. Christmas in purgatory, Ab thought.

The preaching was coming from a man with a microphone standing next to the truck. "Jamu Jago!" he exclaimed, "for seminal weakness, for tuberculosis, for smoker's cough, for all your beauty aids." Ab strained his understanding of Bahasa Indonesia to the limit, attempting to make the words say what they obviously didn't. "Now take this product here," the man went on, as if expounding the second point in his sermon. He held up a bottle. "Made from natural oils, will make your skin smooth and clean."

Nancy squeezed his hand. "Good preacher?"

He put his arm around her and held her close. "Yeah, good preacher. I'm convicted already. Where do I go to be saved?" He dropped his arm. Every time he thought he understood this culture, he was brought low.

The preacher went on for ten minutes and then his voice seemed to give out. Very loud disco music blared over the speakers and Ab stood transfixed as three dwarfs appeared on the roof of the truck, in floodlights, dancing ludicrously to the music. They jiggled and jumped for five minutes, at which time another preacher took over, to expound on the virtues of some other products.

He felt his arm being squeezed. "They travel around the country. Later, there will be a Karate film, from Hong Kong." She paused. "A Chinese film but the words dubbed into Bahasa Indonesia, so not really Chinese, you know? That's important here." The squeeze on his arm tightened. "Come on, let's go buy some beauty aids."

She pulled him to the nearest booth. As they approached, a very raggedly dressed man with a persistent, harsh cough was talking with one of the two white-shirted young men behind the counter. The salesman pulled a bottle from the shelf and showed it to the man, who nodded. The salesman then pulled a glass from under the counter, poured some of the brown liquid into it and handed it to the customer. The man horked out a fierce, deep, phlegmy cough, spit on the ground beside him, then drank the liquid in one gulp and handed the glass back to the salesman, who wiped it off with a towel and set it back under the counter for the next customer.

"Good way to keep yourself in business, passing around dirty glasses like that."

"Yes, but all natural," said Nancy. He wasn't sure if she was joking.

"I wonder if a guy could sell sunflower oil at the Red River Exhibition in Winnipeg that way."

"What's that?"

"Never mind. I'll have to take you some time."

She smiled. "Perhaps you will." She turned to the man at the counter and bought several small bottles from the shelf. "Can I put these in your pocket?" She placed them into his jacket pocket. "What's in there, your birdseed?"

He reached in, took out a handful and examined them. "My version of Jamu Jago. My culture. They give me power. Without them, I am nothing." He stared absent-mindedly toward the truck, then realized that George was over there, talking animatedly with John Schechter.

"Wrong. Like all cultural artefacts, you give them power."

She followed his gaze. "Mr. George knows a lot of things and a lot of people." She took Ab's elbow and guided him toward the dark edge of the field.

"In this country knowing too much can be fatal," she added as they stepped back into the full darkness of the lane. Ab felt her hand settle comfortably into his as they entered the laneway.

He frowned. "Do you mean Claudia?" They could hear the party already from the end of the lane.

"No, I didn't mean Claudia," Nancy said quietly, but his mind was already elsewhere, thinking about Schechter's temper outbursts, and her comment didn't really register until much later.

They walked slowly, and when they returned, the crowd was more boisterous, and was gathering for a parlour game of some sort at one end of the room. Nancy went off to the bathroom. Ab elbowed his way to the punch table and downed two glasses in quick succession. To his surprise, George was at the table, filling his glass. "One more drink and I've got to go," Ab said. "I've had about all my little culture-shocked brain can handle. That was quite a show up at the field, eh?"

George spilled part of his drink and wiped at his mouth with his shirt. "What show? Oh, that. Listen, come out with me to the car for a minute." They walked out to George's truck. He reached into the passenger side and pulled out an ornately etched, tarnished brass sheath with a knife handle protruding.

George placed it into his hands. It felt warm.

"Where did you get it?"

George pushed the truck door shut and leaned against it. "I was looking through our locked supply shed and found it back behind some boxes of antibiotics, kind of stuffed down under a pile of rags. I didn't tell anyone. Well, only you and Schechter."

"Jesus, George. You stole it? What did Schechter say?"

"I didn't steal it. It was just there. Schechter said something cryptic about backing off. Whatever the hell that means. Anyway, I hear that Soesanto, the guy you work with, is a bit of an expert on these things. I wondered if he could check it out. See where it came from. How authentic it is."

Ab stood there, staring down at the knife in his hands. "You said you think you found Susilo's body at the farm. Do you think it's the murder weapon?"

George lifted his cowboy hat and ran his hand back over his head. "Listen, Susilo was an old Communist. If it *is* the murder weapon, nobody really wants to find it. They'd want it to disappear, just like Susilo disappeared, don't you think?" When Ab didn't say anything he seemed more agitated and went on. "Listen. Who would know? Can you imagine what a great souvenir it would be? Something with a real story. Anyway, can you check it out?" He walked around to the driver's side of his truck and opened the door and climbed in. Ab recalled what Sarah had told him. He signalled for George to open the passenger window, then leaned forward, the knife pressed between him and the door.

"On the way back from Cilacap the other day, Soesanto and I stopped at the black sand beach near Wates, those terrifying monster waves, the howl of the hot wind from the South Pole. Said every year there were tourists who thought they could swim in it. Bodies never found. He told me that maybe I should leave the cattle epidemic alone, both the poisonings in Boyolali and the anthrax at the main farm. I should steer clear of this whole business."

George started the motor. "We can't really do that, can we? It's our job. Just have it checked out, okay?" He pulled away before Ab could answer.

Ab put the knife into his car and then turned back toward the house. Nancy was standing at the door, watching. He had a sudden dizziness and pain in his head. He bent over. Nancy came up and rested her hand lightly on his back. "I think you've had enough," she said. "Better get away while you still can."

It was only later, much later, that he understood what, exactly, she meant, and by then it was too late.

Chapter Five

Ab awoke with his head throbbing. He rolled over to hug his long, firm, cylindrical pillow, what the local Javanese called a Dutch Wife, no doubt after considerable colonial experience. He rolled over the other way and sat up on the edge of the bed, rubbing his eyes with the back of his hands and running his hand back through his hair.

Nancy. They had gone for another walk after George had left. She had talked about her childhood. Her grandfather, imprisoned by the Japanese during World War II, had later joined Sukharno's forces against the Dutch and had had some influence in government when Indonesia gained independence. In the 1966 Night of the Generals, when an alleged Communist coup led to a very real and very bloody counter-coup, her parents had been murdered at a road block while walking home from a political meeting. Her grandparents, fearing for their lives, had left six-year-old Nancy, the only child of an only son, to be raised by a white missionary family. Her grandparents had separated and gone underground to hide from the terror. The Chinese were targeted during the rampage, and her extended family thought that she would be safer with a white missionary family, ostensibly an adopted orphan, rather than remaining with her grandparents, running from vigilantes in the countryside. After the coup and during the subsequent chaos, with his old mentor Sukharno under house arrest, her grandfather had managed to travel at night, cross-country, and eventually in a fishing boat, to the island of Bali, where he had found refuge with a sympathetic Buddhist family. Her grandmother had made her way through family connections and a series of small, well-paid boats across the water to Singapore.

Nancy's grandmother eventually moved back to Java and made contact with her husband, but remained estranged from him, and lived in a separate house, albeit one of his traditional family homes. Nancy's grandfather, ever the resourceful survivor, had done well in business as the political situation stabilized and was regaining some influence with the new government of General Suharto in Jakarta.

"I didn't know any of this until a couple of years ago. I spent all my formative years thinking I was an orphan. The missionaries who raised me left the country when I was sixteen. I thought my grandparents were dead. They had no idea if I was dead or alive. If I was alive, they didn't know how to track me down. We only rediscovered each other, through a network of Chinese business connections, when I turned twenty and was looking for money to open a computer shop. Now I spend my life trying to discover who I am, to recover something I lost." She leaned against him, not looking at him, talking quietly to the space in front of them.

When they returned to the house, the party was still in swing. They stood in the entryway. He felt their bodies soften against each other, and turned to face her for a kiss, and then said, "So, are you looking for a man to help you escape from this place?" And she pulled away. "Not a slob who eats sunflower seeds," she said, standing up and walking with a slight, graceful sway back into the party.

Why had he said that? Why did he always sabotage his potential relationships? Was he so afraid of landing somewhere after years of flying?

He pulled on his clothes and walked out into the main part of the house. The terrazzo floor was cool under his feet. He had managed to get a rented house from the university; it was in the older, Dutch style, with high ceilings and over-head fans, and, out back, servants' quarters, which were empty. There were two washrooms, one with the usual western-type shower and toilet, and the other with a squat toilet and a *mandy*, a deep concrete tub which you filled with cold water. You then used a pot at the end of a long handle to give yourself a splash-bath. Both the storage tub and the acting of splashing water over yourself were called *mandy*. *Mandy* and *to mandy*. He wasn't the first expatriate, nor would he be the last, to have tried to use the mandy as a very awkward climb-in bathtub.

He went into the Asian bathroom, where he brushed his beard and his teeth, pouring boiled water into his cup from the gallon jug he kept there. At least this place had a yard, with several trees in it. That was one of the advantages of some of the older houses. It was a colonial advantage, he thought, as he pulled the gate open, feeling satisfactorily guilty, but what could be done about it now, in retrospect? Who was he to reject a house the university had offered him, slighting his hosts? Once a week the neighbour's gardener would, for a fee, cut the lawn and trim the bushes.

He slipped quietly out into the street and felt a weight of worry lift like a huge bird away from him. He headed out to the main road, wondering about Nancy. He wondered what he wanted to have happen. He wasn't sure he could deal with all the complications of sharing his life with another person. He made the old deal with himself, the kind of deal he had made all through his growing up. If Nancy somehow came back into his life, despite his rudeness, then he would know that God willed for him to woo her. Otherwise, well, God willed something else. It was all up to God. As he walked, he pushed his hand into his trouser pocket, played with a handful of sunflower seeds he found there, then, impulsively, emptied them all out into the open ditch beside the street.

At the office, Ab looked over to where Tri was typing the paper records into the computer.

"Tri?"

She turned and flashed him that wide-eyed wide-mouthed smile. "Yes, Dr. Ab?"

He stood up and came to her side, almost put his hand on her shoulder, reached for the pile of files instead. "Do you mind if I look at some of these while you type?" He placed his hand on the files. "Are you finished with these?"

"Yes, finished. Anything else?" She rested her hand an inch from his and leaned forward slightly. From where he was standing, he could see down inside the front of her loosely fitting sun dress, way too far down, far enough to see that she wasn't wearing a bra. He could see, as he and George would have said in high school, everything. He turned his head away.

"Dr. Soesanto has not come in yet today?"

She smiled brightly. "Maybe he went to visit his mother in Surabaya," she said, touching his arm, "Or maybe at the bird market. He sometimes goes to look at sick birds at the bird market. Have you been there?" Ab took her hand gently off his arm like a small animal, set it down, and patted it lightly. He shook his head.

"You should go. The Yogyakarta bird market is very famous."

Ab didn't know that Soesanto had a mother in Surabaya. He never talked about his family. He'd never make a good Mennonite.

Ab was trying to avoid looking at Tri. Her hand seemed to be creeping back towards where his rested on the folders. He slipped the folders out from under her hand and went back to his desk and began reading the reports. "Um, thanks. Maybe I will some day." It took a few minutes to get his mind to pay attention to the words on the page in front of him, until the silence at his back was broken by the sound of typing again. Restless, he got up and went down the hall to the library, where he was allowed through the locked doors to actually handle the books. Most readers had to request something specific, which they were then allowed to look at in the room, under the vigilant eye of the librarian. Books were a guarded commodity in the university. Ab was looking for a toxicology text.

That evening, Ab drove to Soesanto's house. Dusk was falling quickly, and restaurateurs were setting up tents, lighting lanterns, getting their grills started and rolling out mats that spilled off the sidewalks and into the main roadway. Ab noticed several large snakes slither out from the open sewer at the roadside and across the road. Soesanto's street was a mixture of sand and mud, as if it had once been finished with a fine graded surface, and then left to sag and wrinkle in rain and sun. Ab stopped in front of the small, low house, half-hidden among papaya and banana trees, overgrown with bougainvillea. The ground trembled slightly, as if a truck was passing, and he steadied himself against the car for a second.

A short, wrinkled woman wrapped tightly in a bright green and blue sarong, grinning toothlessly, met him at the door. He touched her hand lightly and brought his own back up to his heart in a gesture of greeting. He was led into the small front room, set off from the main house by an ornately carved wooden screen, decorated with a scene dominated by Hanuman, the monkey king from the Ramayana. This waiting area, common in Indonesian houses so that strangers at the door would not have visual access to the main dwelling, contained a small bookshelf and a glass-topped coffee table with legs consisting of teak cobras. Javanese seemed reluctant to invite foreigners into their homes, and this was Ab's first time in Soesanto's house.

He had, in fact, driven over without an invitation, and wondered if this was what he should have done much earlier. He also wondered if this was a terrible blunder of etiquette and if he would be invited past this waiting room. He stood with his back to the room and perused the books. They all seemed ancient, worn, well-used. There was Wallace's *The Malay Archipelago,* Raffles' *History of Java*, Blood and Henderson's *Veterinary Medicine*, as well as some novels by Promoedya Ananta Toer. Maybe Sarah and Soesanto should have a book club.

Ab could hear the thump of the cane on the terrazzo floor, followed by a moment of silence as the good leg moved forward, and then the thump again. He turned to meet Soesanto, dressed in a traditional black shirt and brown-and-white Yogyakarta batik sarong and cap. "Ab! What a pleasure!" They greeted and then he waved toward where the old woman disappeared. "My housekeeper. Stone deaf. Hardly speaks. Lost two kids and a husband during Suharto's housecleaning in 1966." He stood for a moment leaning on his cane. "You like my books?"

"I thought Toer was banned."

"Depends."

"On what?"

"On the year, the time of day, someone's whim, whether or not your visitors read, or notice books. He's been banned by every administration since the Dutch, and is the most widely read novelist in the country."

"You keep them in full view? Why not back in a library somewhere?"

Soesanto smiled. "If someone is out to get me, I doubt they'll check my bookshelf first. Anyway, when the thought police come looking for evidence, they'll ransack the place until they find something. There is no point anymore in hiding who I am."

They sat down on the brocaded, over-carved chairs, and the woman brought in a tray with a bottle and two glasses. "A perfect housekeeper," he added, as she retreated. He poured the glasses, raised his and signalled for Ab to do the same. "Two-day-old palm juice. Getting a bit ripe, but good for the stomach, and the spirit."

"To the spirits," said Ab, taking in a big mouthful and feeling it hit his gut like a large, live fish. "Ha! Ripe is right." He held the glass down to his lap and stared at it. "If she's deaf, how did she know I was here?"

"You felt the earthquake?"

"I saw the snakes moving first, or I would have thought it was a truck passing."

"I have to double check sometimes too, although we don't get many trucks here. I looked out the window about the same time you arrived."

They finished their glasses and started on seconds before Ab reached down to the bag he had set on the floor at his feet. "So, I have something I would like to show you."

Before Ab could zipper open the bag, however, Soesanto stood up. "Ah, you are my guest. Let me first show you something. Please, follow me."

He led Ab back through a large room, almost the full size of the house. In the corner was an ancient writing desk littered with papers, and a glass case on the wall, similar to the one at Wilkinson's house, with many traditional knives in it. The case still had spaces for more. They passed a wooden dining table, and then walked out through the kitchen with the cement counter-tops and a door leading off to the side, a general washroom and mandy, and out into a backyard. Ab was hit by a wave of red-green-yellow-black feathered air, resplendent with screeching, high-pitched whistles, melodic songs, the stifling stench of feathers and bird-shit, an exuberance of colour and noise. It was the biggest aviary he had ever seen, the whole back yard screened over, tree to tree to tree. Soesanto leaned on his cane and grinned at Ab's shock. He stuck his finger through the screen and a small parakeet flew over, landed on his gnarled finger, and bent over to chew at it with his beak. They couldn't talk for the noise and just stood there, as in the midst of an off-beat opera chorus. Ab felt simultaneously stunned, asthmatic, and elated.

They retreated to just inside the door and watched. Soesanto said, "You know how we Javanese love birds in cages?"

Ab laughed. "I noticed. And only in cages. Never flying free."

"So I go to the bird market, as I did today, and buy as many as I can and bring them here," he paused, "where they are half-free, at least."

"And why not let them go completely?"

He sighed. "Because they will just fly back to the cages for food anyway, and be caught again, or killed in the attempt."

Ab stared. "What's that red and purple and green parrot-looking one?"

"Black-capped Lory."

"The one with the long silky tail over there."

"Lesser bird of paradise. You don't know birds very well?"

"I'm from the prairies. I recognize the chickens scrabbling around in the bottom of the cage. I know about crows and meadow larks. And Canada geese. A few ducks." Then, under his breath added, "Mostly members of my own family."

"Next time, I'll walk you through the names of these birds, something to remember me by when you leave, something learned from a poor third-world veterinarian educated by Communists. But you said you had something you wanted to show me. Come, let's go back to the front room."

Soesanto topped up their palm wine and when they had sipped, and sat down, Ab pulled the kris from George out of his carry bag. He laid it on the low table before them. Ab felt as if he were laying a precious gift before a king, an old knife in its ornately etched brass sheath. He could hear a sharp intake of breath from Soesanto as he gently touched the finely etched metal lying before him. Slowly, he pulled the knife from the scabbard. "Look," he said, his voiced hushed into a hoarse whisper, "look at the damascene, how finely it is decorated. I have a whole collection, but none like this one."

Ab had not looked closely at it until now. He bent over to get a closer look. A snake wound its way up the wavy blade to the hilt. The blade had an intricate lacework of what appeared to be dwarves, monkeys, and Hindu figures, with Sanskrit words inscribed on it, polished to a fine thin-ness as if by much use.

"This kris is very old, back several hundred years, maybe more. Let me check something." He pushed himself to his feet with his cane, went to the bookshelf, and pulled down a dark, well-worn leather-bound volume. He flipped through the pages, then stopped and put his finger on a section of text. He leaned over to look at the knife again, muttering to himself. He looked carefully up at Ab. "Where did your friend get this?"

Ab shrugged. "He…he said he found it in a shed. Why?"

Soesanto scanned Ab's face, then picked up the knife and fondled it. "This kris is very special. Very special. If it's the real thing, and I think it is, it goes back to the 13th century. It was commissioned of the *empu* Gandring by Ken Arok. He was driven mad by the thighs of the beautiful Ken Dedes, which he saw when her dress caught as she descended from her carriage. 'Her lap radiates a blaze,' he is said to have written. 'Her feminine organ glows like fire.'"

He paused and Ab looked up. "That's pretty high up her thigh he was looking."

Soesanto grinned. "I have your attention now?"

"I'm that obvious?"

"Don't ask."

"The story?"

"Ah, Dr. Ab, listen well. Ken Arok used the kris to kill the husband of the beautiful Ken Dedes so that he could marry her. But Gandring was rushed into finishing his work because Arok was so anxious. A good craftsman does not like being rushed. So he put a curse on Arok, so that he and his children and his children's children would be killed by the kris."

"And?"

"And Arok killed the husband, married the queen, ascended the throne at Janggala. With the support of the clergy, he revolted against the sovereign Kediri and set up a new capital at Singhasari."

"I'm not surprised about the clergy," murmured Ab. "America. Pakistan. Afghanistan. Israel. Countries run by fanatical clergy. And then there's the story of King David, the man after God's own heart, who lusted after his neighbour's wife." He paused. "Makes you wonder about God."

"Arok was, in the end, assassinated by a kris."

"Almost the same story. God is a passionate and tragic lover. That's the message. Figures." Ab was stroking the oily damascene of the blade. "Did you say Gandring?"

"I did."

"Like the village we were at a few days ago. Gandringan."

"You noticed."

"Any significance?" He looked at Soesanto, who shrugged. Ab gripped the blade between thumb and forefinger. "Yet it seems flimsy for a weapon. I wouldn't want to do an autopsy on a buffalo with it."

Soesanto picked up the knife and held it high over his head, then broke in one motion into a choreographed forward-reaching stance, the knife held out at arm's length. "For thrusting, if you are Javanese. And then," he circled behind Ab, "there is the Balinese execution style." He stood silently behind Ab, pulled a handkerchief from the sash under his shirt, and laid it with a flourish on Ab's right shoulder. He rested the point of the blade on Ab's right shoulder. Ab stayed frozen. "Then with one quick motion, he takes the 18-inch straight Balinese blade, plunges it down directly into the heart, withdraws it in a clean movement, wipes it on the cotton cloth, and replaces it. Merciful. Bloodless. Also an effective method if you're sneaking up behind someone." He returned to the other side of the table, resting the blade in one hand, grinning. "Of course, this is a Naga kris, Javanese, not quite as long as the Balinese type, probably a bit messier if used for those purposes, but effective in skilled hands." He set the knife down on the table again and sat down, hands folded in his lap. "And then there are the Bugis, as in the Bugi-men. Here, let me read from Wallace." He retrieved an old book from the bookshelf behind him, and flipped it open.

> *A Roman fell upon his sword, a Japanese rips up his stomach, and an Englishman blows his brains out with a pistol. The Bugis mode has many advantages to the suicidally inclined. A man thinks himself wronged by society—he is in debt and cannot pay—he is taken for a slave or has gambled away his wife or child into slavery—he sees no way of recovering what he has lost, and becomes desperate. He will not put up with such cruel wrongs, but will be revenged on mankind and die like a hero. He grasps his kris-handle, and the next*

moment draws out the weapon and stabs a man to the heart. He runs on, with the bloody kris in his hand, stabbing at every one he meets. "Amok! Amok!' then resounds through the streets. Spears, krisses, knives and guns are brought out against him. He rushes madly forward, kills all he can—men, women, and children—and dies overwhelmed by numbers amid all the excitement of a battle...It is a delirious intoxication..."

Soesanto closed the book, sighed, stood up to replace it on the shelf. "Running amok: our great contribution to the global vocabulary. Useful for describing British football matches. And then there is the modern corruption, we Javanese or Bugis or Sumatrans get upset by a newspaper report and rush in a riotous mass into a town and massacre a few hundred or a few thousand or maybe a million Chinese or Communists or anyone we don't like. Then we stand amid the blood and silence and weep crocodile tears for what we have done." He stroked the blade, as if remembering something.

"Now sit back. See this." Soesanto, suddenly changing his tone, stood the knife very carefully on its tip.

"Good trick," Ab started to say when the knife catapulted suddenly into the air, flipped over several times and slammed into the white-washed plaster wall, driving itself in up to the hilt. He was aware that Soesanto was watching his face very carefully as this happened; what he felt was a thrill of fear, confusion and scepticism. This could not be happening.

"If one thinks the right thoughts, the Naga kris will transform itself into a snake," Soesanto said, looking at the knife in the wall.

Ab cringed internally, as if a small fierce animal were cornered at the back of his mind. "Do you believe in this...this...?" He waved his hand vaguely in the direction of the wall.

Soesanto stared at Ab. "You mean, as a scientist. I don't seem like a fool or a sorcerer, do I? Well, as a scientist, I study the average. I study large categories of things. Any good scientist acknowledges that there are *always* exceptions. Never say never and all that. No hypothesis is ever proven true, only not proven false, for now.

Every good biologist knows this. Our theories explain ninety-five percent of the data. But it's the five percent that is interesting. In fact, you could even say that free scientific thinking demands that these kinds of odd events must take place. If they don't, then either we have perfect understanding, which given our evolutionary origins as great apes is unlikely, or that the world we live in is a perfectly predictable clock, which is also patently false. That's what makes something interesting. It's what demands that we use statistics—if there were no variation, exception, oddity, then you could study one animal and know all animals."

"Some would say you can," Ab interrupted.

"Do you believe that?"

Ab thought. "Only at a trivial level, like where is the heart and number of legs. But every animal is particular, a product, necessarily, of an individual history."

"Okay, and the second rule is like unto the first, that science, at least experimental science, is not designed to study exceptions." He paused. "It is not something to believe, or not to believe. Always defer to the evidence, even if it defies theory. Some things have power because you give them power, and some things have power in themselves." He paused. "This one is also said to be full of mischief."

"Full of mischief?"

"Once it is drawn, it likes to draw blood."

Ab stared at the knife in the wall and finished his glass of palm wine. "I think I should go home now." Soesanto looked thoughtfully at the knife. "Would your friend mind if I keep it for a few days? I just need to check a few things more about it. If it is genuine, then it should probably go to a museum or...in any case, it is not every day I get to handle such a kris. Don't worry. I'll keep it locked in my case, the one you were looking at it when we passed through the house."

Ab hesitated. "Sure. I guess so." He was not sure he wanted to have the thing in his house anyway. "What about the mischief?"

Soesanto walked over to the wall and rested his palm on the handle. "I shall go catch a chicken out back for tomorrow's supper."

At the door, Ab turned again. "Really, Soesanto, you flipped that knife, didn't you? It was a trick, wasn't it?"

Soesanto smiled. "I'd better go find that chicken before the knife gets hungry."

Chapter Six

The following day, Ab took the white powder from Boyolali over to the laboratory at the medical school. They agreed to test for strychnine, but said it would take a few days. Then he returned to his office. From the shelf above his desk, he took down his copy of Blood and Henderson's *Veterinary Medicine*, and a book on tropical diseases of cattle. Maybe he was missing something. He flipped through the books, checking out every possible acute disease he could find. Nothing made sense. He set the books aside and began flipping through the paper files from the project.

He stared at the files, his mind drifting back to the previous evening at Soesanto's. Almost without thinking, he picked up the phone and called George at his office out at the farm.

"George, we have to talk. About that knife."

"Great! You have something on it I assume. Is it genuine?"

"Very. But you need to know a bit more about it before you get too excited."

"Why don't you come for supper tonight? I'll call Sarah and tell her. Six o'clock? It's the end of Ramadan. We can have our own feast."

It was late afternoon when Ab took a becak back to the house. Old Pak Budi, the night watchman, was dozing in his stool by the gate, which stood open. There was a motorbike in the carport next to his car, and Nancy was sitting on the front steps, a newspaper in her hand. "We need to talk," she said, "about last night."

Their eyes met and Ab felt his body want to reach out and touch her. "Last night. Yes. I was drunk."

She stood up. Standing on the stair, she was exactly his height. She folded the paper and rested it on his shoulder, as if knighting him. "We were both drunk. I told you things I should not have." Her hand dropped and she looked over his shoulder toward the street. "There are things in this country that should never be spoken aloud."

Ab was thinking that there were things between a man and a woman that should never be spoken aloud as well. What he said was: "I am going to George and Sarah's for supper tonight. Do you want to come? There will be children. George and I have some business to talk about. We won't be drunk. Maybe we can re-start this…this…" He couldn't think of how to finish the sentence. "Relationship" seemed too strong a word. "Maybe it would be good to just have some normal conversations."

Having a telephone in Java was reserved for village heads, police, bureaucrats, and others with some political clout. In Yogyakarta it was a luxury reserved for those who could pay the several thousand dollars to the right people to have it installed. This house came with one. It was assumed expatriate visitors would need one. Or maybe they were all tapped. A way of keeping tabs on foreigners. Right now, Ab just wanted to sit down with a cold beer and not think about anything.

George answered the phone. "George. I know this is last minute, but do you mind if Nancy, the girl I was dancing with last night, comes along for supper?"

"Ab and Nancy. Lucky man! Hey, the more the merrier. I'll tell the cooks."

Ab looked over to the wicker couch where Nancy, head tilted slightly forward, was reading the newspaper. Her shiny hair fell like black silk to her shoulders, where it broke cleanly into two flows, one to her back, and one along the slender creamy ivory of her neck, skirting the low, V-shaped neckline. "George says it will be fine," he said, his hand resting on the phone.

Nancy looked up and immediately smiled, her eyes fixing directly and uncompromisingly on his. When she set down the paper, Ab noticed that it was open to the article about the execution.

Ab and Nancy, Ab and Nancy. He said it over a few times to himself as he went to wash up.

He poured the cold water from the deep, concrete mandy over himself with a small cooking pot. Ab and Nancy. Was that how it was going to be? He tried saying the words out loud. "Let's see if Ab and Nancy can come over for supper tonight."

When Nancy climbed into the car beside him, he sat quietly for a moment without starting the motor, without looking at her.

"If we come back here afterwards, I can pick up my motorbike," she said.

Ab's mind fixed on the "coming back here afterwards." He rested his hand on the key, still without turning it. "I'm sorry about the other night."

She spoke to her reflection in the car window. "You should know that in my culture, personal relationships are like contracts. We just set out some negotiating positions." She paused and weighed her words out, one by one, like fragile eggs taken from a nest. "The other night...I have never told anyone outside my family about my childhood like that."

"I am flattered."

She laid a hand on his arm, tightened her grip, and waited until his eyes met hers. She seemed to be both deeply full of emotion but also incredibly under control, wound up, dark, dangerous, sad, on the verge of tears, on the verge of a predatory leap. "I don't want you to be flattered. I want you to be serious. That was very dangerous information. My life depends on it and now, maybe yours. I am sorry. I had too much to drink. I didn't intend to endanger you."

"So you are here now to make sure that information doesn't get any further? Is that what this is about?" She looked away, and he thought there were tears at the corners of her eyes, and cursed himself for his insensitive stupidity.

"We'd better go now," she said quietly.

George and Sarah lived in a white plaster house with red clay tile roof and columns out front that was both traditional and somewhat pretentiously new. It was not a house of their choosing, but had been selected by the Indonesians as being appropriate for them.

Nettie, six years, and Frieda, eight, circled around Ab at the door. "Uncle Ab!" they screamed in unison. They immediately took his hand and led him into the house. "Come see what we've made!"

Uncle Ab. Ab and Nancy. Ab could sense a life constructing itself around him, with or without his own consent. Sarah appeared just behind the girls. He stood there, awkwardly, the girls tugging at his hand. Always on the bosomy side, Sarah had gained weight since she had come to Indonesia, and seemed to have lost a little more of her thin blond hair on top. Ab thought she looked more worried than usual this evening. He recalled their brief exchange at the grocery store and pulled himself free of the girls to give her a hug. Sarah's hug almost degenerated into a cling, and he had to resist the urge to pull her whole body against his. He sniffed at her neck, the rich, sweet scent of Opium perfume, mixed with the clean, bitter smell of gin. She wore a loose-fitting, strapless batik dress. He looked over her shoulder at George, then gently pushed her away. George, chatting with Nancy, seemed oblivious, distracted, jovial.

"Gin and tonic?" Sarah offered. Ab went over to where the girls wanted to show him their work. He eyed Sarah. She seemed to have had her quota of gin for today. "Sure," he said.

"And who do we have here?" Nancy crouched down to look at what the girls were making with their plastic building blocks.

"Oh, I'm sorry, I should have introduced them. Nettie and Frieda? This is my friend, Nancy." They looked up at her and returned to building their complicated-looking structure. "This is *kraton susu*, the milk castle," said Frieda matter-of-factly. "It is where the cows live."

Nancy examined the castle closely. "And what do the cows do in the castle?"

Frieda looked at her, as if unsure she could share this information. Then she leaned over and whispered loudly, "They die, and then the snakes come and take over."

"Ah," Nancy nodded.

Sarah, returning from the sideboard with their drinks, clinking with ice, laughed lightly. "I think we've all been a little depressed lately. It seems to have rubbed off. Frieda's been having strange dreams, snakes and death."

Ab laughed gently and laid a hand gently on her arm. "Sounds like normal Freudian to me." He tried to sound light. She was silent, serious. He withdrew his hand. "In case you were wondering," he said, turning back toward Nancy, "I'm only an honorary uncle."

"Uncle Ab!" Nettie looked up suddenly from her work. "Do you know where we can get fireflies? Mom said you might know."

"Sure, I know a place. Maybe we can go out a bit later and catch some. Would you like that?" Frieda came over and pulled playfully at his beard. "That is, if it's okay with everyone else." Ab looked around at Sarah and then at George.

The girls turned quickly, in unison, and descended first on George, whom they had tagged as the chief potential obstacle to this enterprise. If they could convince him, the rest would follow. "Oh please, can we?" George looked over their heads at Sarah, winked, and said quietly, "Okay, but you have to be very good during supper. No complaining or fighting over who has too much or too little. Now go back to your blocks and behave until supper."

The girls returned to their play, and Nancy and Sarah remained standing above them, conversing quietly. George tugged at Ab's arm and led him over to an alcove with a couple of wicker chairs, near the cool breeze coming in the door. He set his drink down on a glass-topped coffee table in front of him, and brought his palms up in front of himself into a tepee.

Ab sat across from him and looked up at the bright Balinese paintings on the wall. Balinese paintings both intrigued and bothered Ab. He marvelled again at how they completely lacked perspective, as if there were no past, and no future, only the eternal *now*. He wondered if that was not only a romantic ideal, but also how one survived under a dictatorship. The past did not exist and the future was not acknowledged.

George leaned forward in his chair. "And?"

Ab was startled from his reverie. He took a sip from his drink, looked over to Nancy and Sarah and the children, and then lowered the glass to his lap. "Soesanto showed me some weird things last night. The kris is genuine, but it apparently is very valuable and has a bloody history behind it."

George smiled. "Damn, that's great. What is the story?"

Ab set his drink down on the table. "George, you don't understand. It was part of an elaborate Macbeth or Hamlet-like royal massacre seven hundred years ago. You would be stealing a priceless cultural artefact."

George glanced over at Sarah and Nancy and the girls. They seemed preoccupied. He leaned forward and lowered his voice. "Listen, I told you that we dug up Susilo's body, right? Anyway, it really was him, that body we found."

Ab narrowed his eyes and took another drink. Where was this going? "Soesanto knew him. Says he was a toxicologist. From what Soesanto said, he didn't seem like one to just run off because he doesn't like the job, not after all these years."

"And then there's Waluyo, the new farm manager, who was hand-picked by someone. No one I ask will tell me who made the appointment. Which I guess in this place meant that Susilo had to be retired, which in Java, for an old Commie, means he had to be killed." He picked up his drink from the table in front of him, swirled it around a few times, and set it down. "I think Waluyo is a spy for someone in Jakarta, to watch his investments. And I would guess that the person pulling the strings is General

Witono, who has been delegated to sign all the approval papers for this project."

"I thought the project money was put up by that wealthy Chinese businessman, Sani Sentosa."

"Pak Sani. But I suspect that Witono wouldn't approve the deal with Sentosa unless Waluyo was hired."

"George, where are you going with this?"

George rubbed his hands nervously, looked over at the women, and dropped his voice to almost a whisper. "It's like I said at the party. If this is true, and if that kris is the murder weapon, wouldn't everybody just want it to disappear? Why else would it be stashed in an old storage shed?"

He coughed and raised his voice out of a whisper. "Anyway, the cattle up at Gandringan, in Boyolali, that's a different problem. Opportunist. Somebody's getting that butcher the poison, the magnets, and he is taking advantage of the already troubled project to get a little cash. The farmers are probably in on it. If a project animal dies on their farm in the first six months, it gets replaced at project expense. I would have thought that Susilo might be doing it, but it hasn't stopped since he was killed."

"That's Waluyo's home village."

"There you go then. Motive, means. That one should end after Eid al-Fitr, so, day after tomorrow. But the anthrax at Susu Senang is something more. I don't know what. The cow deaths discredit the project, so the government, Witono in particular, but his boss Suharto as well, looks bad. This is Suharto's home territory. He doesn't like trouble here. He or Witono may have to come out himself to settle things."

"An assassination plot maybe?"

George paused and looked out the window. "Jesus I hope not." He played with his glass some more, frowning at it. "That would really complicate things."

"You mean it would make it almost impossible for the project to carry on."

"Yeah. The project. It would really complicate the project too."

"I took the stuff into the lab at the medical school to have it tested. But let's suppose we are right, that the deaths up at Gandringan are strychnine. Maybe if I can track down the source of the poison in Gandringan, it will also lead to the people who are responsible for the anthrax outbreak on the mother farm."

"Yeah, maybe, but you told me at the farm the other day that if you crowd a bunch of cows into a small space and add some drought and then some rain and some stress, bingo, you get an anthrax outbreak. The spores could have been there for a century, waiting for a crowd of foreign cattle to give them an opportunity to germinate."

"But you were giving vaccines and antibiotics."

"Yeah, if they work." George paused. "If they're not being tampered with."

The cook looked in from the dining room. "Ready!" she called.

"Well, let's change the subject for supper," said Sarah. "I've been hearing this cow story all day and I think it's time for a change." George looked up with a start. Nancy and Sarah had been standing just within earshot, nursing their drinks.

"I'm game for that," added Nancy.

"Here's a change of subject," said George as he stood up. "At the Wilkinsons' the other night I was talking with John Schechter. He said there's no political opposition to Suharto in Central Java. It's all in Jakarta. He was adamant about it."

Nancy laughed.

"What's so funny?" Ab asked, turning to her.

She shrugged her shoulders. "Ideological Americans," she said. "And gullible Canadians."

The table was set out with a steaming plate of rice, mixed, stir-fried vegetables, saté, deep-fried shrimp, and a kind of beef stew. "This looks fantastic," Ab said, pulling up a chair between Nettie and Frieda. "Is it all right if I sit between these two pretty girls? Or do they already have boyfriends?" The girls giggled.

Sarah held out her hands. "Let's all hold hands for a short grace."

During supper, they could hear the home-made bamboo fireworks exploding and music coming from various directions. Eid al-Fitr, the feast day at the end of the month of fasting, was starting. The celebrations would go all night and all the following day. From every mosque the chanting and singing blared out over the city through the megaphones. A banging of drums approached down the street and they all got up to stand in the front yard and watch a procession of young girls in long white gowns and head coverings, chanting in Arabic, "There is no God but Allah! Allah is great! Allah is our God!" They passed by bearing torches and banging on make-shift drums.

"Which brings me to something maybe Nancy can help me with," said George as they returned to the table. "One thing I must get before leaving this place is a kris. Nancy, what I want to know is how you know if you're getting a genuine article, or if someone is just putting one over on you."

Nancy played with her fork, turning a shrimp over and over. "You can buy them on Malioboro Avenue."

George laughed. "Yeah, but those are the cheap ones for tourists. I'd like the genuine article. Say I had a chance to buy one privately. How would I know it's the real thing?"

"I think you should stick to the tourist versions," she said quietly. "One should be respectful about things that are important in someone else's culture, don't you think? Anyway, with a kris, it may not be the knife itself that creates problems, but who owns it. These aren't tourist antiques. A real kris has history and in Java history means..." Her voice trailed off.

George cleared his throat and scratched the back of his head uncomfortably. "Of course, I'm not saying I don't respect it. That's not the point. I mean, people hang icons and crucifixes in their homes, or even family Bibles and doilies from Russia, don't they?" He looked at Sarah, as if continuing an argument with her. "And that doesn't mean they don't respect them. In fact, I could make a good argument for saying I'm the only one here who really does respect them. Other people collect meaningless trinkets. In my travels, I collect icons, crucifixes, old Buddhas. I want to add a kris to the little multi-cultural shrine I'm building. I'm a firm believer in keeping all my options open. What could be more respectful than that?"

Nancy set her fork down with a clink on the plate and her voice turned suddenly sharp, an edge of anger to it. "The trouble is, if you keep too many such options around the house, perhaps one day, when it's too late, you will inadvertently find that one of them wasn't an option you really wanted. Maybe it's not your option. Maybe it's somebody else's. To be blunt and to finish my sentence, history in Java means blood." She took a deep breath and her voice turned soft again. "I'm sorry. That was a bit of an outburst, wasn't it?"

Ab, whose mind had flung itself back to the display at Soesanto's, stood up suddenly from the table. Friend or no friend, he was tired of George and his endless games. "Time to go get fireflies," he announced. Everyone agreed readily, as if relieved to change the subject.

They packed into Sarah's mini-van, which she drove, and bumped down the crowded, pot-holed narrow streets to a dirt track just outside of town, a quiet, dark road between rice fields that Ab often visited when seeking out the nearest thing in Java to a starry prairie night. He stopped the car and turned off the lights. They could still hear the pop of the fireworks in the distance, but close at hand was a display of a different sort. "Look." He pointed to the fields beside the road. A great sheet of fireflies twinkled and shimmered over the top of the water. They climbed out of the car and stood momentarily in silence. It gave Ab a sense of standing on some fragile foothold in space, with stars scattered in the darkness all around. He felt suddenly incredibly isolated and lonely. Sarah stood still in the darkness while George rummaged in the back of the car for a butterfly net. Nancy was already out along the ridge between the paddies, the two girls in tow. Ab stood next to Sarah. He could feel the warmth of her body. "It almost looks as if they're synchronized. Look, see how one area lights up, and then goes dark, and then the next?" He was silent a moment, then added, "Nature's illusion of meaning."

George, Nancy and the girls mucked around the edge of the field, awed and excited, filling their jars. Ab and Sarah stood quietly watching the others. "What's up, Sarah?" he asked quietly.

Sarah leaned back against him and gripped his hand, furtively. "Oh Ab, Ab, I'm miserable and afraid and I don't know what I'm afraid of. I know George found that awful knife. It's a murder weapon for God's sake. Sorry. I should leave God out of this."

"If it's any consolation, I did talk to him. And Soesanto has it now. Maybe we can just leave it there."

She squeezed his hand, let go, and wandered off a short distance. "That would be just fine with me. Delay a while. Tell George you are still investigating. With all this other stuff on the farm, he doesn't need any extra problems."

She sighed. "And I don't know what I'm doing here. Nothing."

"Raising daughters."

"Yeah, well."

Ab moved closer and she leaned against him. "You know that's not what I was talking about. That's not what my life was supposed to be. At least not my whole life."

"Hey guys, come out here. Look what we've got!" George called from the glittering darkness. Sarah walked out toward the field. Ab followed. "We got our feet a bit wet, but don't yell at the girls. I take full responsibility." George was in a state of elation. "Anyway, don't look at their feet. Look at the fireflies. And look at the moon just coming up behind Merapi. God this is a beautiful place."

Frieda and Nettie were excitedly showing their little jars of glowing flies to Sarah and Nancy.

Ab stood next to George, a little ways off, looking up at the sky, his voice a bare whisper. "Maybe Susilo brought in an animal he knew had anthrax to start the outbreak. Sani got wind of it, killed off the old Communist. That restabilized the situation." He looked again at the sheets of fireflies turning on and off across the paddies. "Doesn't explain the ongoing problems, though." He kicked at the dirt in front of him. "Do you worry about yourself in this?"

George laughed as he turned toward the car, where the others were waiting. "That night at the party, Schechter told me his protection could only go so far, whatever that means, but I'm guessing a dead foreigner is too much trouble. The Indonesians would never risk it. Besides, if your theory is right, the killing in Boyolali should stop now, and I should get all the help I need to stamp out the anthrax at Susu Senang."

Ab stared a moment at the fireflies. What if this is a way to get at Suharto or one of his friends, he thought.

When they arrived back at the house, the children were asleep, and they carried them from the van into their bedroom and tucked them in.

Ab followed Sarah into the kitchen to help prepare some tea. She was in a meditative mood. She drummed her fingers on the counter, waiting for the water to boil. He put his hand on her moist shoulder, but she shrugged it off like a fly.

"Don't." She turned around. "I have this whole sense of not belonging here. Home is where you know which objects and people have power over you, for good or ill, and how to deal with that power. I guess that's followed me from when I was a kid. We didn't even belong to one of the main Mennonite migrations from Russia in the 1870s and the 1920s. Did I ever tell you? My brother and I were born in the mountains between the Soviet Union and India. My parents were trekking out of Russia after Stalin died. My Mom died in childbirth. I was raised by an Indian nanny. And then, when we finally got here, I mean there, to Canada, that promised land, we didn't even belong among the Mennonites, never mind all those *englische* folks. And then I go off and marry an *Englische*...and end up..." Her voice trailed off and she turned back to watch the tea water.

"Well, not exactly English, with a name like Grobowski."

She looked back at Ab, brushing her hair back with one hand. "You know what I mean. An *Englische* like everybody else in Canada, including the French. And George, well, he's even more *englische* than the English, he tries so hard. I really do weary of it sometimes."

Ab laid a hand gently on her shoulder, then withdrew it. "So what is it that he really wants?"

She leaned back against his hand. His fingers tingled. "I wish I knew. I wish I knew." When they turned back toward the living room with the tea tray, Nancy was standing in the doorway. Ab thought she looked more vulnerable and lonely and beautiful than anyone he had ever seen.

Later, driving home, Nancy wrapped a shawl tightly around herself. Ab smiled. "If you want to come to Canada, you must realize that this is not a cold evening. This is warm."

Nancy said nothing until they were back in the driveway. She seemed distracted, almost angry. He turned off the car and sat quietly again. Nancy started to get out, hesitated, then stayed. "You know, I really envy people like you and Sarah. You grew up knowing who you are. You take it for granted. You quarrel with your past. But it is *your* past. It is the roots from which you have sprung. Whatever the soil and the rain, you grow into some form of the same plant.

"I, on the other hand, don't even know what happened to the people who protected me and who raised me. I lost touch when they went back to North America. I barely know my own grandparents, who barely seem to know each other. I have only just recovered my past, and it is a stranger to me. My parents are a collage of stories and vague memories."

When they got out of the car, she came around to meet him, rested her hand on his chest, and kissed him lightly on the cheek. Her hand trailed down his side and he reached for her waist, but she pulled away. "George shouldn't mess around with that kris he gave you at the party," she said, "or with politics. Things aren't always what they seem in this country."

He watched her walk over to her motorbike. His mind was racing. How did she know about the kris? It had been dark in the street when George gave it to him and he and Nancy had not discussed it afterwards. "I don't have that kris anymore. Soesanto is examining it for a few days."

She swung her leg up over the seat and rested her foot on the pedal.

"Do you want to meet tomorrow and go for a walk on Malioboro? We could meet at Superman's." She seemed to ponder this. "Ten o'clock?"

"Okay," she said, as she pushed down the pedal to start and drove out into the street.

"I gave up my sunflower seeds," he said, quietly, to himself, into the darkness, as Budi pushed the gate shut and sat down again on his stool.

Chapter Seven

That night, Ab stared up at the slowly circling ceiling fan, and thought about Nancy. After years of mulling around in the past, his fear that this relationship might actually lead to something, some unexpected landing in a strange place, fed into a vague, almost disturbing, sense of excitement. He spoke to the ceiling, as he sometimes did, a kind of prayer, but just talking out his sense of never being at home, neither in the land of the English and French in Canada, nor here, and asked out loud if this was just the human condition, to feel marginalized. Everybody thinks he is on the outside, even all the insiders. Maybe even especially the insiders, since they have worked so hard to get there that they can't believe that they are there. "There" must be somewhere else. History played tricks like that. Maybe Nancy and he, two outsiders, were made for each other. Maybe here was "there."

He recalled something Nancy had said on the way home from George and Sarah's when he asked more about her parents and grandparents.

"Please don't ask me about them. If I tell you more about them, the way you have talked about your family, then I shall have to kill you, and I really don't want to."

She had reached over and rested her hand on his thigh at that point. He remembered that touch, and held his Dutch wife pillow more closely, and fell asleep.

The next day was Eid al-Fitr, the big feast day. He took a Colt down to Malioboro Ave, the big tourist street leading down to the *kraton*, the sultan's palace. The bus was stifling, and filled with smoke, and he was glad to be back out in the open air when it finally stepped down near the flower shops. On impulse, Ab stepped into the nearest flower stall and bought a large bouquet of orchids.

Nancy was waiting for him just down the street, leaning against the whitewashed wall in front of the Garuda Hotel. He saw her first, looking the other way down the street. Set against that white wall, her black hair still wet from a mandy, she was striking. In a long, loose dress made of the local black and gold batik, which set off both her hair and her pale skin, she looked both strong and lithe, vulnerable and on guard. It sent a quiver through him. I don't deserve this, he thought. He handed her the orchids just as she turned to check his direction.

"These are kisses, which I cannot give you here in the street or we'll be arrested for pornographic behaviour."

God what a stupid thing to have said. She looked at him, quizzically, seriously, then leaned up and kissed him on the cheek. "Let's go get a cup of coffee." She waved her hand toward the other end of the street. "The crowds are gathering up toward the kraton. Looks like it will be a very dense crowd today."

Superman's was an eating place down a small alley just off the main street of Malioboro. They played 1960's rock-and-roll and served food palatable to low-budget western travellers. Ab sometimes went there to just sit and listen to the music and drink the gritty coffee. Today, he ordered himself a tall glass of hot orange juice and a banana pancake. Nancy ordered a soda. Ab looked around. The place seemed fuller than normal, and the white, low-budget travellers looked very young. He could be a father to half these kids. He felt as if they were staring at him, a wealthy foreigner with a young Indonesian woman. What did they know about anything? Only what they saw. And what they saw was not what was. He wondered if Nancy sensed this as well, but he did not wonder for long.

After one glance around the room, she stood up and yanked Ab after her, announcing, so that everybody could hear, "Oh, forget this food. Let's go back to your place. I can give you *exactly* what you want." She winked extravagantly, grabbed his crotch, and then turned to walk out of the restaurant.

Back out in the alley, she put her arm through his. "Sorry. I don't know where that came from. Let's go stroll down towards the parade. Maybe we'll get to see the prince."

As they rounded the corner of the old Garuda Hotel on to the main part of the street, they were suddenly in the chaotic press of a crowd. He took her hand as they pushed their way toward the kraton.

They passed a man sitting on the sidewalk with a large wooden box full of black scorpions. Several scorpions were crawling on the pavement before him. He picked one up and allowed it to crawl across the palm of his hand. In his other hand, he was holding up a jar and explaining something to interested by-standers. "It's medicine," Nancy whispered into Ab's ear. "Scorpion oil. In small doses, good for eye infections and impotency."

He pushed his body back against Nancy and pressed his hand against her belly. She guided his hand gently away. "In high doses, it kills," she said. "Does it seem strange that one thing could do both?"

"No. As a matter of fact, we make use of such properties commonly in medicine. Nux vomica, for instance, is a seed which we use to stimulate a cow's stomach when she has indigestion."

"And the active ingredient is the poison strychnine."

Ab turned to face her. "How did you know that?"

"The tree is native to south Asia. We use it commonly here, both for its stimulation, and for its poison. Life is a matter of harmony, of balance, yes?" She smiled brightly and continued on down the sidewalk and he hurried after her.

"So strychnine is readily available?"

"Of course. Why?"

"Just thinking. Like you can get large quantities?"

She pondered whether to say anything, her face softening as she considered Ab. "If you know the right people. Your butcher in Gandringan for instance, or the farm manager Waluyo, if that's what you are wondering about."

The heat was blazing, suffocating. The sidewalk and street were full of large groups of students, as well as families, hawkers, becaks, bicycles, and the occasional foolish car. They passed a thin, wizened old man, with no legs, sitting on a straw mat on the sidewalk. He was holding out his hand and looking up plaintively, trying to catch someone's eye. His little tin bowl had a handful of rupiah coins in it. Nancy leaned down and set the orchids Ab had given her into his lap, and said something.

"What did you tell him?"

"A kiss for you, old man."

Ab put his arm around Nancy's waist and gave her a squeeze. He began to believe, after all these years, that he might even be falling in love, that maybe there was life beyond obsession or lust. Maybe this wasn't just an emergency landing because he had run out of fuel.

As they neared the palace, the crowd pressed in around them tighter and tighter. A parade was emerging from the palace grounds, a parade of flowers, mountains of food, local dignitaries and members of the once-grand and still-respected royal family. They were decked out in full Javanese regalia. At first, Ab felt the ripple of excitement in the crowd, body to body, a kind of public orgy, as the parade neared. Then, as the pressure increased, he had trouble getting air, as if he were a beach ball, the last air being squeezed out, ready to be stuffed away into some dark corner of the basement. He struggled, unsuccessfully, to move. The police were keeping the crowd back with whips, which they lashed out over the people's heads. He felt his hand and Nancy's being pulled away from each other, even as they grasped for each other more tightly. The air was thick with sweat and clove-scented tobacco. He tried to fight back, but found himself buffeted from side to side by the dense crowd of bodies, out of control. A whip flicked over his head. Someone behind him cried out. He felt as if he were drowning. With a sudden, fierce burst of energy, he elbowed his way back away from the palace until he was free of the crowd.

He found her back outside the Garuda, looking worried.

"Did you get whipped?"

He shook his head, wiping the sweat from his forehead with a handkerchief, still panting.

He bent over to his knees and breathed deeply and she rested her hand on his shoulder.

"Some people feel it is an honour to be whipped by the royal guard."

He straightened up. "I am not one of them."

She rested her hand on the sweaty small of his back. "Why don't we go back to your place? Have you ever had a good Indonesian massage?"

He lay on the bed, face-down in his sarong. She had tucked up her dress and was barefoot. He was not sure what to expect, something to do with sex, he thought, and then he thought how strong her hands were as she began working the rosemary-scented oil deeply into the base of his skull and down his neck. When her fingers dug into the muscles where his neck met the shoulder, he flinched with pain. I didn't have any pain there until you made it, he joked into the pillow, and then sank into a kind of pleasurable torpor as she encouraged the pain down his arms, into his hand, into her hands. It seemed at one point that she was walking on his back, her toes digging into all the painful sulci between the ribs, wiggling into the small of his back, her hands kneading his buttocks. The hands gripped his thighs and milked all the tension down toward his feet, pressing, wringing out all the tension and pain he never knew was there. The fan turned slowly overhead in the afternoon heat, barely stirring the air.

When he awoke, she was gone, and his mind was pleasurably empty. He found a business card with her name and the address of her computer shop on his dresser.

Chapter Eight

The next day, Ab went to his office at the university. The laboratory report from the medical school lay on his desk. It was positive for strychnine. No surprise there. When he turned on the computer, the files came up. Tri had already typed the data in again. Maybe it was a technical failure. Maybe there was no conspiracy. On the other hand, the dead cattle were all up around Gandringan, and at Susu Senang. They were all imported cows. Tri was at her desk, working on some other reports. She didn't know where Soesanto was. At another job maybe. What were Soesanto's other jobs? Ab realized that he didn't know. He didn't really know if Soesanto *had* other jobs, just that it was probable: a private veterinary clinic maybe, or selling drugs or feed.

Ab started going through the cattle disease and shipment records related to Boyolali, and Gandringan in particular. The deaths all fit the pattern, and in some ways it was just a straight-out case of butchers trying to make a little extra money in a place where a little extra money was hard to come by. He could hardly blame them. Yet there were oddities that made Ab nervous, things that seemed to speak of other, deeper currents in a cultural and political landscape he didn't understand, and, after what Soesanto and Nancy had said, wasn't sure he wanted to.

The cattle deaths had started only after Waluyo became manager. Ab thought he should go up to Gandringan, to talk to the Lura again, and explain his and Soesanto's theory. He could phone, but his Bahasa wasn't *that* good, and he didn't want to be making serious accusations without seeing the man face to face. In any case, if this theory was right, the outbreak up there would be over now, and there was no rush. The anthrax, on the other hand, would probably linger until…until what? He felt a mixture of inertia and anxiety. Where would he start working on this?

Tri left the room and then returned, and stood in the doorway. Ab looked up at her. She seemed nervous. For a moment she just stood there. "Dr. Ab?" She seemed to be struggling with what she was about to say. Then she took a deep breath and said all in one breathless sentence, "Dr. Ab please be careful, General Witono and Pak Sani are not playing games." Then she disappeared. Ab stared after her. What was *that* all about?

Tomorrow he would go to Gandringan, maybe nose around some other villages in Boyolali. Then visit the Susu Senang and talk to George again. It was, he thought, a plan. He felt better already. He returned to going through the files.

Later, he stopped in at Nancy's computer shop. It was a small store, sandwiched between a stationery store and a tape shop. The disco music from the tape store blasted out into the street, serving both as an advertisement for the store and as a sign of good will. At Christmas, the shops would be decked in bright lights, have a fake tree in the corner, and be blaring Christmas disco hits out into the street, a way of sharing their joy in the season. He could see several people sitting at counters listening to tapes through earphones, their heads bobbing up and down.

He pushed open the door of the computer store, and was relieved at the silence and the coolness. The shelves were well-stocked with IBM and Apple imitations, many of them made in Indonesia, with names like IBS and Appel. One shelf was filled with bound copies of just about any hardware or software manual you could imagine. The programs themselves could be had for the cost of the disk, and were not sold so much to make money as to keep customers happy. Not signing the international copyright convention had its advantages.

Nancy was at the back of the store, talking with Peter Findlay and Gladys White. "Well, I thought I recognized the car outside. This is the place to come then, if you want to buy a computer?"

"It's the place all right." Peter, suave and self-controlled as ever, reached for Ab's hand. Ab kissed Gladys on both cheeks. Even here, in a computer store, she exuded a kind of musky energy, not the languorous, indirect Indonesian kind; it was more blatantly intense and invasive, thought Ab, and he didn't like it.

She brushed her blond, curly locks away from her eyes. "Are you in the market for a computer?"

"I'm looking for some intelligent software to help me solve a deadly political outbreak in cows." Nancy gave him a don't-mess-with-the-customers look, which he tried to avoid.

Peter laughed. "Ah, a lifetime of fruitless work, I can assure you, in this country. Best to leave politics to the professionals."

"Well, when animals die on a project where I'm the vet, it is suddenly my job as a professional. I figure if I can trace the strychnine back from Boyolali to Susu Senang, I might be able to solve the anthrax problem as well. Unfortunately, the causal pathway may take some political detours."

Peter became suddenly solemn. "Ab, this is not a very good time to be prying into these kinds of things."

"Meaning what?" Ab was annoyed, and could feel his temper rising.

Peter eyed him coolly. "Several months before an election, the whole world is looking this way. The government will give the appearance of clean living and integrity." He paused, then added, "At any cost. Whoever is causing these problems with the imported cows is not playing games. I would just leave that problem alone and deal with parasites or something."

Playing games. It was the second time he had heard that today. He wondered if someone was trying to send *him* a message. "It's just a bunch of cows, Peter." But he wondered: how did Peter know that the deaths were only in imported cows? He tried to remember with whom he had discussed this: George and Soesanto. He couldn't remember if he had told Nancy, but she might have overheard George and him talking at the dinner. And the killer obviously knew.

Peter paused, weighing his words carefully. "The farmland those cows are on is a piece of fertile land on the most densely populated island on earth. This is all about control, Ab. It's all about power."

Gladys put her hand on her husband's arm and squeezed it. "I think we've had enough of that," she said brightly. "So, how is Tri working out in the office? She used to be *so* loved at the Australian consulate, I tell you, and they were sorry, well, I think a lot of the *men* were sorry, to lose her." She laid her head against Peter's shoulder and winked at Ab as she said this. Her husband pulled away, annoyed.

"People's previous work records are not a matter of public discussion," he said through his teeth.

Nancy continued to focus her I'm-busy-with-a-customer-who-might-actually-buy-something look on Ab.

Ab thought he had heard enough, and didn't want to upset Nancy. "Yeah, well, maybe I'll go listen to some tapes next door for a bit."

Nancy relaxed and smiled. "Good idea. I'll come around as soon as I take care of these customers."

Ab walked next door to the tape shop. What was that about Tri? Had she been a plant by the Australians? That would explain how Peter knew that only imported cattle were affected. Jeeze these spooks had their hirelings everywhere, and if they thought that a few sermons about danger would somehow stop him, well, then they didn't know him very well, did they. He had grown up with sermons about the dangers of hell. Suharto's dictatorship was nothing.

Selecting several tapes of traditional Javanese music at random, Ab inserted one into an empty player, put the earphones on, and closed his eyes. The ringing, percussive sounds of the gamelan filled his head. The notes seemed at first to be random, leading nowhere, deep, sinister gongs and lighter, bell-like rings scattered in a dark space. He tried to imagine the slim, dazzlingly clad dancers of the Ramayana or Mahabharata tales gliding or leaping across a stage, each slight, improbable motion of the finger or head bearing great significance. It seemed like life here—the random events of millions of people on a small island, the pregnant nuances he was sure he was missing. The crashes and gongs in his head gathered momentum, and from the sounds came images of dead cows, Sarah, George, and Soesanto, Nancy arose serene as a Buddha, signalling something of life-and-death importance with a slight movement of her wrist.

When he felt the real Nancy's hand on his shoulder, he almost jumped off the stool. He pulled the earphones off. "God, you scared me."

She picked up the tape box and turned it over in her hand. "You like the gamelan?"

"Like. Don't like. I don't understand it. I think if I could understand gamelan music, I could begin to understand this place. Understand you. It's all or nothing, I think, on this one. If I can solve one, I will have solved them all."

She laughed lightly. "Moonlight and running water."

"Moonlight and running water?"

"That's what they say the gamelan sounds like. If you understand moonlight and running water, you will understand me also. You want to go out for supper?" She rested her hand on his shoulder and then massaged the back of his neck.

He turned the tape over in his hand. "I think I'll buy this. A souvenir to mull over on cold prairie nights." He motioned to the girl behind the counter that he wished to buy the tape he had been listening to. She filled out a bill, which she handed to Ab to take over to a cashier wicket, where he paid out the equivalent of three dollars, which was slightly more expensive than, say, a tape of the Beatles would be, since foreign-music tapes in the country were mostly pirated, while Indonesian ones were actually recorded here, with paid performers. From the cashier, he received a receipt, which he took to a pick-up counter. By the time he had made this little circle in the store, the tape was waiting for him, wrapped in brown paper.

"Talk about labour-intensive systems," he said as they went to where his car was parked. "They'd never get away with that in Canada. Management would say it's inefficient."

"Did you have to wait long for service?"

"No."

"Was the tape expensive?"

"No."

"Do you think somebody's losing money on that business?"

He laughed. "Okay, okay, so it's efficient. I'm just saying, in Canada..."

"In Canada, perhaps you don't value people. Perhaps your economy is based on the stupid notion that people exist for the economy, and not vice versa. Perhaps you do not depend on each other to survive. You depend on *things*. Here, if you do not have people to depend on, you have nothing. You could begin by understanding that."

"Are you sure you are just twenty-two? You seem to understand way too much."

She smiled slightly. "A short life, but very intense. Before you get into the car, we'll need to load up my motorbike."

His shirt clung sweatily to his back as he loaded the motorbike into the back of the car. *So who am I depending on?* They got in and Ab pulled out into traffic, almost bumping a becak bearing two blond-haired camera-laden tourists, all legs and elbows like a couple of large, bony, Charolais calves stuffed into a baby carriage.

"Dutchmen, come back to see the old colony," he mumbled.

"They're harmless now. They can come back and spend all the money they want. At least they haven't come back to try to save us from something." It was a dig, and Ab knew it, but he bit his tongue. Nancy watched the becak stop while one of the men climbed out to take a picture of the other.

"You know, all those people who are telling you to back off? You should listen to them."

"You mean I should listen to you?"

"Of course. And Peter."

"And Soesanto."

"Him too? So you see."

She watched a becak full of flowers careen around a corner and barely miss ramming into a bicycle. A funeral wreath flew off the top and landed on the cyclist. The becak driver and the cyclist both laughed. "He has the kris right now, right?"

"Who, Soesanto? Yeah. Yes, he does."

"Good. At least you and George are not mixed up in that." She gently massaged the inside of his thigh. Ab wondered if she realized what that gesture did to him. She seemed to be lost in thoughts entirely different from those going through his own mind.

They were at a red light. He watched a girl walk by with a tray of saté on her head. She had that slow, languid walk that seemed like pure sexiness to Ab, but must surely be just a slow adaptation to the heat. Her hips moved rhythmically.

"Do you like it?"

He startled, blushed. "What?"

"The way that girl walked."

"Oh. I was just thinking how someone like me could easily misinterpret it."

"Yes. As you probably did. Like many other things. Did you know that, besides being a veterinarian, Soesanto was an active socialist intellectual in the early sixties? He did popular adaptations of the wayang kulit shadow puppet plays in the villages. He was a *dalang,* singing and playing all the parts."

"Soesanto?" Ab tugged at his beard, wishing he could chew on some sunflower seeds. He tried to imagine Soesanto singing. "I thought everyone who works for any government institution was screened for latent communism. How could he get through that? An American degree and a gimpy leg would hardly hide such blatant latency."

She was silent a moment. "The handy thing about latency is that those who have power can use it to whatever ends they please. When people say 'veiled' this or 'latent' that, it's a cover for manipulation. The government needs educated people. Not many left after 1966." She paused. "Or maybe he is a right wing plant to expose real latent Communists."

"I don't think I believe that."

"Which could just mean he's good at his job." She paused, as if wondering if she should say something more, then added, "Or he has had friends in high places."

"Who?"

She shrugged, waved her hand in the air. "High places. That would explain a lot."

"Yeah, but a theory can explain a lot of things and still not explain the crucial things."

Nancy shrugged her shoulders. "One way or another, I only want to say, if Soesanto tells you to stay clear, he knows something."

"If Soesanto were a plant, this whole cattle-poisoning business could be a big frame-up to set somebody up. George suggested there's a plot afoot to assassinate Suharto, or, at the very least, one of his generals, like Witono. But maybe it's really all just a sting to catch the plotters."

"Could be."

"If Soesanto is genuine, then he himself could be in danger if he gets too deeply involved."

"Could be."

"Could be, could be, could be. But what is?"

She reached up and massaged the back of his neck. "Soon, if you continue to think like that, you will understand the gamelan," she said.

He reached past the stick shift and rested his hand briefly on her knee. "But only if I persist, and ignore all this advice I've been getting to back off and leave."

"Sometimes your life is worth more than understanding music."

"And sometimes, understanding the music is the whole point of life. What else is there?"

They ate rice and fried chicken, cooked over an open grill, at a sidewalk restaurant on Jalan Kaliurang, the main road from the city center going up the slope of Mount Merapi. The street was filled with people talking, smoking, debating. Ab was watching people go by. A three-year-old with a cigarette in her mouth. Three young college students in white shirts and dark trousers, their heads together, looking over their shoulders as they talked. Four young girls with Muslim headscarves, several steps behind the boys, giggling. When he looked up, he found Nancy staring at him. She reached over and touched his hand where it lay on the table.

"I'll miss you," she whispered.

Startled, he turned to face her, took both her hands in his, and leaned across the table. "What do you mean?"

"When you leave," she said.

"So come with me."

She pulled her hands away and, it seemed to Ab, brushed a tear from the corner of her eye, then reached forward and patted Ab's hand. "Ah, Ab, Ab, I wish. If you only knew how much I really wish."

"What?"

"I think I'd better go home. Help me get the motorbike out of the back of your car."

He was left, sitting by himself, wondering what had just happened. His heart felt wrenched. At home, he lay awake for a long time, and had just drifted to sleep when the call from the minaret startled him awake again. It still looked dark to him outside, but the muezzin singing through the loudspeaker must have been able to distinguish the dark thread from its background, his sign that sunrise had begun. The first, faint, unseen rays of the sun must be creeping into the sky. Ab closed his eyes, and drifted off to sleep again.

Chapter Nine

The sun was already baking in through the window when he awoke again. It was now two days after Eid al-Fitr. If he went up to Gandringan this morning, he could at least sort out the mechanics of the outbreak. Get the easy part out of the way. He could stay overnight, get some fresh air, and maybe get a handle on the more difficult part. He rolled over to get out of bed, then looked back at his pillow and remembered Nancy, the way she had pressed against him before she got on to her motorbike, how much he had wanted to invite her over for the night, and his confusion.

He slipped on a sarong to go to the washroom, splashed cold water over himself, dried off, slipped into his jeans and a clean cotton shirt. He realized with a sudden pang how much she had suddenly become part of his life, how he missed her when they weren't together. Did she feel the same? But where was she now? Work? He didn't want to be checking on her too much, didn't want to scare her off with his nosing around, some kind of control freak. Still, what did he *really* know about her? He sat on the edge of the bed with his head in his hands for a moment before going out to the dining room.

He could hear Tina, the housecleaner, busying herself with cleaning up food crumbs in the kitchen. He poked his head out into the garage. Pak Budi was sitting on his stool by the gate. He stood up when he saw Ab. "Selamet bagi," Ab said. *Good morning.* Budi grinned, toothlessly. Ab had never had a conversation with the old man. He realized how invisible Budi had become to him, so that he hardly noticed when the gate was opened for him, and closed, as if the man was simply another sort of automatic gate opener. Ab had no idea what the old man did when he wasn't sitting at the gate. Where was he from? Did he have a family? Kids? Grandkids? He probably only spoke Javanese. Ab went back into the house and Budi sat down. Ab wondered what exactly this old guy could guard him against, but he remembered Sarah's argument about servants. This wasn't about somebody doing work for you. This was about spreading the wealth. He sighed.

Ab fixed himself a plate of greasy fried eggs and rice, drank a cup of the black sludge that passed for coffee, and left the dishes in the sink for Tina. He was already at the car before he turned around and went to the kitchen to tell Tina that he wouldn't likely be back until the following day, so she could also take the day off.

It was going to be a hot day. He could feel it in the air, already now at eight-thirty. At the office, he dug into his own personal cupboard of supplies: needles, micro-hematocrit tubes, a microscope, a portable centrifuge. Not much. The Canadian International Development Agency representative in Ottawa had said that they were not to be providing supplies. That was an Indonesian responsibility under the contract. George had said that General Witono, the project overseer in Jakarta, had bought himself a new tinted-window Toyota Camry. All Ab knew was that none of the money for improving the diagnostic facilities actually materialized in Yogyakarta. It was just him and Soesanto and a computer. The university itself was broke. How was Ab supposed to do his job? He loaded up his car, and then realized that he had forgotten to talk to Soesanto about this trip. He had been busy with Nancy.

At Soesanto's house, the old lady didn't come to the door when Ab shook the gate. He could hear the birds, a tumbling wave of whistles and rustles and screams from behind the house, but nothing else. It was already nine o'clock. If he wanted to get anything done up around Gandringan, he had better leave soon. Depending on traffic, it could take two or three hours.

He scribbled a note and stuck it to Soesanto's gate with bandage tape. Soesanto could come up later on his own. Ab wondered if he should be worried, but set that thought aside. If anyone could take care of himself, it was Soesanto.

He passed Nancy's computer shop. The shutters were up and the shop looked open. He thought about stopping, but recalled how she had reacted when he came into the shop yesterday. Best to keep love and work separate. He had barely gotten to the edge of town when a police car with its siren screaming barrelled down the middle of the road, clearing away traffic. He pulled off to the side. In a few moments a single black Mercedes limousine sped by, heading toward Klaten and Solo. Another police car was close behind it. Ab pulled back out into the stream of traffic that closed in behind the speeding dignitary. He pulled over at a police kiosk at the next intersection to ask who had passed in the car. Ab could see his reflection in the policeman's sunglasses.

The policeman shrugged. Someone important.

"How important? General Witono? Pak Sani? President Suharto?"

The policeman then decided he had said enough and, as if Ab no longer existed, went back to stand by the road with his thumbs under his belt.

Ab shifted into gear and sped off down the road, his mind churning, his heart pounding. What if the assassination plot was in progress? What should he do? Stay out of politics, said the clause in his CIDA contract. He knew he was in denial. He didn't want to think about it. After passing Klaten, he debated with himself whether to continue on the main road or take the scenic, pot-holed, barely passable scenic cross-country route. At the intersection, he pulled off to the side and took a deep breath. He was a god-damned veterinarian. He would work on animal diseases and leave the rest to someone else.

He headed cross-country. The road wound up, away from the sizzling, dusty heat of the plains. He swerved to miss a big pothole in the middle of the road, and then again to miss a horse-cart.

The sun was hammering down mercilessly when he pulled into the yard of the Pak Lura. He stopped in the shade near the edge of the yard and climbed out. The Lura came out to greet him, shaking hands and then touching his breast. Ab did the same.

And to what did the Lura owe the pleasure of this visit?

"I just wanted to check if there had been any more deaths. I hadn't heard from you and hoped you didn't forget." He realized that he could have phoned, if that had been all there was to it.

The Lura laughed. No, he didn't forget. Yes, there had been a couple more die the day before Eid al-Fitr, but since then, nothing. He smiled at Ab and added that in neither case had he known beforehand that they were going to die. When Ab asked if it would be possible to talk to the farmers, the Lura called in one of his helpers and discussed the matter vigorously in Javanese with him for a few minutes. Then he switched to Bahasa Indonesia, and explained that the Canadian who lived where there was snow and ate birdseed wanted to speak with the farmers who had lost some cattle. Ab wondered what the Javanese part of the discussion had been about.

Ab went with the Lura as translator. At the first farm, they stood with the wiry, shirtless farmer, leaning on the bamboo rail outside an empty cattle shed. The old man's cow had died like those of the other farmers. It was late at night, so suddenly. It was lucky the butcher, Pak Sumiarto, happened by when the cow died, or the meat would have been wasted.

So the butcher came by?

The Lura asked again, to make sure. Yes, the butcher had come by just as the cow was dying and had bought the meat from him, so he could at least have some money and not lose everything.

"Just like with Pak Machmud. And what time of day was this?"

"It was before first light."

"Just when you would expect the butcher out wandering around, yes?" The old farmer stared thoughtfully at Ab.

Was there anything else? Ab wished Soesanto were here to help him probe a little deeper. Finally, after a long pause, the farmer added that this disease was never seen here before the new dairy cows started coming in, the ones that came from America. He had heard that they had a similar disease down at the main farm. Was that true?

Ab shrugged. "They have a different disease."

"I think we will not take cows from that place again," said the old man in Bahasa Indonesia.

Every farm was the same story. Either they died without anyone seeing, or they were very stiff and then fell over and had convulsions. With a few exceptions, mostly occurring early in the course of this "epidemic," they reluctantly admitted that the butcher had come by and purchased their meat at salvage prices. It wasn't much, but was better than nothing. Yes, they had received replacement cows as well. And in the days since the feast at Eid al-Fitr, there had been no cows dying. They all said they had no interest in that development project anymore.

Ab turned to the Lura as they drove back from the last farm. "I cannot think of very many diseases that strike only in the evening or at night, or that take a holiday at Eid al-Fitr. I do not know very many butchers that wander around the village at night, doing good deeds for farmers."

"There *was* a high demand for meat at Eid al-Fitr," the Lura commented. He paused. "Perhaps it would be good for me to have a little talk with the butcher."

"Yes," Ab added, "before he slips away to visit his grandmother in Jakarta."

The Lura laughed.

That night, Ab lay down on the hard bed in the guest room of the Lura's house and hugged his Dutch wife. He rolled over on to his back, loosened his sarong, and watched a *cecak* stalking a moth on the ceiling. He tried not to think about the scenario of plots and counter-plots that George had laid out for him. What could he do? It really wasn't his business. The *cecak* zapped the giant moth and slowly drew the struggling insect into its mouth. The lizard sat there, perfectly still, with the wriggling tail and wings protruding from its mouth.

It was still dark when he was awakened, not by a call from the mosque, but by the blaring of a radio into the cool mountain air, and by the persistent crowing of a kampung rooster just outside the open window. He stood up, stiffly, and pulled the shutters open. Yes, it really was Abba resonating among the trees. *Mama Mia*. He tightened up his sarong, slipped outside and walked to the roofless, concrete-walled washing-up area at the corner of the yard. Someone was in there already bathing, a kerosene lantern set on one corner of the four-foot wall. Ab could just see over the top of the wall. A woman stood up and poured water over herself, a glassy stem of water breaking with a splash of light over her sleek black hair and then down over her low-hanging breasts, the nipples long and pulled-at looking. Twenty-something and a mother several times over no doubt. He looked away and squatted down on the ground just outside the entrance. In a few minutes she came out. She stared at him for a minute as if trying to figure out what kind of lowly pink-skinned animal he might be, lurking around the washing area in the morning. Then she walked away, rubbing a towel in her hair.

Ab poured a bucket of the icy water over himself. The sharp slap of water caused him to suck in his breath and shiver. The bar of soap that sat on the edge of the mandy was small and hard. He soaped himself up and then rinsed. Wrapping himself back in his sarong, he stepped back out into the open air. The music was still ricocheting off the walls of the little gully the village was in. He returned to the house, slipped into his clothes, and walked in the direction of the music.

About fifty yards away, he followed the music down a mud path and along a bamboo fence to a pole barn. There was a dairy cow tied to one corner of the barn, and a kerosene lantern hung up above. Just below the kerosene lantern, on the wall of the barn, was a big poster of Michael Jackson: *Thriller*. Barely out in North America, already pirated into the back country of Java. Hunched beside the cow on a three-legged stool, the farmer was milking his cow. Beside the farmer, a radio was blasting the music. Some extension agent must have once told him that if cows are played music they give more milk. No one ever told him the difference between music that was jarring and music that was soothing. Maybe all western music sounded the same. Like gamelan to Ab.

Ab approached him and greeted him with the few words of Javanese that he knew, then pointed at the cow and made signs of milking. The man nodded and continued milking. No, he interrupted him again, *he, Ab,* wanted to milk. He pointed at the cow and then at himself. The man laughed, thinking this hilarious. *Maybe he thinks I think I am a cow? Maybe he thinks I want to breed her? Whatever.* Ab shrugged his shoulders and walked away, the music thudding after him like thrown rocks.

Breakfast at the Lura's, at least this morning, was a full plate of fried rice with an egg on top. The Lura's wife served and then, as always, withdrew to eat by herself in the kitchen. The Lura apologized for not having any bread and then remarked, with approval, again, as always, that Ab was already eating rice.

Yes, Ab assured him once again. He was already eating rice.

After breakfast had been cleared away, the Lura spoke. "We had a discussion with the butcher yesterday evening." Ab searched his face, in vain, for what kind of "discussion" it might have been. "He insists that the killing of the cows started before he was involved, and that, at first, he only walked the streets at night looking for dying animals, to salvage them for meat." He paused. "Later, when he needed more meat, he used some strychnine to make some sick."

"And do you believe him?"

"We asked the questions in such a way…yes, I believe him."

"So where do we go from here? Does the butcher know who else had killed cows before he started, or in neighbouring villages? Did he say who provided him with magnets and poison? His cousin from Susu Senang maybe?"

The Lura arose. "I think it is better that you leave now. Thank you so much for discovering the cause of this illness." Ab thought his voice was strained, but there seemed to be no room for argument. He got up to leave.

"Well, we know at least part of the story."

The Lura herded him toward the car. "I think we know enough now. I hope you have a happy trip home."

Chapter Ten

Ab took the long way home, the Boyolali-Solo road, and then the road that would take him past the Susu Senang turn-off outside of Klaten. Driving down to the plains, Ab felt as if he were sinking into a hot, hazy soup. Behind him, the mountains wavered and disappeared into a blazing blue haze. He rolled up the windows and put on the air conditioner. Well, that part was settled. Now, what to do about the anthrax at the main farm?

Through the haze in front of him Ab saw a truck and a Colt running toward him side by side. Looked like they were coming at about eighty kilometres per hour. He swerved between two mahogany trees at the side of the road, slalomed around them, and skidded back on to the road. His heart was racing. The trouble with this country was you never knew when people were actually trying to kill you and when this was just the normal course of events. He wiped the sweat out of his eyes and turned up the air conditioner. He reached instinctively over to the passenger seat and wished he hadn't given up sunflower seeds. He passed the turnoff to Susu Senang and kept going. He was thinking about Nancy.

It was noon when he arrived back. Old Budi opened the gate for him. He had barely stepped into the coolness of his living room when the phone rang. He sat down. He could hear Tina in the kitchen.

The phone rang twice, three times, four times. One thing Ab had learned in veterinary practice was that telephone ringing, like hemorrhaging, eventually stopped without any human interference. He stood up and was going to reach for it when it stopped. Beside the phone, on the buffet, was a package, something loosely wrapped in newspapers. Something Nancy had left lying around? Slowly, he opened the paper. It was the kris. The phone rang again. He picked up the receiver. It was Sarah.

"Ab? Listen. George went to see your friend Soesanto last night. He seemed very upset when he came back. He said he dropped something off at your place, but you weren't there and he needed to talk to you as soon as possible, that you shouldn't under any circumstances sleep at home tonight. You might be in danger." She was quiet. "Ab? Are you there?"

"I'm here." He was staring at the kris.

"He said you should talk to him before you see Nancy again. He didn't explain. He told me to keep phoning until I talked to you. He seemed in such a rush. He had to go out to the farm early today. One of the big shots from Jakarta, rumour had it maybe even Suharto, was supposed to visit, and he went out extra early to make sure everything was okay. He said he'd be back well before noon. I'm worried. When he said he needed to talk to you, he seemed really agitated. He wouldn't tell me anything. I tried calling earlier but you weren't in. I phoned John Schechter. He said he would check, but said George might just have gotten caught in the middle of a traffic jam or something."

Ab picked up the kris, turned it over in his hand. It felt warm. "You phoned Schechter? Why?" He pulled the knife partly out from the sheath. There seemed to be flecks of rust caught on the etching.

"He and George seem to have been talking a lot lately. Why? Shouldn't I have?"

"Sure. That's fine. Schechter's right. It's probably just the traffic." Or maybe the Jakarta General took up a lot of time. The escorted car had been yesterday. Witono must have arrived a day early. If there had been a plot, it had probably been foiled. So why did George go today? Had he not been informed? And what had upset him at Soesanto's? He put the knife back into its paper wrapper.

George had said something about Nancy. What? Ab would love to just take the day off and spend it with her. Maybe he could give *her* a massage this time, maybe they could finish that dangling conversation from the other night. Sarah sounded really worried. Maybe Nancy could go along with him. He picked up the wrapped kris, walked out to the car, and threw it into the back seat. Budi smiled and bowed as Ab backed rapidly out into the street.

Ab took a brief detour to check on Soesanto. He'd try the house first, as he seemed to have been avoiding the office lately. Maybe he could fill in what George wanted to say. Ab's note from two days ago was gone. The house looked shut up, the birds quiet at this time of day. He rattled the gate. No answer. On an impulse, he scrambled over the gate and wandered around the side of the house toward the back. The birds were everywhere, in the trees over his head, on top of the screen, climbing up and down both sides of the open wire-mesh aviary door, squawking, singing, ruffling feathers.

"Soesanto?" No answer. The back door to the kitchen was open and he stepped inside, waiting until his eyes grew accustomed to the dimness. There were two small parakeets pecking at something on the counter. "Soesanto?" His voice hung heavily in the air, like a wet towel on the wash-line with a bird sitting on it. He walked slowly into the house. The next rooms were even darker. The air smelled feathery and musty. There seemed to be someone sitting at the desk at the far end of the room. "Soesanto?" His voice broke. No answer. Ab walked slowly across the heavy, dark silence of the room. The glass door to the case where Soesanto had kept his krisses was propped open against the wall. A red and purple and green parrot-like bird was scrabbling among the knives. *Black-capped lory. I remember, Soesanto.*

As he walked over to the figure a tawny bird with black markings and long silky white and yellow tail feathers lifted from Soesanto's shoulder, skimmed over Ab's head, the feathers dragging across his scalp, and flew out the door. *Lesser bird of paradise. I will always remember.* He stopped, his heart pounding, and placed his hand on the shoulder. The head fell back as he pulled, and his fingers slipped down into a slit near the base of Soesanto's neck. What had he said? A Balinese execution, also good for sneaking up behind someone. The body was cool and blotchy, beginning to self-destruct in the heat. Ab looked around the room in slow motion, breathing deeply, while a thought formed in his head. There were no signs of struggle. Either someone had been very quiet or it was someone Soesanto knew, and he had sat down at the desk to check something.

Ab sank to the floor, his back against the wall. Call the police? What had Soesanto said about "when the thought police come"? Ab ran his hands back over his head.

"Flecks of rust on the blade," he said out loud. "Mischief, my good friend. No shit." He pushed himself to his feet again and stood behind the body. He hugged Soesanto from behind, the already rank smell of decomposition in his nostrils, a mixture of fear and anger tearing around inside his head, tears forcing their way from his eyes. There was nothing that could save Soesanto now, nothing that could see justice done without also getting Ab into really deep shit with both the Canadian and Indonesian governments. There was nothing.

The ground trembled under his feet and he rolled back on to his heels. "Damn!" he shouted as loudly as he could. And then he thought: George.

The road to Solo was jammed. Buses, minibuses, trucks, people, people hanging out the doors of the buses, herded like cattle into the backs of trucks. Four people to a bicycle. Bicyclists hanging on to the hands of motorcyclists as they dodged and wobbled in and out among the traffic. People walking in groups down the road. And in between, the express buses from Solo and Bali and the Honda Accords and new Toyota Camrys with tinted windshields at one hundred kilometers an hour. There were several dead chickens on the road today. He imagined there were some dead people too, but there was a tendency to clean those up faster. People around here didn't like to see messy things like blood out on the road, out in the open.

◇◇◇

It seemed to take forever to get to the farm. In a few hours daylight would plunge into night. Waluyo came toward him at the gate, waving his hands in the air. "Too many problems, too many problems," he exclaimed. "Yesterday morning, General Witono come. Too many dead cows, he say. Then today Mr. George..." He waved in the direction of the back of the pens. George's truck was parked to one side of the yard. The young cattle were kept in roofed-over concrete pens with feed bunks along one side. The ones that were left seemed sleek and healthy. He walked toward the back, where the bigger cattle were kept. There were several cattle bodies out back, one with her feet straight up, and George bent over her. Ab came up behind him, agitated.

"George! What did I tell you?! No post mortems! Jesus, do you have some sort of death wish? I just saw Soesanto. You won't believe..." He reached to grab George's shoulder and when he did so, the body fell back against his legs. There was blood on George's arms from where they had been inside the cow, and blood on his hair from where it had rested against the incision. There were no autopsy knives visible.

Ab reached down the neck for a jugular pulse. His fingers slipped down into a slit just at the collar-bone. He felt as if his hand were being sucked into the body and held there, against the collar-bone, and he fell into a squatting position. The body was slouched back against him, his hand still in the wound. He couldn't move. Soesanto. George. Jesus. Not this. A noise near his leg startled him, and he turned to see a brightly coloured snake slither into the water of the canal and swim away, head held straight up out of the water.

He turned to where he had last seen Waluyo. There was no one.

Chapter Eleven

Ab knew before he had finished telling his story at the police station in Klaten that he was going to be in trouble. He had blood on his hands and he was babbling on about two murders and Balinese executions. He was a fool, and should have simply phoned the veterinary college or one of the expatriates back in town for help. He did have the presence of mind, before leading the police back to Susu Senang, to go to the bathroom at the station and wash off the worst of the blood.

He led the police between the cattle pens like a zombie, seeing nothing, his mind racing from Soesanto to George and back again. *What's going on here? Soesanto, what does your government not want us to know now? What did George get himself into? What should I have done? What could I have done?*

As the police put the body in the back of their mini-pick-up, Ab came back to the side of the cow and walked slowly around her. George had not been doing an autopsy. He would not have been doing an autopsy on an animal that looked this much like anthrax, not after all they had talked about. It was a set-up. "Dr. Ab! You will come now." The policeman took Ab by the arm and led him to the truck.

In the Klaten station, Ab was given several forms to fill out, and questioned in some detail about what had happened.

After the initial questioning, the police chief left him to sit on a hard bench in the front office, and retreated to his office with several other officers for consultations. Ab went to the bathroom to wash up again. He stared at his face in the mirror, then went out to the secretary at the front desk and asked if he might leave. No, he would have to stay. Could he make a phone call? His wife would be worried. The secretary hesitated, then allowed him access to the phone. He pulled Nancy's business card out of his pocket. She might know what to do.

The phone rang four times before Nancy answered. "Sorry, I was out back doing some inventory."

When he explained the situation to her, she was silent for several minutes. "I thought you were still up in Boyolali," she said quietly. "I'll—I'll see what I can do." He could see the police chief come back into the room and talk to the secretary, pointing at him. He frowned, then remonstrated her angrily. He was stalking over toward Ab.

"Listen, Nancy, I have to go. Please try to do something. Don't you have friends somewhere?"

The police chief took the phone receiver from his hand and set it back down. "According to our information, you do not have a wife," he said.

"Well, she's sort of like a wife, you know?" Ab smiled knowingly at him, but the chief's face was expressionless. He placed a hand on Ab's shoulder and guided him to a small room at the back. "Anyway, in my country we're allowed at least one phone call."

"You are not in your country. You will wait here. No more phone calls." There were two hard wooden chairs in the room, which was bare except for the required pictures of the president and vice-president. In the next room, there was a heated discussion going on. The phone rang. More discussion. They were carrying on in Javanese, so that Ab couldn't understand.

Suddenly the door swung open and the police chief strode in, thumbs behind his belt. "We have decided that Mr. George died from anthrax. It is too bad. You may go now. But you must be gone from this country in one week."

Ab stood up. "But..." Ab was about to say something about the stab wound, but bit his tongue. "One week? What about Dr. Soesanto? He didn't die of anthrax. What about the contract with the government? I am to be helping Dr. Soesanto...helping the veterinary college. I have another full year on my contract. I have to train Soesanto's replacement. I can't just leave like that."

The chief reached out and took Ab's hand, shook it, and then touched himself on the breast. "Do not worry. The police in Yogyakarta have been informed about Dr. Soesanto. They will take care of that. As for the university—it was here before you, and will continue long after you are gone. We all will, insh'Allah."

Ab was sure he was missing something important. It was all happening too fast. He stepped outside, then turned back. "The body? May I take the body with me?"

The police chief looked weary and angry at the same time. "You will leave now. The body is none of your business."

"But he is my friend, and his wife will want to see the body, and she will want to send it back to Canada for proper burial. Do you not respect religious rites in Indonesia?"

The chief scowled, and then seemed to soften. "Listen. This is not my doing. I will see what I can do. We shall seal the body into a proper coffin for transport to Canada," he said. He ran a hand back over his head, and then added, quietly, "If we are provided with sufficient money to do so, I think we can do this."

Ab reached for his wallet. "How much is sufficient? Will a hundred thousand rupiahs do?"

The chief looked thoughtful, as if calculating some costs.

"Here is two hundred thousand. It's all I have." Ab did a quick calculation in his head: two hundred dollars. In Canadian terms, cheap.

The police chief took it, glanced at it and looked around, as if he had lost something. "We shall prepare the coffin for you for shipment. We will even make arrangements at the airport so that you do not have problems. You may pick it up here tomorrow around noon."

The evening prayer calls were blasting out from the mosques by the time Ab reached Yogyakarta again, and darkness was dropping. It was only at this point that he remembered having seen Waluyo, and his sudden, inexplicable disappearance. In none of his reports to the police had he mentioned this. He must have been in shock. His first impulse was to turn around and go back to Klaten, but he stopped himself. They would be closed by now, and it would just make more trouble for himself. Besides, they would surely get around to questioning Waluyo, since he was the head manager—wouldn't they? And what about Soesanto? How would that be investigated?

Ab's mind was racing in all directions. What had George wanted to tell him? What was that about talking to him before he talked to Nancy? Well, it was too late for that, wasn't it? Ab tried to push his mind laterally. Waluyo seemed the obvious choice all around, but he was probably working for someone. What were some other possibilities? What about John Schechter? Would he kill? Ab remembered the look he gave across the dance floor and George's none-too-subtle advances to Claudia. And the heated exchange at the fairgrounds. Ab shuddered. No, that was impossible. Expatriates might fight and copulate, but they didn't kill. Or did they? What if John had found out? How did Soesanto fit into this? Was the kris making mischief? Was 1966 going on and on and on?

Budi answered at the gate. Tina had gone home already, assuming that there would be no cooking this evening. He stood by the buffet a moment and remembered the kris. Returning to the car, he picked up the package from where he had thrown it, turned it over in his hands, then stuffed it into the overnight bag he had taken to Gandringan, and which was still sitting on the back seat. How had the knife ended up at his place? Had George picked it up from Soesanto and brought it over? Was that what he had wanted to talk about? And what did Nancy have to do with this? Why had George said something about Nancy?

He drove over to George and Sarah's house and stopped out front in the dark lane. How do you tell a woman you loved—

love?—that her husband is dead? Do you say, "I'm sorry, but…" Do you just look into her eyes, and then she knows? And you realize that this changes everything about your lives? Every option he could think of seemed trite and maudlin. George was dead. He climbed out of the car and went to the door. When the door finally responded to his knocking, Sarah was there. She threw her arms around him and clung to him and wept into his beard. Over her shoulder, he could see Nancy sitting on the couch. Gently, he stroked Sarah's thin blond hair. There was nothing to be said.

Ab and Nancy stayed late at Sarah's, to keep her company. Frieda and Nettie had been in bed when Nancy had arrived with the news. Sarah said she would tell them in the morning. She had no idea how, none whatsoever. Sarah agreed that Ab and Nancy should go pick up the coffin, while she and the girls packed up to leave. She would arrange for a flight tomorrow afternoon. She gave Ab an extra set of keys for George's truck, which was still out at Susu Senang. They'd have to use the truck to bring the coffin, and would have to go by the main farm to pick it up before they went to the police station. Ab thought Sarah seemed suddenly very clinically efficient, and mused that this ability to act in a crisis would have made her a good veterinarian, better than him. When Ab and Nancy left, Sarah was standing in the doorway to the girls' room, staring into the darkness.

Outside, Ab and Nancy sat on the stairs and he put his arm around her shoulders. "You sure must know somebody, to have gotten me out of trouble that quickly."

She was quiet a moment. "That's just it. I didn't call anyone. I don't know anybody that could have helped you. Someone else didn't want you in trouble." She looked at him nervously, sideways. "Someone a lot more powerful than me."

"Or someone else didn't want a murder investigated. Or just wanted me out of the country. They gave me seven days to get out."

She laid her head on his shoulder. "I'm sorry about that, so sorry."

"Well, it's not your fault, is it." He ran his hand slowly up and down her back. "I just don't understand it. Why kill George? Why kill Soesanto?"

She sat up and laid her hand on his thigh. "Soesanto alive is more of a mystery than Soesanto dead. George, George. I don't know." She stood up and paced in a circle, rubbing her hands together. "I just don't know. It's so *stupid.* So pointless."

"Sarah said he'd wanted to talk to me." He was going to add, "before I talk to you," but couldn't think of a good reason to add that, or to say something about the kris. His mind went numb. "If only I hadn't stayed overnight in Gandringan. If only I had come back a day earlier."

She stopped her pacing. "That wouldn't have helped at all. There was nothing you could have done."

"So who knew he was going out there?"

She was silent a moment. "Waluyo. And, according to Sarah, John Schechter."

Nancy stood still, staring to where old Budi was sitting on his stool, smoking.

Ab shook his head. "But that's insane. I mean, to be killed for your political views, that's one thing. But for philandering? Sarah would be devastated twice over."

"If it's true, you don't think Sarah would have known?" She brushed her hair away from her eyes. "You underestimate her intelligence. But I don't think you expatriates are capable of these things. A planned murder would take a level of commitment and courage..." She waved her hand in the air. "Passion maybe." Her voice drifted off.

Ab thought about that for several minutes, turning the possibilities over in his mind, then reached up to have Nancy pull him to his feet. Nancy straddled the motorbike as Ab stood by his car. "You could stay at my place tonight," he offered.

She was silent, then in one quick motion dismounted, came over, threw her arms around his neck, and kissed him hard, passionately, her whole muscular body pressed against his. Just as suddenly, she was back on her bike, pushing down on the starter pedal. "I'll see you in the morning," she said, and then was gone.

Chapter Twelve

The next morning, Nancy was over early. They drove in the Suzuki out through Klaten and out to Susu Senang to pick up the truck. Ab was relieved that the truck was still parked off to one side, and no one seemed to be around. They drove tandem, with Nancy in the Jimny, back to the Klaten police station. They were given sweet jasmine tea, and then had to sign several forms, and finally had to wait forty-five minutes for the police chief to arrive. He insisted on another cup of tea, and a couple of cigarettes for himself. He seemed in good spirits. At last he stood up, straightened his jacket, and led them around behind the building, where they found a solid teak, six-foot coffin, resting on two saw-horses. It was bound around with metal straps, and there were several official looking seals.

The chief placed his hand on the coffin lid. "This must remain closed, and sealed, until it arrives in Canada."

Ab combed his fingers down through his beard in a gesture he had once used to get rid of sunflower seeds. "And how do we know the body is in there?"

The police chief stared at him, and then turned to Nancy, saying something in Javanese. She laid her hand on Ab's arm. "I think we'd better just go now. I'll tell you later."

The chief dropped his cigarette and ground it into the dirt. "I will get some men to load it into the truck for you."

◇◇◇

Ab pulled the truck around behind the station and watched as two men struggled to lift the coffin and push it into the back. Nancy was standing by his side, leaning against him. He paused before climbing into the cab. "I don't mean to be intrusive, but what of my friend Soesanto? I don't know if he had family, and I would like to be able to do something. I don't know who I should talk to." The police chief glared at Nancy and said something in Javanese again.

She stepped away from Ab, walked around to the front of the station, and climbed into the Suzuki without saying a word. As Ab pulled the truck up beside her, she rolled down the window. "I'll lead. I know where to go at the airport," she said curtly. She rolled up the window and drove away quickly, so that Ab had to scramble to get into gear and stay behind her.

That afternoon, they stood at the fence at the Yogyakarta Adisocipto airport and watched as the coffin was loaded into the luggage compartment of the plane. Sarah, in a black, lacy Balinese dress, her thin blond hair brushed flat, looked both forlorn, and, thought Ab, strikingly beautiful. Frieda and Nettie clung to her, one on each side. Little Nettie was trying to pull away and run back to the terminal. Even from this distance, across the tarmac, Ab could hear her persistent voice, asking, as she had all the way to the airport, "Where's Daddy? When is Daddy coming? I don't want to go!" Sarah picked her up and carried her. Frieda, holding to her mother's dress, was playing the older sister: terrified but dignified.

They entered the plane from the rear. Sarah seemed oblivious to the screech of the engines blasting around her, and exhaust fuming at her face. She did not turn to wave.

Ab stood next to Nancy at the fence. He gripped the metal posts with both hands until his knuckles blanched. "Maybe I'll see you in a week!" he shouted above the din of the engines. He put his arm around Nancy. "Maybe *we'll* see you." But he could feel her body pull away from him.

The plane roared down the short runway and banked up quickly over the river valley and up over the rim of volcanoes. When it had disappeared, Ab turned to Nancy, took her in his arms, and kissed her aggressively, fully, on the mouth. They walked back to the car, ignoring the astonished stares of the other people in the waiting lounge.

In the car, Nancy said quietly, "That was stupid. You shouldn't have done that. I don't appreciate being used in anger to spite my countrymen."

"Your countrymen!" He clamped his mouth shut and put his hand on top of hers. "I'm sorry. I guess I'm a little out of control right now."

She yanked her hand away. "Yes you are," she hissed. "Watch it."

On the way back from the airport, they stopped at the big Ambarukmo Palace Hotel, where many of the expatriates spent their spare time sunning or swimming. Claudia Hernandez was there, sunbathing, and Nancy sat and talked with her while Ab swam. He swam twenty laps of the Olympic-sized pool, trying not to think about Soesanto, or George, or Claudia, or John, the possibilities of espionage or jealousy. As he swam, the image of all the schoolchildren he and Soesanto had seen outside the car window came into his head. Where was their future now?

They went back to Ab's house, where they sat on the couch without speaking, without touching, drinking gin and tonic, watching a video. He had picked out the video a week ago, hoping for an opportunity to educate Nancy about North American Mennonites. It was "The Witness," a murder mystery, in which a small Old Order Mennonite boy witnesses a murder, and how a police officer is drawn to investigate his own superiors. He has to hide out on a Mennonite farm, disguised in traditional black garb, to save his life, and falls in love with a Mennonite woman. But her religious, rural culture is so different from his secular, urban one that, despite their strong attraction for each other, they must, in the end, part ways. Ab did not want to think about that ending. It was not the ending, now, that he wanted.

The television now silent, he rested his hand on her leg. "Thanks for all you've done. I appreciate it. Having one person around I can trust." He could feel his voice breaking, and stopped.

She lifted his hand away. "Now they might connect me with all of this. I can't leave in a week like you. I have to live here."

He took a deep breath. "You could come with me." He was going to add, but didn't, "Isn't that what you wanted out of me anyway?"

She looked pensively at the blank television screen. "It would take more than a week to get all the paperwork done."

He reached over and played with the back of her hair. "You could come with me as far as Singapore, and we could get married there."

She turned to look at him. Tears appeared at the corners of her eyes, and she brushed them away. "I'm in this place for life, Ab. There was a time when I thought I could come with you. But that time is past. I know now that I can't." She took a deep, uncertain breath, and looked again at the screen, as if expecting some new message to be written there. "Oh well, I can get out to Singapore on buying trips for the computer shop.

"What the policeman in Klaten said to me was, 'Don't ask questions. This is bigger than you want to be involved in. Bigger than I want to be involved in. Just go home.' He meant both of us, you and me."

Outside, the mobile food vendors made their rounds, knocking on wooden sticks, ringing bells, making distinctive cries. Each sound signified a different food: chicken with rice soup, beef and noodles, fried fish, rice and saté. The night guards and servants often bought their suppers from these vendors. The vendor had one, maybe two bowls, which he would rinse out with a little dirty water between customers.

Ab felt distanced, suddenly, from his life, as if his own life were a video he was watching. He felt as if he were a man without a country. Where was home now? Southern Manitoba? Central Java? He'd have to leave here soon. He wondered if he was doomed to wander the globe for the rest of his life. On the other hand, maybe it wasn't a doom at all. Maybe he was blessed to feel a little bit at home everywhere. Is this how his parents felt, coming from Russia to Canada? Is this how Nancy felt, alienated from her own culture? He wondered about her. What did he know about her? Nothing. Was she trying to scare him out of the country to save his life? It wasn't working very well. He felt a sense of panic.

"We can make our own home, a new home, away from all this," he wanted to say. "I don't want to lose you. You are all I have left in this mess." His hand was sliding up her leg. She stood up and took his hand, then put the tips of his fingers into her mouth.

"I want to. I want to. But not tonight."

Chapter Thirteen

The next morning just as Ab was finishing his breakfast, Nancy was back. She seemed giddy and excited. "We don't have much time left together, so tonight," she announced, "let's just have a night on the town. Have you ever seen the shadow plays, wayang kulit?"

"The ones Soesanto used to do? No. Only the wayang orang, the ballet version with live people dancing on stage. Once, at the Ambarukmo Hotel."

"Well, you really have been working too much. Yogyakarta is famous for the shadow plays. Your Canadian friends would never forgive you if you missed seeing at least one before heading home. And later, a real treat, a piece of my childhood: a fun house at the annual fair. Would you like that?"

Ab stirred his eggs around on the plate and smiled. "A piece of your childhood. I would love that."

"Great. In the meantime, I imagine you have some things to wrap up at the veterinary college. You have less than a week. I have to go into my shop or I'll go bankrupt. So, dinner and a date?"

He stood up from the table, came around to her side, and tilted her chin up with his hand so she would look at him. "Nancy, really, you could leave today, and meet me in Singapore in a week."

She took his hand away from her chin. "We went over that. Now don't condescend to me, please. It won't make it any easier."

"How can we do this? Soesanto and George are dead. How can we just go out on the town as if nothing has happened?"

Her eyes were dark, soft, steady. "We are going out because everything has happened. Because some things are no longer possible. I am trying to give you some small gifts, Ab. Please." She pushed him gently away. "Meet me at the shop at closing time, say six o'clock."

Tri was in the office at the vet college. Ab could see that she had been crying, but didn't know what to say. She was typing furiously at the computer. He came up behind her and laid a hand on her shoulder. She kept typing.

"I am so very sorry about Soesanto. Has someone told his mother?"

She stopped, her hands resting on the keyboard, but stared straight ahead. "His mother," she said softly. "Yes, someone will have to tell his mother." She fell into silence, and seemed about to start typing, but couldn't get up enough energy to move her fingers.

"I will have to leave the country in less than a week." Ab felt as if he were lying in bed, talking to the ceiling again. "Nancy is taking me to see a wayang kulit this evening. Do you know, after all this time, I haven't seen one yet? Too much work and too little play, says Nancy." Tri said nothing. "And then she's taking me to visit a fun house at the fairgrounds. She says it's an experience I will never forget."

Tri stood up, knocking the chair back against Ab, and walked out of the room. He stood, holding the chair, then pulled it out and sat on it, facing the screen. She had been typing in the Boyolali information. Ab stared at the screen. The answers he was looking for, he realized, were not in the computer. He still had five days to sort this out. Tomorrow he would start looking in earnest, but where?

It was dusk when Ab and Nancy rode to the Arjuna Hotel on Nancy's motorbike, Nancy side-saddle on the back. Seated at one end of a dimly lit upstairs room were half a dozen tourists seated in chairs facing a large screen. The play had already started when they arrived, the gamelan gonging and crashing in the background, the finely cut buffalo-hide figures casting intricate shadows against the screen, accusing, fighting, triumphing. It was the struggle of good and evil played out on the world stage, a Javanese variation of the Indian Hindu Ramayana tales. The dalang was singing all the character voices in different nasal whines, the gamelan orchestra tumbling and battling behind him. Ab tried to imagine Soesanto playing the dalang. A right wing plant, to flush out "latent" Communists? Possible. The dalang was, after all, everybody. Was that how Soesanto had survived, by being everybody?

The tourist version was shortened from an all-night tale to a one-hour Reader's Digest Condensed version. Back outside, they paid the *parkir*, one of the ubiquitous parking attendants, and climbed onto the motorbike. Nancy drove this time. As he climbed on behind her, he asked, "Did you understand what the singer was actually saying?"

She laughed. "No, it's old Javanese, which no one ever taught me." She turned around for a moment. "It's easier to express the nuances of Indonesian social life in Javanese than in Bahasa Indonesia." She sighed before she started the motor. "Or at least so I'm told."

She plunged down her foot, the motor snarled into life, and she wheeled the cycle abruptly out into the street.

They left the motorbike with a *parkir* in front of the old post office, about a block away from the fairgrounds in front of the sultan's palace. A plywood archway had been constructed over the entrance to the grounds, painted with the bright, gaudy colours of circuses the world over. Ab could see Ferris wheels going around, and carousels. Except for the sidewalk vendors selling essence of spider and scorpion, and the density of the crowd, and the stifling heat and dust even this late at night, it seemed to Ab that this could be a fair anywhere in the world.

Nancy guided him silently between the rides and the booths, the hawkers calling and the speakers blaring. The front of the fun house looked like the front of a fun house anywhere in the world, painted with pictures of ghoulish faces laughing. Music, screams, and laughter blared from the speakers out front. "A fair and a fun house unlike anything you would know," she said, as if reading his mind.

They bought tickets, and stood for a moment, watching the people going in the entrance. Nancy suddenly gripped his arm and pulled him towards the door, laughing. "I think you are in for a real surprise."

"But you'll be with me." He tried to reach for her, but she slipped in the door away from him.

"Catch me if you can," she called over her shoulder. "But watch your step. It's dark."

She was right about the dark. And Ab was wrong about this being like a fun house anywhere in the world. He realized this as soon as he had entered and his eyes tried to adjust to the lack of light. This place, rather than just having the appearance of being old and haunted, really was run-down, ready to fall apart. They began by climbing steep stairs made of rotted wood, with planks missing. Nancy stumbled in front of Ab and he propped her up. At the top of the stair, a bright light shone in their faces, and a ghoulish, deformed creature leaped out at them, garbling out a preposterous song. Ab nearly fell back down the stairs. The creature laughed uproariously.

Ab pushed on quickly and caught the back of Nancy's jacket. "Hey, that thing was real. What…?"

"A dwarf. They paint themselves up. It's not a bad-paying job."

He thought he would be ready for the next one, but was carefully avoiding gaps in the rotten wood floor. He could see through the floor to a level below with scenes of evil-looking creatures and strange noises. "A person could actually, really, fall through here and break their legs," he called to Nancy above the din.

"Or their neck," came her voice from a pitch-black spot, slightly ahead and below him. "Watch your step," she added, as he suddenly dropped half a metre on to a platform of sagging plywood. At that moment four evil-looking beasts seemed to dance out of the thin air and reach for Ab with a blood-curdling cry. He pushed himself quickly to his feet, bumped into a wall directly in front of him, and turned through an opening that led on to a narrow walkway along the outside top of the fun house roof.

Nancy was standing there, her hand pushing lightly against a very rickety-looking hand-rail. She was grinning. "Are we having fun yet? By the way, don't lean on this," she said. "You might fall over." He looked over the edge into what looked like a series of bamboo frames and broken boards.

"Is this still part of the fun house?" he asked.

"Ah, yes. We have to walk along here and then enter again back there."

"You've been here before."

"Of course. Like I said—a piece of my childhood. I don't think they have repaired this in twenty years I've known it. It is one of the constants in my life."

Three children came out of the fun house door and passed toward the back, laughing excitedly, gabbing about what lay behind and what might lie ahead. Nancy followed them and disappeared. Ab was about to follow when he felt a body pressed against his back and a hand on his arm. He turned. It was Tri. "Dr. Ab. Please. Be careful of Sani Sentosa and his family. And this house. It is not safe."

"Ab, you coming?" Nancy had poked her head out of the door at the back, then disappeared again. He turned to where Tri had been. She was gone. What the *hell* was that?

He grabbed the flimsy railing and made his way along the walkway. From inside, he could hear a loud crashing noise, and shouts, but he was not sure if it was part of the normal fun house noises. Suddenly anxious, he hurried after Nancy. Almost immediately, he was set upon by a small, hard body, and sent stumbling headlong down a set of rotten wooden steps, tripping and falling down a full metre before he hit a platform.

When he landed, someone was clinging to his leg, about the size of a child but with a grip of steel. He swung his arms and legs violently in the dark and the grip loosened. He yanked himself away and stumbled on. The downstairs of the house was more of the same: dead ends, screaming dwarves and children, loud, beastly cries played over the speaker system. Something clutched at his beard, but he yanked it away and plunged through a pitch-black spot and out through a series of wet curtains into the air outside. Nancy was standing there, staring at a dense knot of people that was slowly moving toward the fair exit. She turned when he came out. He thought, for a moment, that she was both surprised and relieved to see him.

"The house owner said there has been an accident," she said quietly. "They say they are taking the injured woman to the hospital." For a second, as the small crowd turned a corner under a light, Ab glimpsed the body on the stretcher. It was Tri. Nancy turned and put her head against Ab's shoulder. "Such a dangerous place, that. Maybe I shouldn't have brought you here."

He could feel her body against him. "But it really *is* so much fun, yes? Do you want to try some rides?"

Ab looked around. All the rides looked home-made and genuinely dangerous. "No, I think I want to go home. I think I have had enough of your childhood." He reached around her from behind and squeezed.

They were back at the motorcycle before either of them said any more. "Are the dwarves in there supposed to actually try to kill you?" he said.

"Sometimes it feels like it. That's what makes it exciting."

He paid the *parkir* and climbed up behind Nancy on the motorcycle. "This was more than feels like it."

"Sani Sentosa's family," he mused out loud.

Nancy turned around with a start. He could feel her body stiffen.

"What?"

Even there, in the half dark of the street-lamp, he could see her pupils widen. "Oh, nothing. I was just wondering out loud if the infamous Pak Sani has a family." She turned, and, without answering, started the motorcycle. He had to grab on quickly as she sped into the thick of the traffic.

Back at the house she didn't say anything. They did not turn on any lights, but went to the bedroom and lay, fully clothed, in the dark, quietly staring up at the ceiling, the overhead fan circling. She went to the living room. He could hear her rummaging through the drawers of the buffet, yanking them open and then slamming them shut. She came back and stood in the doorway for a moment.

Ab propped himself up on one elbow. "Did you lose something?"

She seemed to consider this for a moment, then opened her hand. She was holding a cigarette, which she lit up, and then came back to lie down on the bed.

"I didn't know you smoked."

She didn't answer.

Ab waited a moment. A car drove by outside.

Nancy leaned over the edge of the bed, stubbed out her cigarette on the terrazzo floor, and then turned back and put her leg up over his thigh. She played for a moment with his hair and beard. Then she rode up on top and leaned over, pinning his arms back. "Promise me two things. One, that you will never, never mess with that kris Soesanto had and two, that you will leave the country when you are supposed to." She was leaning over him, pinning his arms back, deadly serious.

"But..."

"Promise!" Her voice was almost at a scream. He tried to sit up, but she held him. She leaned forward so that her hair fell around his face like a tent. "Promise, please." She was pleading now, quietly, her voice quavering, her eyes fixed on his. The urgency of her request and her physical strength surprised him.

He lay back. "Okay, I give up. I promise."

She rolled back and lay beside him. "Good," she said. Ab wondered if now was the moment he had been waiting for, but with two friends dead, and a hard promise extracted from him by a woman who pushed him to the edge of passion, and held him there, at the rim of an abyss, the time just didn't seem right. He lay awake, breathing slowly, deeply, feeling his own tense muscles slowly retreat into themselves, listening to her uneven breathing, not daring to look if her eyes were open or shut.

Chapter Fourteen

Harry Loewen doesn't whack the rabbit hard enough on the back of the head, so that when he goes to skin it, the animal twitches and screams like chalk screeching down a blackboard. I shudder and Harry drops the jerking body. Pete Patterson, the oldest of the three Patterson boys, grabs it in a flash and hits it firmly and quickly behind the head, so that it falls immediately still.

He hands the carcass back to Harry, whose face is ashen, his long curls clinging, wet with perspiration, to his temples. His hand shakes as he takes the slender warm body by the long hind legs. "Listen, you either do it, or you don't. There's no in between," says Peter gently. "And there ain't nothin' bad about it either way. You just have to make up your mind."

The Pattersons, Paddy and Claire and their three boys, live in a double-wide trailer set up on cinder blocks in the bush. They make their living doing odd jobs for the oil drillers, and by having a small, custom-kill abattoir, where local farmers like Harry Loewen, this back-to-the-land former Toronto philosophy student, can bring their animals to be killed and inspected by a government-certified veterinarian.

I am the veterinary inspector, fresh out of school. I am here to ensure that the kill is proper and the animals fit for human consumption. I stand in the background, whetting my knife, getting ready to check the offal for infection. In the twinkling of an eye, that's what the apostle Paul had said. That was the divine way to die. Like a rabbit at the Pattersons'.

"Yeah, city boy, look at this." Billy-the-Bear, who once killed a bear that fell through their trailer roof onto the kitchen table, pulls a rabbit from the crate by the hind legs and whacks it once, quickly, decisively. He holds it up and slits the skin. There is no child-like cry. No struggle. Just life, and then a brief terror, and then death. But you have to decide what you are going to do, and then you have to go for the head. Anything other than that will just increase the suffering.

Harry looks at the body in his hands, lays it down on the concrete floor, and goes outside. We can hear him retching.

It took a few moments for Ab to remember where he was. He was in bed. He turned to look over to where Nancy was. Gone. Something was ringing. The phone. He walked into the living room and steadied himself against the couch. He sat down next to the phone as he picked up the receiver.

It was Sarah, her voice crackling through a mist, far away. "Ab. Thank God. I've been trying to get you for hours. The phone lines are so bad."

"Sarah, where are you calling from? Plumstein? Listen, I haven't been able…what? Yes. Yes."

"The coffin had rocks in it." Sarah's voice seemed to be coming through from another planet. He felt a darkness close around him. "Ab, are you there? Ab, George's body wasn't there. The coffin was full of rocks. Can you find out what happened?"

"Sarah, I've only got a few days here myself. I'll try."

They were both silent for a moment. "Ab, you're not in danger, are you? I…I care about you."

"Thanks, Sarah." He took a deep breath and found himself thinking the words of St. Paul about prayer, that *through our inarticulate moans the Spirit speaks for us, and God knows what we mean.* The darkness seemed to ease away a little. "No, Sarah, I don't think I'm in danger. I'll do what I can. See you soon. Take care." Why would they kill him if they could just ship him out of the country?

He hung up the phone and leaned back on the couch, pulling at his beard. Then went back to the bedroom and looked at his bedside clock. Five A.M. Had Nancy said goodbye? He looked into the garage where she usually parked her bike. Gone to work? A bit early. Budi was slouched over in sleep at the gate.

Time to act decisively. But what to do? He considered going past Nancy's shop, but recalled how she had felt about being dragged into this mess earlier. He was on his own. Against his better judgment, he drove by her shop anyway. It was all dark and the door and windows had metal shutters pulled over them. So where was she? He had somehow assumed that she lived above the shop, but the truth was, he now realized, they had never actually talked about where she actually lived.

The Klaten police station was not officially open yet, but there was a car out front and Ab could see a light on inside. He skidded to a halt in the dust, walked into the station, straight through the empty front room and into the chief's office. "I need some answers. Two of my good friends have been killed in Balinese kris execution style, and I want to know why."

The chief was sitting behind his desk, rose as Ab entered the room, saw who it was, then slumped back down. He lifted his hat, ran his fingers over his hair, and put the hat back down. Then, as if terribly weary, he stood up and turned to look out the window. "You are a very brave man, Mr. Ab, to come into my office like this. I could accuse you of murder." He was silent, as if pondering this option, then turned around. "If I question you, will I find motive? I think so. Will I find a weapon? What veterinarian does not carry a knife? You do not understand, Mr. Ab, what is happening."

"You are damn right I don't. So tell me. I've got a few hours." Ab lowered himself into a chair, remembered the kris in his car, dug his hand into his empty pocket. He should take up gum, like ex-smokers. He ran his hand back over his head. What had happened to his baseball cap?

The policeman sighed. "Unfortunately, Mr. Ab, I also do not know what is happening." He reached into a box at the left side of his desk. "There were more cattle that died at the mother farm. We asked Dr. Arsentina from the Livestock Office to come look. She will replace Dr. Soesanto."

"You didn't ask me."

"She did not need you. We did not know where you were. These are the reports Dr. Arsentina did." He handed Ab some pathology reports, which he scanned, rushing to the bottom line. "Anthrax," he read out loud. "Well, that's no surprise. Question is, why didn't the vaccine or the antibiotic protect those cattle? Who has been sabotaging the project? Who killed George and Soesanto?"

"Dr. Ab." He leaned across the desk. "Why must you persist in reading the darkest motives into everything?"

"Into murder? Executions by kris? I can tell you George's wife is not too happy about receiving a coffin full of rocks, either. We may have an international incident over this. Do you know what happened to the body?"

The policeman shrugged. "That, perhaps, I know."

"And?"

"What I can tell you, Dr. Ab, is this. I am bound by decisions that are made," and here he waved his hand noncommittally, "elsewhere. In any case, it is not permitted, I am told, to ship a body of a person who has died of anthrax across international boundaries. We are sorry. We are deeply sorry that your friend George has died. I can also tell you that Dr. Soesanto was fortunate to have survived as long as he did. His colleagues all disappeared years ago." He paused. "It is true that he was a good man."

Ab slouched back into his chair, staring at the man across the desk from him, an ordinary Indonesian police officer, doing a job. *Deeply sorry. Right. So he knows.* It was no use. There was no getting to the bottom of it. He leaned forward again with a sigh of despair.

"Well then at least tell me this: Is *my* life in danger, and if so, from whom?" If he could find out from whom he was in danger, then he could find out who murdered George.

The policeman shrugged.

"If you don't know, who would? Sani Sentosa?"

"Maybe."

Ab got to his feet. "I want to tell Mr. George's wife something. Can I tell her that you disposed of the body properly, not in a dump somewhere, but properly buried?"

The police chief stood to see Ab to the door. "You may tell her that," he said.

As he climbed into his car the police chief came over and pushed the car door shut after him. "Mr. Ab, be careful," he said quietly.

Ab sat at the wheel without starting the motor, his anger seeping away, the vague fears returning. "Where can I find Pak Sani?"

The policeman looked at him long and hard. He said nothing.

"Two of my good friends have been murdered. I have to leave the country in about four days. You must understand. I need to find out something. I can't go home empty-handed." He was pleading now, feeling hopeless. This was his last chance.

"He has a summer home in Bandungan," the policeman said finally. "You can sometimes find him there."

Ab started the car and headed back to Yogya. Where the hell was his baseball cap anyway. He turned the gamelan tape back on. It still sounded like a confusion of a million voices, all going their own way. Yet they were held together by something, and they seemed to be moving, if only in circles, or batik-like patterns. But in all the noise, he could not discern that pattern.

It was late morning by the time he got back to Yogya. Shops would still be open for a few hours before closing during the hottest part of the day. He drove by Nancy's computer shop again. Still dark and shuttered. His stomach tightened another twist. Where was she?

Ab pulled up to his house and honked twice. It was only when he got out of the car and rattled the gate that he realized it was open and unlocked. No Budi. Nancy's motorbike was not there, as he knew it would not be but hoped it would. He picked up his overnight bag from the back seat and carried it into the house.

The house was dusky, heavy with silence.

"Nancy? Budi? Anyone?!!"

His voice fell like a dead cat to the floor.

He set down his bag, felt for the kris, then gently lifted it out. His baseball cap was there, in the bag. A stupid, small thing to worry about, he thought. He took it out and put it on, backwards. Then he slowly drew the kris out of its sheath, marvelling again at the snake and complex damascene. He took it to the kitchen and found a bottle of cooking oil. Using the thick palm oil, sold as "Genuine Corn Oil," he polished the blade to a sheen. No flecks. He caressed it, as one would a small kitten, and wondered which other hands had done the same. Unthinkingly, he reached up toward his throat and thought of George and Soesanto. He pushed the blade back into the scabbard and placed it back into his bag. Motive. Opportunity. Weapon. Go home Ab. What had Sarah said was George's message?

I can't sleep here tonight. He dug around in his chest of drawers and threw some fresh clothes into his bag on top of the knife, then threw the bag into the back seat of the Suzuki. He walked out to the street to the warung with the poster of Lake Louise where he used to eat and ordered a big bowl of soto ayam. He watched the people and becaks passing, then walked home. He lay on the bed for an hour, staring at the ceiling. *What has power for us now that we have overthrown all the old idols and icons? Words? But those too we have undermined and overthrown. Money? Power itself? For what do we kill?* Dusk was falling.

Shops opened up after being closed between two and five in the afternoon, and the mobile food vendors were wending their way up and down the alleys making their distinctive noises. Enterprising cooks spread out across the sidewalks with make-shift canvas-covered restaurants that advertised Pak Pujo's Bakso, or Bu Nona's Saté. It was a bad time to be driving, as many of the pedestrians spilled out onto the streets, and the becaks, motorcycles, and bicycles which flocked everywhere carried no lights.

He passed Nancy's shop again. He stopped and rattled the shutters. No one. As he headed out of town, he sensed that he was being followed. But that was silly. How could he, manoeuvring through that sea of vehicles, get any sense of being followed? And yet it was there. He carefully scanned his rear-view mirror, then drove alternately fast and slow, and went around one block three times. It was a thin man on a motorcycle, wearing a dark brown batik shirt and sunglasses. The Waluyo-type. Somebody had seen too many American movies.

Chapter Fifteen

Ab drove up the highway skirting the west side of the volcanoes, the side away from Klaten and Solo, for half an hour, then pulled over to the side under some trees next to a small warung and fell asleep. The next morning, he awoke feeling rumpled and foul. He put on his baseball cap, and had some soup at the warung. Then, feeling half-civilized, he drove north up the road toward Semarang through the blinding white haze of heat and dust and diesel fumes, on a road that climbed steadily, smoothly upward. For the first half hour or so, he tried to listen to his gamelan tape, but the music only jarred and perplexed him, so that he turned it off. He was even further from understanding anything now than when he had started.

After a drive of about an hour and a half, he turned left at the small town of Ambarawa, up a narrower, more winding road that could take him, if he cared to keep driving for a day, to the ancient sites of the Dieng Plateau. At the mountain resort town of Bandungan, he drove over to the market to buy some fruit and take stock of his situation before proceeding to find Pak Sani's house.

Here in the mountains one could find fresh carrots, bright red tomatoes, green, but juicy oranges, apples—all the things that had to be trucked down to Yogyakarta and which deteriorated rapidly in the intense heat of the plains. He strolled leisurely through the market, savouring each cool moment, pacing himself, trying not to think about the fact that his life might be in danger, or Nancy, or what might lie ahead. He was just beginning to relax, to almost forget why he had come, when a voice behind him startled him.

"Well, Ab! If we'd have known you were coming, we could have come together!"

It was John and Claudia. "Didn't know you were a Hasher," said Claudia, leaning up for her kisses. "If we'd have known, we'd have done this more often. We almost never come to these British events, but John really wanted to this time, so…here we are." She looked around.

"Where's Nancy? Did you bring her along?"

"A Hasher?" His mind raced. Damn, he'd forgotten. It *was* Sunday, and Marie had said something about this at her party. It seemed aeons ago. "I'm not actually. Is that today?"

"Don't tell me you didn't know!" John put his arm around Ab from the left side. "Just came up here to get away with Nancy, did you?" John's squeeze seemed painfully hard. "Good idea, to get away from all that stuff down there."

Claudia took his right hand and held it against her as they walked, so that his knuckles brushed against the side of her breast. "Where are you guys staying? We're at that great old Dutch place on the hillside, with the cottages and white rose bushes and the big trees. A bit run-down but the view down over the valley and the lake is incredible."

The two of them seemed to be dragging Ab along between them. "You mean you really didn't know that today is the Yogyakarta-Semarang Hash Bash?" John asked. "The place will be crawling with expats within the hour. We're running over at the temples. No sneaking away, ha! Hey, there's Peter and Gladys!" He let go of Ab to wave down the minivan that was slowly pushing its way through the market crowd at the corner.

"See you later," Claudia waved as she ran after her husband.

Ab returned through the market to where he had parked his car, distracted, his mind racing. The Hash, especially a joint party like this one, was a bit rowdy for Ab, like a Wilkinsons' party in the open air. But now that they'd seen him, how could he not go? And how could he explain Nancy's absence if he did go? Ab didn't know if he could stand it. And yet, if his life were in danger, there would be safety in being in a large group of expatriates.

He climbed into the car, pondering his next move: how to find Sani's house. The policeman at the main kiosk in town gave him vague starting directions. But at least it was a start, he hoped, in the right direction.

From the main intersection in town, he turned right, and then left and up a very narrow, winding road out of town. Large sections of the road seemed to have been washed away, so that he had to drive slowly not to break an axle in the potholes. A steady stream of people hiked along the road and then headed up various side paths, bearing wicker baskets piled with produce on their heads, or in cloth slings over their backs. At one point, the road turned sharply to cross a deep ravine. The bridge consisted of rotting planks and logs with no side rails. Ab got out and tested it with his feet. Near the middle, one complete plank was missing. He walked back to the car.

Two women, their slings full of vegetables, had watched him with some amusement. He pointed to the bridge and then at his car, and shrugged his shoulders sceptically. They nodded and laughed. Did they know if Pak Sani Sentosa had a house up here? They conferred a moment on this, then smiled and waved on ahead. Three, maybe five kilometers. Near where they lived. Could they have a ride? Ab looked at his little Suzuki. Packing into a small space wouldn't faze them. He looked at the bridge. After he was across the bridge, he said. The car bumped slowly over the boards, and slumped precariously at the gap. Sweat was leaking around the rim of his cap and trickling down his back when the car reached dirt again. The ladies climbed into the back.

The road seemed to get much steeper after the bridge, and a series of switchbacks tilted the car up at ninety degrees and put him into four-wheel drive. It felt like ten kilometres before the ladies touched him on the shoulder and indicated that they wanted to get out. Pak Sani was over there, the next road left, one of the ladies said.

The next road left was a deeply rutted dirt road that switch—backed down into a ravine and up the other side. He passed through a small village, and asked at a shop about Pak Sani. Further on, just a little, he was told. Maybe a kilometre. After another kilometer of road which turned suddenly into sharp stones, he stopped beside a young boy tending some zebu cattle. Pak Sani? Not far. Maybe five or seven kilometers.

He was beginning to think that he should turn around and head back while he still could, when he came over a rise and saw, on the next hill, cutting through a heavily wooded area, a brick and plaster wall. The wall was a good ten feet high, with broken glass worked into the plaster all along the top. Above that, short iron poles bent outward, and four strands of barbed wire were strung along the length of the fence.

He pulled up to the black, wrought-iron gate. There seemed to be no one about, and the roadway beyond looked like simply more of the same going up over another hill and into another set of woods. Ab shook the gate and called greetings in Bahasa Indonesia and Javanese. There was a buzzer beside the gate, which he tried, but had no way of knowing whether or not it was working. Knowing how things worked here in general, he suspected it didn't.

He climbed back into the car, and, after five minutes of persistent honking, saw a small dark man in a tattered T-shirt and shorts come running over the rise in the road from the inside. The man peered at Ab through the bars of the gate. Ab asked him if this was the house of Pak Sani.

"Pak Sani? Yah, yah." He nodded and smiled. Ab proceeded to explain, in Bahasa Indonesia, who he was and what he wanted, but the little man just nodded, smiled, and repeated, "Pak Sani, yah."

While he was a very agreeable person, it was quite clear that he did not speak Bahasa Indonesia. Eventually, with a considerable dose of gesticulations, Ab managed to convince him to open the gate and let him in. He drove through and up over the rise. There, set among the trees, was a sprawling, white plaster-walled house with an orange-clay tile roof. The yard immediately in front of the house was swept clean, and the garden of shrubs and flowers looked bright and well cared for. There were no cars that Ab could see, and the place appeared deserted. He took off his cap, set it on the passenger seat, and smoothed down his hair with his hand.

With a sinking feeling, he stepped on to the cool, terrazzo-floored porch and pressed the buzzer at the front door. The wind pleasantly brushed against his face; from where he was, he could look down over the entire valley. Off in the distance, he could make out Merbabu, and beyond that, Merapi. The bottom of the valley itself seemed to shimmer in a haze. From here, it was hard to imagine how very hot and how very crowded it was way down there. Nearer by, he could make out some temple ruins on a series of hills just below the peak on which the house stood.

The guard, in the meantime, had run back from the gate, and disappeared into a side door of the house. In a moment the front door opened.

Ab had expected the gate-guard to be opening the door from the inside. Instead, an ancient, white-haired lady in a bright, many-coloured silk batik dress stood there, smiling, motioning for him to enter. Her skin was smooth, almost translucent, the texture of polished jade, the colour of honey, and her hair, not a strand out of place, neatly back in a roll. "Good day," she said in perfect English. "Or would you prefer that I speak in Dutch. One is never sure these days."

"I...English is fine." Ab was flustered as she waited for him to take his shoes off at the door. This was not at all what he had expected. Was this the villain's mother?

She guided Ab into a large sitting room with fine, antique batiks hung on the wall, and rich, silk covered couches. She motioned for him to sit down. "Please, have a seat Mr..."

"Dr. Ab, Abner Dueck." He turned to shake her hand. They touched hands and she returned her hand to her breast in the gesture of respect.

"I am Mrs. Sentosa," she said. "But then I suppose you already know that, or you wouldn't be here. If you will be seated, I shall order some tea." She rang a little silver bell which had been resting on the ornately carved coffee table at Ab's elbow. They waited in silence until the maid came and departed again.

Mrs. Sentosa's face wrinkled into a toothless smile. "Dr. Ab, I am very pleased to meet you. I have heard my husband speak of you."

Ab found himself, against his will, hypnotized, lapsing into pleasant tea-time talk. "Good things I hope?"

She laughed, a light, chuckling laugh. "Oh yes, very good."

The maid came in with the tea and a tray of sweets. She poured them each a cup and disappeared. For a moment they sipped at the sweet, hot ginger tea.

"I hope you like ginger. At my age, I feel it clears my thinking."

Ab could feel the hot spice lift up into his sinuses. "Yes, it does clear the head, doesn't it?" They were silent, then he continued. "You speak English very well."

"Thank you. I have heard that you speak Bahasa Indonesia very well also."

"Would you prefer that I..."

"No, please." She waved a frail hand. "I so seldom have the opportunity to practice my English." She paused to muse a minute and then added, "These days."

Ab wondered where she had learned her English, but was not sure if it was proper etiquette to ask directly. "Your husband, is he home?" he ventured at last.

She seemed momentarily lost in thought, rubbing her hand back and forth along the edge of the divan on which she was seated. The silk there was almost worn through. She must sit there often, thinking and remembering, Ab thought. Remembering what?

"Mr. Sentosa is right now in Bali," she said dreamily. "I am sure that he would be pleased to talk with you if you should visit there."

Ab felt his heart rise and sink at the same time. Bali? He didn't have time for another trip. He unravelled one of the rice sweets, wrapped in a leaf. He realized that he was hungry and had not had any lunch. "Would it be possible for you to let me know how I can contact him there? It is a matter of some urgency that I talk with him in the next day or so." He stuck the rice cake into his mouth.

"Of course," she said. "But why don't you eat with me first. Do you have time? The cook is already preparing. Then I shall give you everything you need."

"Tell me." He set down his tea glass. "It seems so isolated up here. So difficult to get here—the road was hardly passable. How do you manage?"

She laughed. "Oh, you must have come in the old back way. There's a perfectly good road that comes out by the temples just below."

He felt his ears get hot. Sitting there on a silk couch talking with a very old and obviously very civilised lady, he wondered suddenly if he had been too close to the real picture to see it. Had George just got caught in a skirmish between the old Communists, like Soesanto and Susilo, and the new economic masters, Suharto and Witono and their lackeys? Were Sani and his family, being ethnically Chinese, simply used as convenient scapegoats whenever necessary?

Ab wondered how much of this he could talk about with Sani's wife. "Ready," the cook said, sticking her head through the door.

"Tell me," Ab said impulsively as they stood up, "do you have a collection of kris?"

She patted him on the arm and sighed. "We have a very good and very old collection of kris which we keep in our house in Bali." They entered a formal dining room, with two place settings at one end of a long table. "We used to have them here," she went on as she sat down, "but during the time when there were serious troubles in Java, it was not safe to keep them here."

"Not safe?"

She looked directly at Ab, as if unsure how much of this knowledge to trust him with. "Some of the very old kris are things of great power. If they get into the wrong hands..." She raised her hands.

She ladled soup out for both of them.

"After 1966," Ab said, playing with his soupspoon, "were you... how did you survive?" He was looking down into his soup.

"Look at me," she said firmly. "What do you see?"

He set down his spoon. "I see a very lovely and dignified Javanese lady."

She fixed a steely gaze on him, which reminded him suddenly of Nancy. He thought: it is a look that can seduce and kill all at the same time. And then banished the thought as she spoke.

"You see a very Chinese old lady, a very old Christian lady, a very Communist old lady, a very dangerous old lady. You see a lady to be shunned by friends because to be associated with her is to risk your life. You see a lady to be hunted by enemies she has never met and never wronged." Her voice had risen and was trembling. Her hands were trembling, and she spread her fingers out on the table on either side of her plate. "Do you believe what I am telling you?"

Ab felt as if he were staring right deep inside of her, and as if, in turn, her gaze cut to his very heart. "I see a very dignified and beautiful and very wronged woman," he said quietly, wondering if, once again, he was being blind-sided by his weaknesses around women.

She was rubbing the table on either side of her plate, firmly, persistently. "You see a lady who had to change her name, who had to shun her own grandchild in order to save her life."

She was staring now toward the steaming rice on the table, but in reality at a space both far away and incredibly close.

"I'm very sorry," he whispered.

Abruptly, she changed her mood, picked up her spoon, and began to eat. "Please," she said, "eat. To allow the evils of the past to spoil the present is to give them a power they do not deserve."

For the remainder of the meal, they ate silently. When they were finished, she stood up and became very business-like. From a desk, she took some paper and wrote a message, which she inserted into an envelope and handed to Ab. Then she took out another sheet of paper and very carefully wrote an address and a telephone number. "When you get back to Yogyakarta," she said, placing a hand firmly on his arm, "go to the Garuda airlines office and ask for Jacobus. Give him this envelope. You will be leaving for Bali the day after tomorrow, first flight in the morning. Before you leave, telephone—you have a phone, yes? Good. You telephone this number." She pointed to the phone number she had written. "Tell them that Heimun said to call, and that they should make arrangements for you."

She guided him to the door, but stopped him just before they arrived, and held him firmly, with both hands, at arms length. "You be very careful. And the kris, do not play with them. They are not for foreigners." Ab stooped to kiss her on the cheek, then, on impulse, totally improperly, pulled her against him and hugged her closely. She felt thin and frail against him. The image of his mother came suddenly into his mind, and he felt an upsurge of regret for having ignored her all these years. He wondered if she would welcome a strange Chinese man into her home the way this woman had welcomed him. It surprised and pleased him to think that yes, she very well might.

"I'll tell the guard to show you out the proper way," she said as he opened the door, and then shouted instructions to the little man who had first let Ab into the premises. He smiled and motioned that Ab should take the drive around the house. Ab looked over his shoulder as he guided the car around the corner. Mrs. Sentosa stood alone in the doorway. He took a deep breath and followed the guard, who was running and gesticulating ahead of the car. He drove between the house and a barn.

A small, sturdy brown horse was tethered outside, grazing. It had a peculiar snake-shaped white blaze down its nose. As Ab drove by the door of the barn, a man stepped out, saw the car, and then quickly returned to the shadows. But not before Ab had seen him. It was Waluyo.

Chapter Sixteen

Driving down the smooth, but almost perpendicular road to the main entrance of the Sentosa residence, Ab felt confusion rising up again. Waluyo seemed to be everywhere. If he was working for Sentosa, maybe he had killed Susilo and maybe even Soesanto, just to keep the peace. But would he have killed George? Sani was a businessman and a survivor. He would be too savvy for that.

If George had accidentally stumbled into the middle of this, and was killed because he knew too much, did he, Ab, also know too much? How much was too much?

What did Nancy know? Did she know too much as well? Ab felt his chest tighten, and realized again how much he missed her. Was this love, this intense sense of loss when someone was gone? Was love something one only knew by its absence, like home?

By the time the guard pulled open the gate and waved him through, Ab was already back in turmoil, arguing with himself. Once out of the yard, the driveway continued to plunge down, and, after passing through a clump of trees and down through a gully, joined the main road. Ab looked back from where he had come. From where he was now, the entrance to the yard was invisible.

He turned left and almost immediately passed the entrance to Gedong Songo, the nine-temple Hindu complex, built up over six hills, where the hash was to take place. Just past the main entrance, a small, hand-painted sign read: *Yogya-Semarang*

Hash. He turned abruptly left and drove a short way up a gravel road. The road opened into a small field, where numerous cars and minibuses were parked. Knots of people, many of whom Ab recognized from Yogyakarta, were wandering in among the cars and trees. While some were dressed in actual jogging outfits, the majority wore only casual clothes with running shoes. He pulled his cap firmly on to his head and climbed out.

"Hey, Ab, over here!" Claudia called to him. Harold Wilkinson was there talking with John, but Marie was nowhere to be seen. She was not a runner, and her drinks ran to the harder stuff. Beer was not, she would giggle, her cup of tea. John and Harold paused in their conversation, and looked over at Ab, as if they had been talking about him. Ab nodded, raised his cap, smiled, then looked away.

"Should we ask about Nancy?" asked Claudia.

"I will need a lot of beer this time, if that answers your question," he said. He was about to put his arm flirtatiously around Claudia, met John's steely gaze with his own, and resisted the impulse. Could John have killed George out of jealousy? But he wouldn't have killed Soesanto. Could there be two things going on? Could John have used the quarrels over land and politics to cover a personal revenge? The way the butchers in Boyolali had used the situation?

He suddenly wanted to run, and to drink, and to sleep. And, he realized, eat sunflower seeds. He dug into his pocket. Remembered that he had quit. That Nancy was the reason.

"How come we start here and not up from the real temple entrance?" he asked Peter Findlay, who had strolled up beside him.

"I guess because it wouldn't look good to have a beer truck in the official government parking lot."

Someone was blowing off-key on an old cornet. "Okay hounds, off we go," a strongly accented Australian voice called. "Looks like we may have some rain, so try to stick close and don't get lost."

In a minute, the first keen joggers set off, soon followed by some eighty others in a long strung-out line. Ab took off after the last stragglers. "Save some beer for me!" he hollered back to the two Indonesians standing by the Bir Bintang truck. They laughed and waved.

The first part of the trail wound through the woods and upwards. Ab was panting within minutes, and had to stop periodically to catch his breath and walk. It was pleasant under the canopy of trees. John Schechter was the last of the runners ahead of him, but Ab quickly lost sight of him. The marked trail veered away from the main trail temporarily and zigzagged up an old stream bed before cutting across to the next hill. Ab kept his eyes out for the bits of paper that the hares had planted. The trail wound steeply upwards and he found himself suddenly at the first of the nine temples. He stopped momentarily to look at the delicate stone carvings, and then ran to the valley's edge. The sun was low, and a slight mist was gathering in the gullies below. It was cool and fresh and beautiful. He took a deep breath. From the top of the hill, he could see some of the other temples rising up on rocky peaks nearby. He plunged down the trail into a ravine, where the mists were already rolling in. They were now following the main tourist trail and had to be careful to watch for horse droppings, since guides regularly brought city tourists through here on horseback.

By the time he was climbing the second hill, Ab was panting seriously, and a light pattering of rain was coming down. Physical exercise was not one of his strong points. Was it not St. Paul who wrote that "bodily exercise profiteth little"? A person had to keep some shred of moral integrity in his life. Not exercising was Ab's little corner on the moral market. He stopped to take off his jacket and tie the arms around his neck. He wiped the sweat from his forehead and climbed the twisting path up to the second temple. By the second temple, the clouds had rolled in and he felt the moisture washing over, a combination of mist and light rain. He could only see a few steps ahead of him.

"Ho! Ho!" called some of the runners. Ab followed the sound. They seemed to have cut away from the main trail, down into a ravine, and were now moving along another old stream bed.

His foot slipped on a wet rock and he slammed down on to his side. "What ho!" someone called from somewhere in the mist. "Watch for slippery rocks!" Ab pushed himself to his feet and rubbed his painful thigh. "Thanks a fucking lot," he mumbled to himself. He put pressure down on his foot and winced, then hobbled on after the sound of the hounds. The air smelled thick and sulfurous. He bent over to look at the stream which he had thought he was beside and realized that he had almost slipped into a steaming, bubbling pool of sulfurous water.

The cloud was thicker now and the drops of rain were bigger and heavier. He heard the voices of the runners in the distance, but could not place exactly where they came from. He thought he remembered that, at the top of this ravine, there was another group of temples. From there, he could catch the main walking and riding trail and make his way back to the parking lot, and from there back over to where the hash started. He began to clamber up the slippery rocks, pebbles clattering eerily down into the sulfur pools below him.

At the lip of the ravine, he was greeted by an eerie silence. He could just make out a grove of trees in the gulley ahead of him, and what appeared to be a path down into it. Out in the open, the rain was now pelting down, and, passing into the grove, he was glad for the shelter of the branches. He was now clearly on a path, heading back downhill, walking among the close, ghostly trees. The path was wet and muddy, and he was soaked through. A little way into the grove, a circular, grassy space opened up, from the middle of which arose a grey stone statue. He approached for a closer look. It was Hanuman, the monkey god and great warrior. There were little baskets of flowers scattered around the base of the statue, now being washed into the mud. Down on the plains, where Islamic sensibilities prevailed, one would not see such signs of continuing veneration around Hindu statues. Here, the mountain people kept their own counsel on religion.

Ab placed his hand on the stone and caressed it absent-mindedly, then sat down. Either the rain had let up, or the surrounding trees were sheltering him from it. He listened for the sounds of the Hashers. He thought he heard something in the distance, but could not pinpoint where the sound was coming from. He stood up. Soon it would be dark, and then he would really be lost. When he looked around, he realized that the only way out of the grove was the way he had come. He heard a clattering, and something hard and sharp struck him on the shoulder. There was more clattering, and a small shower of pebbles came down on him. In a moment, he heard the sound of a horse blowing its breath out through its lips, stepping its way carefully down from the lip of the ravine above him: one of the guides, no doubt. For a price, Ab knew, he would be given a ride down. He was not beyond such cheating on a Hash run.

Ab recognized the horse first, that peculiar, white, snake-like blaze. Then horse and rider materialized from the mist, as if the cloud had taken solid form. For a moment, Ab was even relieved to see Waluyo's dark face, a familiar landmark in this unnerving fog, but then realized his precarious situation. What if this man was the killer? Ab had just begun to back away when he felt the sharp sting of a horse whip across his cheek and neck. Stunned, Ab stumbled and then turned to run off the path and into the trees. He could see Waluyo reach around behind him, and draw something from behind his belt. He heard the snap of the whip again and the cloppering of the horse. Ab slipped, scrambled to his feet, and clawed into the underbrush, where he froze. Waluyo could not see him in the thick fog, but Ab could make out the silhouette against the paler mist where the path entered the grove. Waluyo had a hand raised over one shoulder, and Ab could see the gleam of steel. A knife. In a minute, Waluyo's eyes would adjust. Ab made a lunge through the underbrush, heading downhill, and heard a whizz and a thunk over his head. He stumbled and fell and scrambled down the steep slope between the trees. "What ho!" he shouted. "Hashers, where are you! What ho!" His feet fell out from under him and he scudded two meters down a gravelly rock face into a cloud of sulfur. He landed at the very edge of a bubbling pool, got to his feet, and stumbled down the ravine. An old stream bed, it would have to go down the mountain. That was where he wanted to go.

Lunging through the mist, he tumbled headlong into the horse and rider. There must be a zigzag path down. He rammed against the horse, screaming, "What ho, Hashers!" at the top of his lungs. The horse reared just as a hand grabbed his jacket. The jacket arms pulled away from around his neck, the horse stumbled, and Ab plunged on down the ravine, still shouting the same refrain at the top of his voice.

His chest hurt. His sides hurt. His legs hurt. His eyes were stinging from the sweat. The ravine seemed to broaden out and open into a field, but he could not see anything clearly through the cloud. His breaths coming in great, heaving gasps, he sat down on a rock. Everything was still. No, wait. Down and to the left he could hear, "Abner Doo-eck, calling Mr. Abner Doo-eck." The voice had a strong Australian accent. In proper form, the hares were out looking for stragglers.

Ab pushed himself to his feet and walked down in the direction of the voice. "Halloo down there, Duck here," he called, mocking himself. In a minute, he could see the bobbing lights of two lanterns.

"Got a little off the trail, I see," laughed one of the two hares as he approached Ab. "You're the last one. We were beginning to get a little worried. It's going to be dark soon."

Back at the Hashers' camp, Ab took a beer and leaned back against the truck. Most of the runners were gathered in a big circle, already drunk, in high spirits, singing "down-downs"; if the object of the down-down didn't finish his drink by the end of the song, he would have to pour the remainder of the drink over his head. Ab's hands were trembling. He felt his whole body beginning to shake uncontrollably. "Ab, Ab, where did you get off to?" Claudia pushed up to him good naturedly. "And where did you get that mean welt across your cheek and neck?" He threw his arms around Claudia and hugged her, wordlessly, tightly. When he let her go, she stepped back.

"Ab, is there something wrong? What's going on? I mean, we're friends right? Can we help?"

Ab ran his hand over his head. His cap was gone. Damn. That was the last straw. It was ridiculous to even worry about it, yet somehow it seemed to him that he had lost the last, small remaining scrap of what passed for normality back home. Fuck it. There was nothing left to lose. He took a long guzzle from his beer. "Do you have an extra couch or a piece of floor I could sleep on in your cottage tonight?" he said. "I can't explain. Don't ask."

"Down-down for the last straggler!" somebody called from the group. "Where's that Duck fellow, out swimming in the rain again?" This was followed by uproarious laughter.

Ab set down his bottle on the edge of the truck. They were already pouring him a fresh drink for the down-down. Claudia put her hand on his arm as he started to walk to the circle. "Yes, of course, you can stay with us."

He finished his beer before they had finished the first line of the song, opened a second, finished it, and finally, at the end of the song had part of a third bottle left to pour over his head. "You guys are going to have to learn to sing faster," he said, returning to the darkness away from the lanterns and the singers.

That night, he lay awake on the lumpy couch in the large family room of the cottage which John and Claudia had rented. The building was old, of yellowish plaster and a high, clay-tiled roof. Rust-coloured stains spread across the walls, and mildew crept up from the corners. It reeked of urine. From outside, faint sounds of Indonesian music wafted up from the town and through the leaky windows. Claudia and John were creaking and thumping with suppressed squeals in the next room. Ab stared at a cecak, motionless on the ceiling. *My Zen master. Dear lizard. Enlighten me.* His body ached all over, and his mind was in complete turmoil. He wished this place had a big bathtub with hot water, maybe even a bubble bath, instead of the cold, dank concrete mandy and a metal bucket to pour cold water.

He drifted into a fitful sleep, his mind racing in circles through the phantasmagoria of possibilities that could explain his current predicament. He was awakened in what seemed like minutes by shouting in the next room, and crying.

"Oh go fuck yourself. I do my job, and you do yours. Yours is fucking around, isn't it? So why don't you just go in there with him, take your mind off fucking George!" This last whispered in a sharp, intense, growl. Ab, strangely, found himself wondering whether fucking was used as a verb or an adjective.

He waited to hear more, but heard only quiet weeping. Just before dawn, he fell asleep again, and then was awakened moments later when a young boy clattered open the front door, without knocking, and carried in a tray of coffee, toast, and boiled eggs, which he set on the table. The boy looked around. *No, Claudia isn't up and about in a towel or something. We all wish, kid.* The first rays of sunlight were just paling the sky. It looked as if it would be clear and hot. Ab sat on the edge of the couch, pulled his sarong tight at the waist, and stood up. If only Nancy were here to help him sort this out. But his only hope now seemed to be to go to Bali and meet this Sani once and for all. The sooner he got back down to Yogya, the sooner he could begin to find some more answers.

Chapter Seventeen

Ab left before John and Claudia had made their morning appearance. He drove back to the market at Bandungan and bought some fruit to eat on the way, and then down to Ambarawa and the main highway. It was eight in the morning, and the air was already hot. He was daydreaming his way through the dust and fumes and haze, so that he didn't see the two buses coming at him until almost the last second. He veered sharply to the left, bumping a motorcyclist and sending him crashing into a fruit vending stall. Ab's car knocked over a couple of chairs next to the stall, ran over a chicken, barely missed a tree, and jerked back sharply on to the main road. He looked in his rear-view mirror. The two buses had scraped each other, and one went sailing off the side of the road and into a rice paddy. Gripping the wheel until his knuckles ached, and concentrating with all his might, he drove on another ten kilometers. Then he pulled off to a side road into a grove of trees, and stopped the car. He climbed out of the car and sat with his back against a tree, looking out over the rice-fields, breathing deeply.

If he had stopped at the scene of the accident, he would have been mobbed, since, being a foreigner, he was *de facto* at fault. He had to keep going. When he had stopped shaking, he climbed back into the car and headed back onto the road. He wouldn't find out much dead, or in jail. He'd better pay attention to the driving.

Ab drove slowly, and then turned on the tape he had purchased from the store next to Nancy's. One small pattern of bells and gongs, a minor harmonic line. But the overall force and direction of the music still escaped him. It seemed to be going nowhere, a random sprinkling of tinkling and clangs and deep gongs, playful innocence and naiveté and something sinister, like a dark fear, momentarily displaced by the investigation, now clawing its way back into his heart. He arrived in the city by late morning. He drove first to the veterinary college, to check for messages. There were none. The office was empty. Even Tri was not there. He wondered if she was in the hospital. Should have asked Findlay up at the Hash.

He stopped off at the Garuda office and asked for Jacobus. The young man at the front desk seemed uncertain, but Ab told him to say there was a message from Heimun Sentosa. In a moment, the young man came back and guided him around the front counter and to an office at the back.

Jacobus was an older man, grey-haired, slightly dishevelled in appearance.

Ab handed him the letter from Heimun, which he took, and then returned to sitting behind a large desk piled high with papers.

Jacobus read the letter carefully, turned it over and read it again. Then he looked up at Ab and smiled.

"So, you are a good friend of Mrs. Sentosa?"

"Ah, yes. A good friend."

"Mmmm. She is a very fine lady, yes?"

"Yes." He suddenly felt tired, and wanted to go home, to his own bed, with no other bodies in it, and sleep.

"And now you are going to Bali...for a vacation?"

"For...yes, I guess so, for a vacation. I will be visiting with Pak Sani."

"Ah, excellent, excellent." He stood up. "I shall have a ticket made for you in a moment, if you will wait."

It seemed like half an hour, but was probably more like ten minutes before Jacobus came back with the ticket. He tucked in the back of his shirt and showed Ab to the door.

"Have a good holiday in Bali, Mr. Ab," he said.

The front gate at the house was padlocked; he didn't remember having had the presence of mind to do this when he'd left. The value of habits, he thought, are to help us survive in chaotic times, when we don't have presence of mind. Or someone else padlocked it, which was a more ominous possibility. The guard was nowhere to be seen. He pulled out his keys, unlocked the gate, pulled it open, and drove in. With the car motor off, he sat for a moment. Everything was quiet. No Nancy. He hoped there were also no dead bodies. He'd had enough. He went back to pull the gate shut, and returned to the front door. It too was locked, as he must have left it.

Inside, the house was silent and smelled warm, close and musty. The drawers of the buffet looked like they had been ransacked, as did his closet in the bedroom. Yet nothing seemed to be missing. Somebody was looking for...what? The kris maybe? He went to the telephone and dialled the number Mrs. Sentosa had given him. A lady answered in English, and, when she heard who it was, immediately asked which flight he was arriving on. The news of his impending trip had preceded him already. The arrangements made, he repacked the overnight bag he had been lugging around; he laid the kris at the bottom, covering it with a few light clothes, his bathing suit, deodorant, toothbrush, a couple of towels. If he was going on a holiday, he might as well play the part. Then, on second thought, he threw all his belongings, clean and dirty together, into his two battered blue hockey equipment bags. One never knew. Maybe he would be leaving the country directly from Bali. He left the bags just inside the bedroom door.

Finally, exhausted after the events of the previous twenty-four hours, he slipped into a sarong and fell into bed and into a deep, dreamless sleep.

He came up through the layers of sleep with a headache. A sharp, metallic rattling hammered in his brain. His body was shaking. A sharp pain in his shoulder jarred him awake. He turned over and sat upright so quickly that he almost passed out and momentarily had to put his head down into his hands. As he did so he thought that he saw, in his half-sleep, a shadow pass quickly from the room. His first thought was that the pain in his shoulder was from an aborted stab from a knife. There was a crashing sound in the next room. He leapt to his feet to run after the assailant, but realized with horror that the floor was shaking under him. Another sharp pain, this time to his back, brought him to his senses. An earthquake! And the ceiling was caving in. He staggered across the shaking floor to the screened back door and threw himself through the screen and on to the grass outside. Handful by handful, he dragged himself across the quaking earth as far away from the house as he could. In a moment, everything was still. As he lay there, he saw a snake coil from the bushes beside the door and slip through the broken screen and into the house. He could hear cries and voices in the street. He thought that it really was a good thing that Java's nuclear power plant was still on the drawing boards. Then he passed out.

When he came to his senses, he was still lying out on the grass behind the house, and the muezzin was calling morning prayers through the loudspeakers from the mosque. It was still dark. He felt stiff all over. "I've got a plane to catch to Bali," was his first thought. He groaned to his feet and looked around. The house looked like it was still all there. A few roof tiles had shaken loose and fallen to the ground. He walked to the screen door and stepped through it. The image of the snake entering the house came to him and he stepped gingerly until he found a light switch. Inside, there was a bit more damage. Pieces of plaster had fallen from the ceiling. Broken glass from vases that had been knocked off coffee tables. Still, the situation didn't look as bad as he had thought it would be, given the size of the quake.

He bent down over the bag where he had stashed the kris. There was a big gash in the leather, and the latch appeared to have been broken open, though he couldn't remember having locked it. He opened it and pushed aside the clothes and towels.

The scabbard was still there, but the knife was gone. Crouching beside the bag, he looked up at the bed. From this angle, he could see the silhouette of the finely carved handle of the kris. It was pushed in up to the hilt at about the spot where his shoulder would have been had he not suddenly put his head down. What had first awakened him? He recalled a loud rattling sound, like sabre rattling, or maybe it was just the falling plaster from the earthquake which had awakened him. He stood up, tightened his sarong, and slipped on his sandals. Then he leaned over the bed and very carefully pulled up on the knife. It had been rammed in with great force, and he had to strain with all his strength before it finally pulled free.

He held it by the handle, and laid the blade across his left hand. The blade felt hot, and his hands were sweating. He fondled the snake and the damascene like a small pet in his hands. Carefully, he slipped the knife back into its sheath, laid it on the bed, and stared at it. Then, as if in a trance, he took the kris and with a small trowel dug a hole next to the mango tree, where he buried it.

It was a moment before he realized that someone was rattling at the gate.

"Pak Ab! Dr. Ab! Everything okay?" It was Tina, the housekeeper, and Budi, the night watchman. They must have come by and seen his car out front.

Yes, everything was fine, but the house needed a bit of cleaning up, and he needed a quick breakfast before catching the plane to Bali.

"To Bali?"

"Yes. I think I need a little vacation."

Chapter Eighteen

Ab arrived at the Yogyakarta airport an hour before the plane was to leave, but it had not yet arrived from Bali. It would be more than an hour before he actually got away. Airplanes did not overnight in Yogya; a flight out to Bali or Jakarta had to await the planes from those places before the first outward flights of the day could take off. He checked in his bags and looked around the small airport.

There were clumps of tourist groups, Japanese and Dutch mostly, people his age and older, loaded with cameras, decked out in gaudy, happy, brilliant tourist-quality batiks. Ab looked at his own modest, dark shirt and brown slacks. Not much fun, a step up from the coveralls he often wore, but, after all, those clothes that seemed gay and clever here, back home would seem gaudy and would end up in the kids dress-up clothes box. Ab was dressed for anywhere. He checked the tourists over again. What was this country to them? To the Dutch, a quaint old colony, now, perhaps, gone to the dogs because they were no longer here. To the Japanese, was it a big market for their goods? A place where friends or relatives had died in World War Two? And then there were the low-budget travellers in cut-off jeans and tee shirts, scorning the tourist groups, seeing the real Indonesia. Which meant the temples at Borobudur and Prambanan, the shadow plays and the puppet plays and the stage performances, all the same things that the other tourists saw, but somehow pure because they were not seen as part of a group tour. And yet, it seemed to Ab, if you did not see Indonesia as part of a group tour, you did not perhaps see Indonesia at all, because everything, everything seemed to be done in groups. Indonesia was nothing if not a group country.

He strolled out of the airport and walked along the road skirting the airport and out along the river valley at one end of the runway. He wandered over the grass away from the road and sat at the edge of the valley rim, surveying the multiple terraces cut into the valley's walls. This was the picture of almost the entire island of Java, with a couple of thousand people per square kilometer. Terraces, everywhere, all linked through one of the most sophisticated irrigation systems in the world. Sophisticated not just in a technological sense, but even more so in a social sense. For the kind of social organization and cooperation needed to keep such a system going must be at least as intricate and weighed down with branches and sub-branches and floodgates and power structures as the agricultural technology it was supporting. It gave Ab the sense of being in the middle of some bewildering, three-dimensional puzzle. It seemed to him that, in trying to fathom Soesanto's and George's killers, he would have to fathom this complex and tenacious web he had fallen into. He wondered if for a simple Mennonite boy from Winnipeg, this would be possible, any more than a Javanese could comprehend the webs of Mennonite entanglements.

A sudden, roaring thunder over his head brought him back to the exigencies of the moment. The plane from Bali had just dropped through the clouds and was landing. He stretched his legs and headed back to the airport.

It was not until he was actually in the plane and strapped into a window seat that he suddenly panicked, thinking that tomorrow was the day he was supposed to be out of the country. But he didn't have anything in writing. Maybe it was only the paper that mattered. For a few seconds he considered getting off this plane and just flying to Jakarta and home. He had heard of people who over-stayed their visas being jailed, or having exorbitant fines levied against them. The last thing he wanted was to end up in an Indonesian jail. And yet, if he got off now, he might never be able to come back, and would spend his whole life wondering why George and Soesanto were killed, what had really happened. He wondered if he would ever see Nancy again, and what she meant in all of this. He was so close, it seemed, to understanding. So close. He settled back and closed his eyes. His official visa, after all, still said he had more than a year in the country. His only deportation order had come from the lips of the Klaten police chief. Wouldn't they need official papers?

The plane was starting to pull out toward the runway. His knuckles tightened on the edge of the chair. The stewardess came by and offered a tray of candy. He picked out a mint and put it into his mouth.

Ab braced himself for the thrill of take-off, the orgasmic rush of endorphins that would course through his blood as the plane would leap upwards and veer sharply to miss the volcanoes. What would happen if you got a combination of a poor pilot and such a runway? He dug into his jacket pocket to make sure his little bottle of gin was there. He tried to think about Nancy, and wished that he had, just that one time after the evening out, been courageous enough to make love to her. Even now, he wasn't sure how she would have responded to more direct advances. He wondered if the Nancy in his head was a fantasy pieced together from fragments of cross-cultural misunderstanding. He wasn't sure about anything. The plane had just lifted clear of the ground when there was a kafuffle in the front of the cabin. The door to the cockpit was open and the passengers and stewardesses were crowding to look into it. The plane circled quickly, and, without explanation, dropped back down to the runway. It was a rocky landing, and the plane swerved sharply once half-way down the landing strip.

Finally, it came to a full halt, and the pilot and co-pilot came quickly out of the cockpit, closing the door behind them.

While waiting for the stairs to arrive so they could open the door, the chief stewardess shouted an explanation to the passengers, who laughed heartily. "A snake has been found in the cockpit, and we must wait for the tamer to come and take him."

"Would that all snakes were so easily tamed," said a deep, clear voice next to Ab.

Ab turned to look at the gentleman sitting one seat over, there being an empty seat between them. He looked Chinese, with pure white hair and a face richly and finely wrinkled like the bark of a maple tree. He was dressed in a bright pink shirt and white trousers, which gave him a striking appearance. He sighed, wearily. "I hope they do not make us sit here in the heat too long."

The door finally opened and several people entered, including a very old, smooth-faced, bony man, who was apparently the animal tamer. He was carrying a large basket.

Ab's neighbour turned to him and the wrinkles in his face moved to create a smile. Like one of those clay-imagination cartoons, Ab thought, almost laughing. "You are going on a vacation to Bali?" said the man.

"Ah, yes. Actually I work here in Java, but I am going to Bali to...to relax."

"An excellent idea. I happen to work in Bali, but it is still, I think, a better place to visit than to work."

"Why is that?"

He leaned conspiratorially toward Ab. "These Hindus, they are very lovely people, so friendly, but every day is a holy day or a holiday or some celebration. It is not so good for getting work done."

The door to the cockpit opened and the animal tamer came out, holding up his basket, triumphantly. The passengers laughed, clapped and cheered. In a few minutes, the door was closed again and the airplane returned to the runway. The stewardess came around with candy again and the take-off, almost identical to the previous one, was again accomplished.

"If we go around a few more times," Ab said, half to himself and half to his neighbour, "I may even get used to it, the landing as well as the taking off."

"Me," said the old man, "I will never get used to it. Maybe I was just born too late."

Ab pondered the possibility that the thrill of taking off might be wearing thin. Like his Mennonite forebears, who had fled over the centuries from country to country and around the world, maybe he would run out of places to fly to. The erotic thrill of being saved at evangelistic meetings had worn off after seven or eight times. And how many times could he run away from his parental home? Maybe Nancy was right about the demons and angels of one's childhood. The beauty of intense spiritual experience, the exhilarating freedom of taking off, both physically and intellectually, was that it was unique, unrepeatable. Maybe he would, finally, have to be at home somewhere and leave God, endorphins, and sex to the teenagers. The thought made him sad. He looked out the window and into the craters of the volcanoes below. The stewardesses came around with the boxes of jasmine tea and a snack that were the hallmark of every internal flight.

Ab looked at the box on the fold-out tray before him. "I wonder which it will be this time, a spring roll or a sweet bread?" he said in Bahasa Indonesia.

"You speak Bahasa." The neighbour opened his box. "Have you been here long?"

"A year."

The man took a bite of his bun.

"You are teaching at the university?"

"Not exactly. I am helping on a dairy development project, and working with the veterinary college to help strengthen some of their programs."

"Ah. You are a veterinarian, then."

Ab swallowed a mouthful of the bun. There was peanut butter inside. "I investigate epidemics and try to prevent them." Having said that, he felt pedantic and embarrassed.

"Mmhmm." The man chewed in silence for several minutes. "And you are finding the work gratifying?"

"It would be easier if my counterpart were around more."

"He is often not there?"

"Actually, he's dead. Died…very suddenly."

The man rubbed his chin as if he were thinking. "That must be quite upsetting for you." Then he sighed. "Well, things must continue, yes?"

"Yes, except that I'm supposed to leave the country very soon."

"Oh?" He looked at Ab. His gaze was penetrating and Ab felt momentarily uncomfortable.

"Uh, yes. Visa problems." The old man continued to stare at him.

"Visa problems. Well, that's too bad. So you are going to Bali for a kind of last vacation."

"Yes." Ab sipped at the cool jasmine tea. It was like drinking perfume. He pulled the straw from the drink box and slipped it into his pocket, next to the gin bottle, then closed up his snack box and leaned back into the seat, closing his eyes.

His neighbour also closed up his box, and set it on the floor at his feet. Then he leaned down and opened an attaché case, pulled out a file of papers, and set them on the tray before him. He pulled a pair of glasses from his breast-pocket and began to read, leaning close to the paper and moving his finger along the line. Ab watched him through half-open eyes.

The gentleman seemed to pause thoughtfully at the end of a line. "So, you came here to help the poor people of the world?" he said without looking up. "Like a kind of secular missionary?"

Startled, Ab opened his eyes. "Uh, yes. Yes, I suppose you could say that." His mind raced backwards. The cowboy missionary: his old joke, a childhood attempt to reconcile what he wanted with what he was told God wanted. Is that really why he had come here? Was he going out to the fields ripe with harvest, as pastor Bill Janzen had exhorted them to? Were all his rebellions and flights in vain? Did God get you in the end anyway? Not much difference between a cowboy missionary and a veterinary development worker, after all. Even the old guy next to him could see it. His mind fought against the thought, but there it was.

The gentleman set down his glasses. "And, do you think you have helped the poor people, by coming here?"

Ab laughed nervously. "You seem as if you have been reading the question on the paper before you," he joked, "like a lawyer." The man did not answer. "Yes, to answer your question, yes, I think I have helped some poor people." He remembered the farmers in Gandringan. That had been something, hadn't it?

The man slipped his glasses back on and looked directly at Ab. "And that gives you some satisfaction?"

"Yes, yes of course it does." *But it would give me greater satisfaction if I discovered who killed Soesanto and George, and where Nancy is.*

"Good. It is good to have satisfaction in one's work. And rare. Especially in the messy business of trying to save the world." He returned to his reading, tracing his finger across the page.

Ab said nothing, but his emotions were turning inside him. *You smug rich bastard. What do you know of suffering, right here in your own country?*

He closed his eyes and tried, unsuccessfully, to rest for the remainder of the one-hour trip. When the plane began its descent into the Denpasar airport he turned to the window and leaned over, pretending to look out, while he slipped the short straw into the gin bottle and sucked deeply on it. He could see the palm-fringed beaches rise up to meet him through the window. He gripped the edge of the seat tightly and took a deep breath.

When the plane had taxied to a stop, he arose and prepared to step out over his still-seated neighbour, and into the aisle. He wondered how he would be met at the airport. How would they know, among the various tourists, which one was Abner Dueck? The old man was groping under his seat for something. He came up with a finely carved teak walking stick. He sat back up and gripped Ab's hand, firmly.

"Could you help me up for a moment?"

Forgetting his earlier anger and seeing only the white-haired gentleman, he helped him to his feet. They waited until the other passengers had passed. The gentleman did not loosen his grip, but held Ab by the arm. His grip was like steel. "I would also appreciate it if you would also be so kind as to walk this old man to the terminal."

"Of course."

Coming down the stairs into the dazzling Balinese sun, Ab looked toward the terminal. There was a crowd of brightly dressed people gathered there. Women in what he assumed were traditional outfits were dancing and holding up flowers, and a full orchestra played crashing, bell-ringing music.

"There must be someone important arriving," Ab said as they stepped onto the tarmac.

"Yes, I suppose there must," said the old man.

Ab waved toward a small executive jet which had just pulled to a stop near the terminal. "Probably some government official in that jet over there."

The old man looked in the direction of the jet. "Yes," he said, "perhaps."

The tourist groups on the plane from Yogyakarta pointed and gesticulated toward the welcoming party. The Japanese took out their cameras. The closer Ab and the old man got to the terminal, the more it seemed to him that the welcomers were looking in their direction. He looked over his shoulder to see if there was someone behind him just as two Balinese young ladies approached and laid garlands of orchids around his neck and that of his neighbour.

"I think," Ab said, trying to pull away from the vice-grip on his arm. "Perhaps there is some mistake?" Cameras were aimed at him and his companion, and even a couple of young travellers in tattered T-shirts stopped to stare.

The old man bowed toward the welcomers, pulling Ab forward with him. He sighed. "In the old days," he said, "the young ladies kept their breasts bare when they welcomed you like this. It was natural and beautiful, like a flower opening or a young rice shoot budding. But now," he guided Ab through the door of the terminal, "now if there are bare breasts, Allah and his helpers in Jakarta are very upset. They are such weaklings, they cannot bear to look on God's beauty. Like all cowards, they prefer guns and knives." He stopped a moment and turned to Ab. "Surely their Allah cannot have created this world, if he so dislikes gazing upon its beauties, don't you think?"

Ab was in a complete daze. Again, he tried to pry the old man loose. "I have to meet someone here," he said. "Really, it is important."

The man firmly drew Ab out the front door of the terminal and toward a waiting black Mercedes limousine, with tinted windows all around. "Yes," he said, "your meeting is very important."

Ab wrenched his arm free and stepped back. "So I must, I am afraid, leave you now," he said.

The driver of the limousine had opened the back door and the old man motioned for him to precede him into the car. "Please," he said, "if you wish to meet Sani Sentosa, then you will come with me."

Ab pulled anxiously at his beard and climbed into the coolness of the air-conditioned car.

"And my bags?" he asked, weakly.

The gentleman made himself comfortable and the door was shut. "Your bags were marked?"

"Yes."

"They will be taken care of. Do you have your tags?"

Ab handed them over to the old man, who leaned forward and handed them to the driver, who returned into the terminal. While he was retrieving the bags, the old man turned to Ab.

"I don't believe you have introduced yourself," he said.

"Ab. Dr. Abner Dueck." He felt hopeless and depressed. Through the tinted glass he could see the driver coming out of the terminal with his bags.

"I am very pleased to meet you," said the gentleman, reaching out his hand. "I am Sani Sentosa. I believe you have met my wife?"

Chapter Nineteen

They sat in silence as the limousine pushed along the highway, scattering chickens and people on bicycles in its wake. Ab stared out the window. He had wanted to meet the infamous Pak Sani. So, here he was, sitting next to him, sitting next to one of probably the richest men in Indonesia, and perhaps in the world, speeding along the highway as tourists in rented dune buggies, peasants on bicycles, chickens, always the ubiquitous chickens and, here in Hindu Bali, dogs, scattered out of their way. Here he was, helping the poor people of the world. Is this what it meant?

Pak Sani propped his walking stick up between his knees and played with it. Ab noted that the head of the stick was the open-mouthed head of a cobra. "You should not let all of this distract you, Dr. Dueck." He motioned with his hand to indicate the luxury of the car interior. Ab noted that his name had been pronounced correctly. "Do not be angry with me on account of appearances."

Ab said nothing, but continued to stare out the window.

Sani continued to fondle his cane. "Just remember that the reason you are here, in this car, today, is because you want to understand why your friends have been killed. And one of the reasons you are interested in that is because you have been concerned about the farmers who are receiving the cows. So you see, you are still helping the poor. Because if you can understand that killing, perhaps you can also help the farmers."

Ab was silent for a few minutes longer. *Yeah*, he thought, *help them by leaving the country*. The car was taking them away from the main tourist beaches and along the south coast road. "I see that you do not like to deal with wealthy people. You do not trust me. Heimun and…and others…have told me that you trusted them." He sighed. "But then that's women. I have had the same failing. Trusting women where I would not have trusted men. Being led by the loins, as it were." He smiled, then immediately turned serious. "Your distrust of wealthy men, is it a part of your religion? Or are you racist too, like," he waved his hand, "like Allah's little helpers in Jakarta?"

Or maybe just an unscrupulous opportunist, like you, Ab thought.

Sani put his strong hand firmly on Ab's knee and gripped it until he winced. "And who do you think pays for the dairy cows? Do you think they drop from the sky? Do you think the American dairy farmers give them away? Do you think, even if your government gave them, and sent us all you experts for nothing, that there would not be political strings attached, strings to make us dance? Look at me!" Ab looked at Sani; his eyes were ablaze, like coals glowing in the wrinkled log that was his face. "If you want to come here and help the poor, sooner or later, you will have to deal with me. You might as well do it sooner."

Ab looked away. "It's too late, Mr. Sentosa. The police say I should be out of the country by tomorrow. There is no point to any of this, really. I don't know why I came." He looked out the window at a Balinese farmer in his dirty shorts guiding the plow behind a pair of Balinese cattle. The cattle were deceptively pretty, brown, with black and white markings, like deer. Deceptive, for they were also very strong and strong willed. Deceptive, like so many things in this beautiful country, because the observers didn't take the time to understand what they were looking at. Deceptive because Ab, like so many visitors to tropical paradises, had seen Java in terms of the illusions he had created, the things he had wanted to believe.

Sani Sentosa took his hand off Ab's leg. Ab rubbed it to bring back the circulation. The old man held his cane firmly with both hands, and spoke in a clear, business-like fashion. "So, your visa expires tomorrow?"

"No, my visa is still good for another year."

"But I thought..."

"The Klaten police chief said I had seven days from the day George and Soesanto were killed. That was six days ago."

"The Klaten police chief." Sani waved his hand dismissively.

"He said his orders came from elsewhere."

Sani turned to Ab and smiled his clay-imagination smile. "Ah, that proverbial elsewhere. You may need me yet, more than you know. With your papers and my money, we may be able to keep you out of jail for over-staying your welcome. Now," he said with some satisfaction, leaning back into the car seat, "think of more pleasant things for today. We are almost at my place. Tomorrow, after we have rested and eaten and played a little, then we can work."

The car pulled up to a large, wrought-iron metal gate, and a guard let them through with a wave of the hand. They wound down a smooth road between overhanging coconut palms. Through breaks between the trees, Ab could see the brightness of the ocean sprinkled with whitecaps. In a moment, they had stopped before a palatial villa, built of orange brick and decorated everywhere with bas-reliefs, grey stone carvings of many-headed gods, monsters and animals engaged in the perpetual struggle between good and evil. The front doors were intricately carved and the lintel was painted in floral patterns of many colours. The driver opened the door for Mr. Sentosa, and another servant came around to Ab's side to open his door. Ab stared a moment at the slim young man in the sunglasses holding the door open for him. He could swear it was the guy who was tailing him in Yogya. Was that because they all looked the same to him, as Nancy had once suggested? He got out of the car and joined Pak Sani before the doors. Sani stood for a moment gazing up at them.

"Do you like them?" he asked. He did not wait for Ab's answer. "They are a reproduction of some doors that have been in the family for centuries. The originals are too small for us now. I suppose we have grown in stature."

"And in favour with God," Ab murmured.

Sani turned. "What?"

"Nothing. Just a quote from the Bible I remembered from my childhood. 'And Jesus grew in stature and in favour with God.'"

Sani paused to ponder this. "Having favour with God does not always help with men, as your Jesus discovered. Anyway, as I was saying, the doors are now too small. We keep them in a special room at the back along with…" The front door was opened and swung inward.

If Ab had been taken aback at who greeted him at the Sentosa place in Bandungan, there was no word sufficiently strong to describe the shock waves that went through him in the next few moments. Just inside the door stood a beautiful young lady in a light, lacy red Balinese dress. "Pak Sani," she said as the old man came through the door. She threw her arms around his neck and kissed him on the cheek. Two thoughts flashed through Ab's mind, one nipping at the tail of the other: Sani had a young mistress. No, Sani had a granddaughter. It was Nancy.

She looked over Sani's shoulder at Ab, her eyes searching his face.

Pak Sani held out his hand in a gesture of introduction. "I believe you two know each other," he said.

Ab stood with his hands by his side, confused, upset, unable to move.

"Hello, Ab," she said quietly, pushing the hair away from her eyes. "May I show you to your room?" She slipped past him and called something to one of the men outside, then returned, putting a hand lightly on Ab's shoulder as she passed. "Excuse me. If you will just follow me, I'll show you where you'll be staying. The helper will bring your bags."

He followed her from the front hallway with its ornate stone carvings, down a carpeted hallway. There were little alcoves at periodic intervals along the hall, each with its own light, each with some precious or beautiful object: carvings of ebony and jade, silkscreen paintings from China and Bali, antique silver work from Java. They walked in silence. Near the end of the hall, Nancy opened a heavy, teak door, carved in patterns of snakes and flowers. The room beyond was spacious and full of light. Large windows looked out across a small park-like space to a wide, sandy beach and the ocean beyond. Ab walked into the room, and the servant followed struggling with the two big hockey bags. He set them down with a grunt and then, silently and discreetly, disappeared.

Ab stood at the window looking out. He was churning inside with anger, love, close to tears and laughter. He tugged at his beard to the point where it began to hurt. He could feel Nancy standing very closely behind him, almost touching, as if waiting for him to turn around. Then, when he refused to move, he could feel her move away. "There is drinking water in the jug by your bed. And the tray over on the small table has tea for you."

Ab's feelings were all over the place. Nancy had been the first woman he had met who had taken his mind, and his heart, away from Sarah. In a sense, she had given him back to himself. And then, just disappeared. He didn't even know, he realized, whether he could trust her. Sani's granddaughter? He even wondered, somewhere deep down, if she could have been a killer. He thought of the kris he had found on the buffet that day. He wanted so much to turn around and take her into his arms, but remained frozen, staring out over the green sea.

"Ab, I know you don't understand, but you will. Right now, if you wish to wash up, you may. We shall have lunch in a few minutes." She started to pull the door shut, but hesitated. "My room is the next one down the hall, if you should need me," she said quietly, and then pulled the door shut.

Ab had not moved from the spot by the window, staring out at the ocean, when there was a knock at the door just a few minutes later. "Dr. Dueck? May I come in?"

"*Silakan*, please," Ab said toward the window, and turned as the door was pushed open. It was Pak Sani. Ab turned to look back outside, and Sani came over to stand beside him. He stood there a moment, also looking out at the sea. It annoyed Ab that the person he wanted to dislike the most was the only person in a decade to pronounce his name right. "If you really want to know, I had to spirit my granddaughter away without telling you, for her own safety. She was supposed to find and return a kris to its rightful owner, but it went missing, and someone else was ready to kill to get it from her. The aspiring killer was convinced that she must still have it." He paused. "It seems to have gone missing at your house. You wouldn't happen to know anything about that, would you?"

Ab fiddled with the inside of his trouser pocket. He had been trying to sort out where his theories of the murders now stood, but it was all hopelessly confused. The man who was now asking about the kris might well himself be a murderer, asking for his own weapon back. Ab was pleased that he'd had the foresight to bury it. "Can we talk about this tomorrow? You said yourself that today was a day for pleasure, and tomorrow was for work."

Ab looked directly at Sani. The old man glared. Then his face broke into something between a deep frown and a mocking smile. "I can see that if you were to stay here just a bit longer, Mr. Dueck, you would fit right in. A pity. Lunch will be served when you hear the bell."

Ab bolted the door and wandered around his room, which turned out to be a kind of mini-apartment fitted with a couch and several soft chairs and an ornately carved low table, on which stood the tea tray. Off one end of this living space was a bedroom, almost equally spacious, with a queen-sized bed, and silk sheets. The bathroom was all of white marble, in western style, with a bathtub big enough for two people, and an overhead shower.

He stripped down and tried out the shower, which did indeed have hot water as the inscription said. The spray pounding against the top of his head felt good and freeing. So, today was a day of pleasure. So it would be. Enough of trying to understand. He was sick of it. Maybe tomorrow he could try again. Maybe after a day of pleasure, it would finally make sense.

He could hear the silver bell ring even from the shower, and when he had gotten out and dried off, he looked around to see how it worked. Small silver bells hung in the corner of each of the rooms, apparently connected by a string which passed from one to the other above the ceiling. At some central place, there must be a master pull-rope to set them all ringing.

He brushed his beard and slipped into a clean pair of shorts, which he very seldom wore on Java, it being considered either too boyish or too foreign, and a pull-over batik shirt with an open neck in the modern, bright, geometric design of the Javanese artist Sapto Hudoyo. He slipped on his sandals and retraced his way down the hallway toward the main entrance. The dining room, he had noted despite his distraction on his way in, was just off the main entrance to the left. The lunch was spread out on the table. There were plates heaped with white rice and rice fried with tiny shrimps all through it, chicken curry and succulent beef stew, steamed Chinese greens and stir-fried broccoli and cauliflower, two kinds of crackers, papaya, pineapple, lichees, rambutan, bananas. There were bottles of beer and jugs of water, cold and covered with condensation.

Nancy and her grandfather were already there, standing by the window and talking. Nancy's hair was brushed back clean and straight, and Ab could see the striking resemblance to her grandmother and grandfather both, now that he knew. She was still in her red dress, which came about halfway down her thighs and clung to her slim body. He had no trouble remembering why it was he had fallen for her, why he still wanted her so badly his gut ached. Her grandfather had changed into a more modest blue shirt, with shell patterns on it.

The sun slanted down between the palms and through the open windows, through which could be heard the recurrent hissing of the waves. The air was warm and pleasant, with a slight smell of salt.

Ab motioned with his hand toward the table. "This is all for just us three?"

Sani crinkled into his smile. "There are many other people in this house who also eat. But for now, yes, this is all for us. Perhaps we can fill our plates and go eat outside on the patio near the beach," he said.

They filled their plates and Ab took a cold beer and they strolled over a grassy knoll down toward the beach. Impulsively, Ab kicked off his sandals to feel the cool prickliness of the grass against his soles. He felt good. They sat on stone-carved but cushioned furniture under a thatched beach-shelter just off the sand. Beside them, in a shed with one side open to the sea, hung a range of snorkelling and diving gear. Below them, the beach dazzled under the bright sun. The beach spread out in both directions in a semi-circle, with the Sentosa house at the centre. To the right, off the point where the beach and the palm trees turned and disappeared from sight, another, smaller island was visible several miles across the water. Several sailboats moved swiftly and gracefully through the channel between the two islands. It was now high tide, but a reef, stretching from one point of the semi-circle almost to the other, was clearly visible beneath the clear water about a hundred meters off-shore.

"There must be a strong wind out there, past the reef," Ab murmured, stretching out his legs and watching the boats.

Sani followed his gaze to the boats. "Yes, the wind seems fine for sailing, but the under-water currents are strong—and more dangerous. More than one boat has come to grief on that reef."

But Ab didn't want to talk about hidden meanings. He reached over and gently touched Nancy's hair, then pulled his hand away. "Tell me, would it be possible to go snorkelling here?" he asked.

"Of course," Nancy said lightly, "we'll fix you up with some equipment this afternoon. You need to stay on this side of the reef to avoid the currents. I'll come with you to show you the best places." She paused. "If you like."

"I would very much like." He closed his eyes and let the gentle nudge of the warm breeze against his skin lift away the little crusts of darkness and worry that still clung there, in shallow crevices.

"Before I go inside for my afternoon siesta, I would like to say just one more serious thing to you, Mr. Dueck."

Ab opened his eyes. "Abner. Call me Abner. Can I call you Sani?"

The old man looked intensely at him. "This is serious. That bit of knowledge that you acquired today, the relationship between Nancy and myself, that is never to pass beyond the bounds of your lips."

"My lips are sealed."

"This is not for clichés or jokes. Many years ago we had to change our names. Nancy was raised by English friends in the expatriate community, and never knew who her real parents were until she became an adult, just a couple of years ago. Because of my ambiguous relationship with the government in power, my family is always under some threat. I don't want Nancy to get caught up as a pawn in this. It is better that she not be closely associated with me."

Ab looked at Nancy as her grandfather spoke. Her eyes were serious and sad.

He pushed himself wearily to his feet with his cane. As he passed his granddaughter, he laid a hand on her shoulder, and she laid her hand over his. "Have a good time, my children. This old man needs to get some rest."

They watched him make his way across the lawn, the rich and powerful Pak Sani, a sad and weary old man. Ab gently stroked the back of Nancy's hair.

"Shall we go for a swim?" she asked.

"I'd love to. I'll just go and slip into my swimsuit. Can I meet you back here?" They walked back to the house in silence, not touching. Coming back from the house in his swimsuit, his feet brushing over the cool grass, the warm wind enveloping his body like soft cloth, he could see that Nancy was already there, her silhouette at the edge of the water, bent over to see some starfish or urchin. He wished the moment would never end. He was surprised at the hot slap of the sun on his back and the sting of the hot sand on his feet when he stepped onto the sand, and couldn't refrain from giving out a little yelp. Nancy turned and laughed. She wore a bright red bikini and had goggles pushed back up on her forehead.

"Grab yourself some gear from the shed there and come into the water," she called. "It's the only comfortable place."

Ab took the largest sizes of everything from the shed, having learned that, in Indonesia, "large" meant "medium" or "small" in Canadian sizes. He stepped into the water and leaned on Nancy to put on his flippers. She really is strong, he thought as he let his whole weight fall against her and she did not flinch.

She picked up a bottle of sunbathing oil from the edge of the sand, filled her hand, and massaged it deeply, firmly, gently over Ab's back. "You can get burnt to a crisp out there before you know what's happened," she said. "And then you wouldn't be good for…for anything…for at least a week." She laughed. Water on stones. Moonlight on stones. He could feel the warm oil melting into every muscular sulcus of his back and he just wanted to fall back into her arms.

They stepped gingerly out into the sea, the coral sand biting into their feet. At waist depth, about twenty metres off-shore, they pulled down their masks, adjusted their air tubes, and floated out over the inner side of the reef.

From this angle, face-down in the water, the sea was an entirely different place. Below them schools of tiny fish like fragments from the same shattered jewel darted in and out of projections from the coral. Angel fish waved past them, graciously nonchalant. Bright blue starfish startled them unexpectedly in dark crevices. They passed close to a high point in the coral, and Nancy reached out and drew Ab to one side. She pointed back to the clump of black, spiny urchins he had almost grazed. Even they, the deliverers of pain, with their fluorescent blue and yellow markings buried deep between the spines, were things of beauty. Time was of no consequence here. Everything was in a soft, blue-green undulating eternal moment.

Ab didn't know how long they had lingered there before Nancy touched his arm and they moved back to the shore. He only knew that his mind was blank, and full of quiet peace. He slipped out of the flippers at the edge of the water, and tip-toed painfully over the hot, sharp sand. Nancy pulled out two folding lounge chairs from behind the beach house where they had eaten and set them out in the shade on the grass. Ab lay down and, in the warm womb of the afternoon air, fell into a peaceful sleep.

Chapter Twenty

Ab awoke to the sun glowing just above the range of volcanoes off to his left. Nancy was nowhere to be seen. He felt pleasantly at ease, and decided to go for a walk to the point of land off to his right opposite the island. The sand was cooler against his feet now, and he sauntered down to the water's edge. The tide had gone out, exposing the rough surface of the coral and leaving strands of seaweed draped over the exposed areas. He thought he could hear music off in the distance, perhaps just around the bend of the beach, and he quickened his pace in the hope of seeing one of the many Balinese festivals he had heard so much about.

From the point where the coast turned, he saw not very far down the beach a knot of people coming out of the palm forest above the sand. They were bearing in their midst some kind of pavilion, all decorated with fruits and leaves cut into intricate shapes, and bouquets of flowers. Musicians trailed behind the main group, beating sharp drums and sounding on nasal-voiced horns and small bamboo flutes. Ab remained, still, at one with his surroundings, where he was. The party stopped near the water's edge and set down their little parade float. More music wafted over the sand to him and he squatted, not thinking, not feeling, just being in this magic twilight. Then, as he watched, the crowd moved away from their flowery creation, and flames blossomed out and up into the darkening sky.

The music intensified, and the flames embraced the pavilion in its entirety, burning fiercely before falling back, like a soul striving for godliness, for purity of spirit failing, falling back to this mortal earth, and then…As he watched, the charred silhouette of a body fell through the flaming platform and to the sand beneath, and then the whole structure seemed to partially collapse and the flames burst upward in another brief, fierce blaze.

He turned his eyes away from what he now realized was a cremation and stared out over the darkening sea.

His father's funeral had not been such a celebration. How stiffly the family stood around the open coffin to have their pictures taken. The pastor spoke, dishing out the false comfort of the bright life to come. The thin yellow face of Gerhard "Gerry" Dueck was couched, incongruously for such a frugal man, in the white satin. Ab thought only of the last year, as his father wasted away, in constant pain, of stomach cancer. He and his sisters had slipped in whispers past the living room where the big hospital bed had been put, where his mother watched night and day, spooning him soup, where the starchy but kindly visiting nurse went to give him his shots. Stumbling headlong, headstrong into the confusions of adolescent life, he was forced, day by day, to live with death. He hated his father for that death, hated the preacher for his optimism, his mother for her selfless compassion, God for His stupidity in foisting this on them. He wished, then, that last year, that he could have burned the whole house down and walked away. Now, looking back to see the last flames of the cremation pavilion die down, he wept, for the first time since the funeral, for his father, for himself, for all of life that he did not understand.

Just before he died, his father said, "You are on your own now, in this place. I can't help you anymore." Ab had wondered what he meant. Now, Ab thought, he was saying, "I am on my own now. You can't be with me anymore." It was as close as he had ever been able to come to expressing both his own vulnerability and his love for his son. And Ab had not been able to hear it. And here he was, so much like his father, unable to make that risky leap beyond his own bounds, no strings attached, which might make communication between people possible. He wanted to love the world and everything in it, desperately, but couldn't, for fear it might forsake him. He was taking off again and again long after the thrill was gone, when all he really wanted was a soft landing.

He looked back out toward the island. The last, faint rays of the sun washed the western sky in watercolour flames. The night would be clear, and the first stars blinked down out of the jewel-like blackness in the east. A young man, a teenager, about the age Ab had been when he was baptized, had walked out from the trees not far from where Ab squatted motionless on the sand. He waded out up to his knees, bent down, and splashed the water over his head. Then he lowered his whole body into the sea and rose again. His shirt and shorts clung to him, and when he again lowered himself into the water, he peeled down his shorts, and then his shirt up over his head, the water running in little rivulets down his slim arms, his sleek, wet black hair, trickling lightly down over his glistening ribs, down to the darkness and the faint gleam of light where his legs came together, down, back to the sea itself down his firm dark limbs. From this vantage point he seemed, if not innocent, at least, quite simply, nothing but a boy. He was held like that by the last light of the sun, in Ab's mind, an image to displace, to stabilize, the reality that, for the past week, had seemed to shift malevolently all around him.

The boy swam a little, holding the clothes in his hand, then arose, like a god from the sea, like a newly baptized convert, wrung his clothes out, and, carrying them, walked slowly back to the shore and into the darkness of the forest. Ab pulled himself stiffly to his feet, stretched his legs, and walked slowly back to the house.

Nancy was standing at the beach house, a strained look on her face. "We wondered where you were. We hoped you hadn't wandered off and got lost. It's supper time." Ab didn't say anything as he approached. He brushed her arm, lightly, and kissed her on the cheek.

She looked at him carefully. "Have you been crying?" He didn't answer and she continued, "You should be careful. We don't think your life is in danger, but..."

Ab stopped a moment as she continued into the house. "But?"

She turned in the light of the doorway. "Yes. But." Then she went in and Ab followed. Ab recalled the incident in Yogyakarta just before the earthquake. Had that been real? Now, in his room, changing into a clean white shirt and light beige cotton slacks for supper, he felt a vague sense of unease, alone in this strange apartment, almost as if he were being watched. The garden outside was pitch dark, and he drew the curtains.

The supper was a spicy shrimp soup, followed by ocean fish and octopus with white rice. Sani was grouchy and distracted during the meal, not saying much, answering questions curtly. He is as anxious as I am to get this business over with, Ab thought. And perhaps he even has more at stake. Ab played with Nancy's foot under the table.

After supper, they went to their rooms. Again, back in his room, he felt uneasy. He sat at the small table and flipped through a copy of *Suara Alam*, the Indonesian nature magazine. He changed into a sarong, lay back on the bed, sat up again. Perhaps he had got too much sun. He opened his door and looked out into the hallway. It was empty, dimly lit by the lamps in the alcoves.

He stepped out, walked down to the next door, and knocked lightly. No response. He was about to knock again when it opened. Nancy was wrapped in a sarong, her shoulders bare. "Would you like to come in?" she said.

"Actually, for some reason I felt very uncomfortable in my room. I can't rest and thought I'd go back out for a little walk. Would you like to join me?"

She hesitated. Ab stood silently in the hallway, making no move.

"I suppose if we go out the back," she said, "and down the beach to the left, there shouldn't be a problem."

She brushed past him, smelling cleanly of scented soap, pulling the door shut after her. Outside, it was cooler, but only just enough to make them walk closely together, and not enough to make them feel uncomfortable. Nancy walked slightly ahead, her feet seeming to know their way through the dark, wooded park without the need for seeing. They walked, holding hands lightly, not speaking, down a small mud path that came out onto the beach several hundred meters away from where they had been that afternoon, away from the point of land where Ab had seen the cremation.

The moon was up and glimmering over the water. They dropped hands and strolled further away from the house, kicking at the sand, still not speaking. "I'm sorry about all the trouble this may have caused you, the way I disappeared," she finally said. Ab was about to say something about being sorry that he had taken and hidden the kris, but something in him rebelled. He didn't want to talk about that now. About George and Soesanto and dead cows.

She stopped and spoke out over the water. "Sometimes I get so tired of this. Of always looking over my shoulder."

Ab came up behind her and slipped his arms around her. She leaned back against him, and his hands slipped up to cup her breasts. She turned to face him and put her arms up around his neck. She laid her head against his shoulder and he held her against him, gazing over her shoulder at the moon on the water, and the dark silhouettes of the volcanoes.

"It's beautiful out here," he whispered. "Can we go for a swim?"

She put an arm around his waist and turned to look at the water with him. Then, pulling her hair away from her face with both hands, she loosed the top of her sarong and let it drop to the sand. "Sure," she said. "Come on."

They swam close together, the warm wakes from their bodies softly pushing against, and enveloping, each other. They went almost out to the reef, and then returned to where they could stand again. He drew her to him, their lips met, lightly, briefly. Her fingertips skimmed down his body like little fish and his mind went blank. He stepped back a little, and reached out, his hands wanting to swim down her body, but she turned away and swam, just below the surface, leaving golden ripples in the path left by the full moon on the water. He swam after her, not quite keeping up, his hand reaching, touching her foot, grazing her leg. This time, they swam almost to exhaustion before turning back. As he regained footing and walked up onto the beach, he felt hot and disoriented, his leg muscles stiff. He bent over for a moment, his lungs heaving for breath. When he looked up, she was already wrapped in her sarong.

They walked silently back to the house. At the door of her room, she looked both ways, as if scanning for someone watching them. She kissed him lightly on the cheek and then went inside, her eyes meeting his as she pushed the door shut. Was it all the way shut? He hadn't heard the click of the latch. He stood there, agonizing as to whether to knock on the door, or push on it. He walked down the hall as far as his door, and then came back, and stood in the dim light of the hallway for several distressed minutes before returning to his room.

He sat on the edge of the bed. There was a glass of what looked like icewater on his bedside stand. He sniffed. It had the sweet bitter scent of gin and tonic. He sipped, then gulped it down, and then sank back against the pillows, and fell into a deep sleep.

◇◇◇

Suddenly, he was awake. Had he been asleep? He looked down at himself. His sarong was rumpled and hitched up around his waist. His heart was racing and he felt a sharp pain searing in his chest. He felt strongly that someone was watching him. Again the pain, like a knife piercing him. For a second, his eyelids felt glued shut by fear, and then, with great force of willpower, he tore them open and stared in horror directly above him. A greenish, translucent face hovered there, a triangular head with long wavy hair slicked back behind the ears, but a male face, a malevolent face, the eyes burning down at him. He gasped out a cry, a choking, fearful-dream, terrified, night-time cry, rolled from the bed, and scrambled toward the door. "Help!" he drew the bolt and fell into the hallway. "Help!" he called and ran to Nancy's door. He beat upon the door, and when it opened, fell unconscious through it.

When he came to his senses, he was lying in a bed, his body aching all over, bathed in sweat. His vision was blurred. His breathing was fast and painful. Someone was sponging his forehead with a damp cloth, and then a hand rested momentarily there. "He still feels very hot," he heard Nancy's voice say before he passed out again. He was in a deep, cold fog. "He's here?" The voice spoke in a forced whisper. "He's an idiot. First, he was just supposed to *frighten* George, not...and now, now this...It *has* to be his doing. Don't these idiots have brains?" And then the fog was thicker, and there was only a soft, cold hissing.

The next time he awoke, he felt cold, and he drew the bed covers up under his chin. He tried to sit up, but a hand pushed him gently back and he was too weak to resist. He fell back against the pillows again with his eyes closed. The bed sheets had a light perfume of flowers. A faint light was coming through the windows. Nancy was sitting at his bedside, and behind her, he could see Pak Sani, leaning on a cane.

Nancy put a hand over his eyes and he closed them again.

"What happened?" he whispered, his voice cracking as if from long disuse.

"We think perhaps you had too much sun. Sun-stroke. It happens here. Foreigners are not used to gauging the heat of the tropical sun." Her voice was firm, re-assuring. But as she spoke, the greenish face hovering above his bed came clearly back into his mind and he felt his heart racing. He gripped her hand and threw himself upright. "No! No, It was...it was...a head, a face, hovering over my bed." He fell back on the pillows again, exhausted at the effort he had made. "I don't believe in this stuff. It was like a ghost," he whispered. "A malevolent ghost. A bad dream. I felt like I was being stabbed."

The old man came closer. "Tell us what the ghost looked like."

"It was a face, a head only. It seemed...triangular...the forehead much larger than the lower half of the face. He...I'm sure it was a he, I don't know why, but I know that...His hair was curly, but brushed back from his face and behind his ears. His eyes seemed as if they were piercing right through me." Ab spoke with his eyes shut, his body shivering uncontrollably as he spoke. "There was a terrible pain in my chest, in my shoulder, like a knife." He pulled the covers more tightly up under his chin. No one spoke, and Ab could hear the swoosh and hiss of the waves through the open window. And the piercing melancholy call of a caged bird.

He opened his eyes. Sani's wrinkled face was leaning over him, gazing at him intently. "You are right," he said. "It was not just the sun. You must rest. We will talk later."

Ab closed his eyes. "He shouldn't be left alone any more, for any reason," the old man said to Nancy. Ab could hear the shuffling steps of Pak Sani across the carpeted floor, the door opening and shutting, and the weight of Nancy's hand resting on him. Then he fell asleep again.

Chapter Twenty-one

There were voices in the room. Sani had come back, and he and Nancy were discussing something—pointing as they spoke over in his direction. He felt better now. Weak, but neither cold nor feverish. He sat up and pushed the pillows up behind him so that he could sit comfortably. Nancy came over to the bed.

"Are you ready for some food now?"

"Actually, I feel quite good now. Yes, thanks, some food would be fine, but I'd better stick to chicken soup and white rice." All of the nightmare last night seemed very far away now, with the sunlight floating in through the window, and the sounds of the wind lightly in the trees and the reassuring susurrations of the waves on the beach. "Maybe I'm just allergic to shrimp, or got food poisoning or something," he said hopefully. "Not that your food is bad. It just happens, especially with seafood. It goes bad quickly."

Sani came over to stand next to Nancy. "We will give you your chicken soup with rice, but what you experienced last night was not some allergy or food poisoning." He paused a moment to play with his cane. "Perhaps we can all eat in here and then we can discuss matters away from…from other ears. Would that be okay with you?"

Ab waved his hand weakly. "Sure. No problem. But I should get up and have a bath first, to soak off all the sweat I worked up."

"Good, I will tell the cook to prepare dinner and serve it in here." He disappeared out the door.

Nancy helped Ab to his feet. Ab sat on the edge of the toilet seat while she filled the big tub with hot water. She then helped him out of his sarong and into the tub. "It's a little hot, so careful."

The water seized his feet with hot teeth and it felt like the hair on his legs was being burnt off. He stood for a moment, leaning against Nancy, before lowering himself into the steaming water.

"Well, I shall leave you for a moment then," she said, withdrawing toward the door.

"Nancy?"

She stopped.

"Your grandfather said not to leave me alone. Could you please stay? It's not that I'm afraid. It's just that, well, could you scrub my back?"

Her strong, slim hands massaged the soap over his shoulders, down his back, down over his chest; his belly tensed, bent back like a bow, as her hand slid down and his body rose up to greet her. She leaned over and kissed the tip of his penis, then she rose up and took a towel from the rack. "I think you'd better rest." She dried him off until his skin hurt, then helped him into his sarong. He was able to walk back to the bed on his own. *I wonder if my mother ever did this for Dad while he was on his sick bed?* The thought made him feel strange all over, and weak. All the things he had never understood.

She brought a shirt and shorts and dropped them on the bed beside him. "We'll eat here in the bedroom. Grandfather and I will eat at the bedside table. Now put your feet up and relax."

The cook brought in several steaming trays of food on a mobile cart, parked it just inside the door, and disappeared. The aroma of chicken soup filled Ab with nostalgia and ravenous hunger. Nancy set his food out in front of him.

"Please, start to eat. My grandfather will be here in a minute."

Ab breathed in the steam from the soup. "I feel like a little boy, staying home from school with the flu. My mother used to do this for me."

"So I remind you of your mother?"

"Not exactly. But your grandmother does." He slurped at his soup while Nancy watched. "Won't you eat too? I'm not comfortable being watched. I feel like I've been watched like a monkey in a zoo ever since I came to this country."

Nancy took a plate and helped herself to some rice and stew, then sat with it in her lap, not eating. "The *organg asli*, the *real* Javanese, watch everyone who doesn't look like them," she said. "Or think like them."

Sani came in shortly, filled his plate, and took a chair next to Nancy. They ate in silence. When they were finished, Nancy took the plates and set them back on the cart.

Then she poured each of them a cup of Chinese tea. Ab sniffed it. "Your grandmother gave me ginger tea."

Sani smiled. "Yes, Heimun thinks strong ginger tea makes you live longer."

They sipped at their tea, then, almost simultaneously, clinked their cups down. "Well," began Sani, gripping his cane before him. "I suppose we should begin. Where shall we begin? Last night, or at the beginning?"

Ab sat back against the pillows. "Why don't we start somewhere in the middle, which is where I feel like I've been. I'll tell you what I know, and what has happened, and then you can correct me and fill in the details."

Sani sat back in his chair. "Good."

Ab closed his eyes as he spoke. Beginning with his investigation of the deaths of the cattle in Gandringan, he recounted his story, ending with the flight to Bali. He included the incident just before he had left, but left out any mention of the kris.

Sani leaned forward on his cane. "Ah, well that explains a few things. I see I shall also have to explain a few things." He paused, as if considering how much he could say, then muttered. "I guess it doesn't matter what you know. You are leaving, and out there," he waved a hand to indicate the non-Indonesian world, "no one would believe you anyway."

He looked at his granddaughter, and she returned his stare. He sighed.

"Both Soesanto and Susilo assumed that they survived the big purges because of their wits. They didn't know that my money was also buying them some breathing space."

"So there's some irony in Soesanto's view of you as a villain."

"It is an irony, yes. But it has also been, for me, some protection. There are people in Jakarta who have looked for ways to get me as well. They don't like it when Chinese people make money. It seems like a kind of moral affront. If they could tie me to the old Communists, they could simply appropriate my assets. If people like Soesanto thought I was the culprit, then I could not be in a league with them, could I?"

"Are you so absolutely sure that Soesanto wasn't playing both sides of the fence? I mean, doesn't it make sense that he would have been kept alive because he had friends or protectors in Jakarta?"

Sani tugged at the cuff of his shirt, then looked directly at Ab. "Am I absolutely sure? No. I am not. But for a person in my position, keeping a double agent alive is one of the risks of protecting my family. For what it is worth, I think Soesanto was genuine." He looked sideways at Nancy, who was looking down at her hands, and then continued.

"The picture has been complicated by something. The kris, which your friend George found, once belonged to Waluyo's family, although it has been residing in someone else's collection. Waluyo was given his current job by General Witono, who must sign all the official approval papers for the Susu Senang project. I think of him as one of Allah's little helpers."

"Allah's little helpers?"

"A figure of speech. If Allah doesn't seem to be doing what some people think he should be doing, then sometimes he needs a little help. So when Susilo is causing trouble, like killing cows with strychnine to discredit the project, then Allah wants him dead. But Allah doesn't actually do anything, so his helpers step in. It's a kind of degenerate view of a jihad, with God as a kind of weakling who needs human help."

"So, Susilo was killing cows even before Waluyo stepped into the mix."

"Yes. Waluyo just carried it a step further, and used it to help his cousins in the kampung. But to return to the kris. To keep things under the table, as you might say, we were called upon to provide a weapon. We gave it to General Witono, who passed it on to Waluyo. After, um," Sani glanced sideways at Nancy, "retiring Susilo, the knife was supposed to be returned. But Waluyo wanted to keep it. At first he tried to hide it in his home village, but his family there were suspicious, and wanted a lot more money, so he kept it in the shed at Susu Senang."

Ab recalled his first visit to Gandringan. Why hadn't he made that connection before? He was feeling again like a stupid foreigner. Sani was continuing.

"Waluyo knew that George had taken it from the supply shed at Susu Senang. He wanted it back. He heard that Soesanto had it, and went to Soesanto's place to get it, but George had already been there to retrieve it. In his anger, Waluyo killed Soesanto. He knew that Witono, his boss, would not be upset about this extra death, and didn't much care about the kris. He had already been directed to kill Susilo. Soesanto was just, what do you say, collateral damage.

"He then went after George. George refused to admit he had it. Waluyo threatened him unless he was told where the knife was. George misjudged the depth of Waluyo's feelings, and scoffed at him. A crime of passion over a knife. Waluyo then came after you. I did not know your friend George well, but I doubt that he directed Waluyo to you. You just seemed an obvious choice, that George must have left it at your house. Nancy also thought this. In fact she thought she had seen it at your place, and then the kris seemed to disappear." Both Sani and Nancy looked expectantly at Ab.

"I found it on the buffet. I guessed that George must have left it there. I taped it to the bottom of the bed."

"Ah." It was almost a sigh of relief, coming from both Sani and Nancy, who glanced at each other. Nancy turned to stare for a moment at Ab, as if trying to read something in his facial expression, then refocused on her hands in her lap as her grandfather continued.

"Waluyo tried to give you all a good fright at the fun house that evening, trying to scare up the kris. His way of scaring is somewhat less than controlled, and could lead to unfortunate accidents, as it had with George, so that I even feared for Nancy's life. That was when I knew that Nancy had to go into hiding for a while. Without knowing where the kris was, we could neither deflect his attention elsewhere, nor bargain with him."

He sighed again.

"That was probably Waluyo at your house before you came here. If not for the earthquake, he would have the kris. And you might well be dead."

"Why kill me? Why not just take the knife? Death seems a hefty price to pay for petty theft."

"For one thing, the military thugs who are running this country right now don't like foreigners interfering with how they run the place. Your death would be an object lesson. More importantly, Waluyo knew it would matter to me. He resents having to working for a Chinaman. And because...I can see I'm going to have to give you a history lesson. This goes pretty far back and sounds like a fairy tale, but that's what popular history is, after all, the fairy tales we tell ourselves to bolster our belief in our own importance. About five hundred years ago there lived in Java an expert craftsman, an *empu*, a weapons maker who was reputed to make the finest kris, the most perfectly suited to their owner, in all of the kingdoms of Java. He was called upon to make a kris for a young Javanese prince to be presented to him on the day of his circumcision. This empu crafted a kris from the finest meteorite iron and nickel of the time; he made a kris of great power and beauty. Unfortunately, the kingdom was overthrown and the young prince killed in battle before the kris was ever put to use. So the empu kept that kris, and used its power in the new kingdom to assure himself and his family a continuing place of honour.

"The kris was passed from father to son, as the art of making fine kris was passed on from father to son. Something over one hundred years ago, the craft of making kris, and the power and sorcery that went with it, were lost. A kris is not much good in battle against a Dutch cannon. The family reverted to farming, and the family treasures, one by one, were sold in the market to buy food and clothing.

"That, then, is how the kris came into another collection. The people who owned it had no idea of its historical importance."

"That's a somewhat different story about that kris than the one Soesanto told me."

Sani laughed. "Well, we each have our own stories, don't we? I am not even convinced that the kris we have is the one Waluyo thinks it is. We believe what gives us power. What gives us energy. The story I told you is the one Waluyo believes, the one he told me this morning when I questioned him. When we hired him, I did not know, nor do I think Witono knew, that Waluyo had grown up as a child with stories about that kris, that he had an image in his head as to what it would look like, as his father and grandfather had described it to him."

Ab sat forward on the bed. "You talked with Waluyo this morning?"

"He came on the flight yesterday afternoon. He said he wanted to talk with me about the shipment of cows coming next week. I knew that was not the reason he came when you told me your dream. So I asked him point-blank. He thinks you have brought the kris here, and that I am protecting you. He thinks that if you are seriously harmed or even killed, I will capitulate and give it to him. I did not know then where the kris was, and so did not disillusion him. But it also means that we shall have to retrieve it from your house as soon as possible, and get it back to its rightful owners. Even if he does not have it in his hand, Waluyo will know that it is safe for now, and not likely to leave the country, but that it is beyond our control. Then he will have nothing to gain. He has been afraid that you are going to take it out of the country and it will end up in some collection somewhere in North America, unreachable. Waluyo has learned the ancient tricks well. The apparition over your bed, Waluyo had called up from the realms of the dead, that was the last professional empu in his family, who died more than a hundred years ago."

Ab's head was dizzy. "You believe that stuff?"

A slight smile played at the corners of Sani's mouth. "After last night, do you?"

Ab recalled the drink on his bedside stand. There might be other explanations, but this didn't seem to be the time for a philosophical discussion. Either way, Waluyo had tried to harm him. Still, something was missing, didn't quite compute. "What about the anthrax?"

Sani waved his hand, too quickly Ab thought, in a dismissive gesture. "A natural outbreak. We shall have it under control shortly." He thumped his cane on the floor in front of him.

"In the end," Sani continued firmly, "this is all about General Witono and Waluyo. Susilo was sabotaging the project, and we couldn't have that happening. Or rather, if it was going to happen, Witono wanted to control it. So I had to hire Waluyo after he killed Susilo."

Ab took a deep breath and looked at Nancy and then at Sani. "So, what happens now?"

"I have arranged to make some special compensatory payments to General Witono for his troubles. They are, officially, profits from the project."

Ab looked from grandfather to granddaughter. "But why?" he asked, already knowing the answer.

Nancy leaned over and put her head on her grandfather's stooped shoulder. "The generals in Jakarta have all the cards. My grandfather has tried to keep himself in the public eye as a way of protecting himself, but it is a weak protection. If the generals and Allah's helpers want something—money, a few dead bodies, this project, and the government and foreign money that comes with it—then they will get it. In the end, it is only our family that matters."

Sani smiled at Ab. "You are surprised? You come from a nation that prides itself on family values. And how much do you sacrifice for your country? How many people? Look at the so-called Great Wars." Now he was pacing angrily around the room, banging his cane on the floor. "Our family has lasted hundreds of years and outlived dozens of countries, and it will outlive many more." He swung around to glare at Ab. His voice fell to a whisper. "A few lives here or there are nothing. Nothing. Family is all that matters. All." He turned suddenly and left the room, then returned as suddenly as he had left.

"I have one favour to ask of you, a small favour for safe passage from the country. Something very direct. That should be a relief, yes?" He smiled. "I want you to deliver some papers to General Witono in Jakarta. Can you do that? He will then make sure you have the proper exit papers."

This time Sani took Nancy by the arm and guided her from the room as he left. Ab stared after them. Nancy had been strangely silent, looking down into her lap, throughout Sani's elaborate—too elaborate?—explanation, Ab thought. She did not look back as she went through the door.

Chapter Twenty-two

Early the next morning, Ab and Nancy were staring out opposite sides of the chauffeured Mercedes limousine. He had said he needed to go to Yogyakarta before going on to Jakarta, just to pick up a few more of his belongings, and to say goodbye to the other expatriates. Nancy had suggested they take a little drive into the countryside on the way to the airport, and had given the driver instructions to take them to a nearby hilltop. Now, in the car, they fell silent, their hands resting next to each other on the seat, separated by some unspeakable gulf. It seemed to Ab that there was a kind of Wallace's line there, demarcating different histories, different cultures. He thought that if they could make that dangerous journey across this line, everything would change. The world would be better, more exciting, full of unheralded possibilities. Hazy dark shapes of cedar-tree-shaped temples slipped past in the early morning mist. Once, a couple of short, swaybacked Balinese pigs appeared abruptly beside the car, snorted, and bounced away into the mist. Ab smiled in spite of himself.

The car stopped beside the road at the rim of a lush valley, and they climbed out. The driver waited in the car. The air was cool and fresh this early in the morning, this high up. There was a small path leading along the edge of the road, and Nancy walked, at first ahead, and then fell back into step with him. Gaunt, bearded, slightly balding on top, in a white cotton shirt hung over his loose trousers, Ab shambled awkwardly beside the lithe Chinese-looking woman in a red silk blouse and black pants. A Mennonite-Canadian was walking with a Chinese-Indonesian. That would be the real Canadian way of saying things. Nothing without hyphens.

He walked closely beside her, their bodies touching with the rhythm of their steps. They wandered over the grass away from the road and squatted for a moment on the packed earth at the rim of the valley. The land fell away from them, in a hundred patchwork shades of green and greenish-blue and brown, cut into sharp terraces down to the river, glistening in the sun, fine-haired paddy rice or adolescently gangly cassava on the flat areas, and broad-leafed banana and papaya trees fringing the ridges between. Nancy put one hand on the wet earth beside her and lightly vaulted herself the four feet down to the first terrace of cassava trees. More clumsily, Ab followed.

He turned to face Nancy, who was speaking. He was trying to reconcile the picturesque postcard around him with the panic that seemed to be rising up in him again. Her voice pushed its way into his frantic, disorganized thoughts. "I can't come with you, Ab," she was saying. "I thought that what I really wanted was to get out of here, no matter how. A marriage of convenience." She looked sideways at him. "Don't take this wrong, but it could have been anybody. And you, of all the people I've thought might be able to help me, are the first one who could really have helped me pull it off. Really. Without faking it." She seemed very quiet for a long time.

"And? But?"

"And until I met you, it was always a bit of a joke. When I faced your question, my question, seriously, about coming with you, when I stared it in the eyes with a clear mind and a clear heart, I began to think about what 'just getting out of here' meant. What I would be giving up."

"Like being watched and persecuted because of your race or your family or your political beliefs?"

"Like everything that I know and love and cherish, my grandparents who are getting old and won't be around much longer, my family who have made me who I am, the sea over the coral reefs and the blistering sun and the volcanoes and ruinous history of this amazing country, and yes, even the things I hate and fear. There is a kind of comfort in being able to identify the things you hate and fear as well as the things you love.

"If I came with you, I would have to start all over again, in a different culture, trying to identify all those things. And when I've identified them, I may find that I don't really love them and I don't really hate them, not in the pure way I can here. They aren't rooted in me the way things here are."

He was facing her now, and his hand wandered from her cheek to her breast. She took his wandering hand and sandwiched it between both of hers. "I have to stay here, Ab." Her voice was like a whisper across the waters of a calm northern lake at dusk, barely hovering above the force welling up inside her. "I have my demons to exorcise, to live with. I'm sure you have your own. You have to leave now. I assure you, the other options are not ones you would like."

As she spoke, his mind was scrambling over what Soesanto had said about hope. His thoughts raced on to all the things he loved and hated in his own country, in his own community, the bigotry, the smug materialism with its masks of piety and concern, the real concern, the real piety. All the things he had run away from to come here. Such petty, stupid demons. Not worth wrestling. His mind was racing wildly in circles, trying to imagine her demons, her family, all the millions of important things he didn't know about her.

She tilted her face slightly forward and then leaned with her back against the earth wall they had just descended, as if drinking in the golden liquid of the rising sun. Her silky black hair fell away from her face like a veil. Ab was standing next to her, his right hand barely grazing the smooth pale skin of her left arm. His eyes were transfixed by a clear pearl of water as it traced a path from the corner of her eye down her cheek, under the curve of her chin, into the shadows of her blouse. His left hand, now hovering a hair's-breadth from the rise and fall of her breasts, was shaking. It would take centuries for such a slender thread of water, running continuously, to make a slight crease in a mountain slope. In one moment, where the tears traced their course, his heart was cleft.

He turned to look out across the valley. In the swirling brown waters of the river, a slim, naked pre-teen boy was bathing his two buffaloes. The buffaloes sank with apparent tropical lethargy into the satisfying mud-warm lick of the current. Only their noses and horns protruded. Ab took a handkerchief from his pocket and wiped the dampness from his forehead. The boy slipped over and around his beasts, his own molasses-muffin bum lifting into the air as he curled his body and raised himself up in a hand-stand and then lowered himself into the water, rubbing the buffaloes, brushing them with a stiff palm-leafstalk brush, scratching the wrinkled, thick skin behind their horns. He clambered atop one of them, his skinny body in a crouch, glistening, then fell with a sprawling splash into the water. He paddled back and, using the buffalo horn as a handle, lifted himself up for another dive. The complex society of terraced irrigation and the social rituals of washing buffaloes reflected underlying biological necessities and complexities. Ab tried to understand this, but his mind boggled. How did one understand anything at all in a world increasingly populated with refugees and misfits like himself and Nancy? All the webs that had given them meaning had come apart. Or maybe there were just so many webs criss-crossing the world from Russia to Canada to Indonesia and back that what they had was something infinitely more wild, intricate and beautiful and resistant to their aggressive desire to understand.

Behind him, he heard the sharp slip of a knife from its scabbard and he turned to see Nancy holding a kris, not *the* kris, but still, a beautiful metallic snake laid across her upturned palms. "Ab, you have no idea. You have no idea at all. We just do the best we can. The world of starting over from scratch is over. We have to start from where we are and move on. Take this little gift to remember me by. My grandfather had other ideas for this knife, but I think you should have it. Hold out your hands." She laid it across his palms, leaned up to kiss him lightly on the lips, and turned to climb back up the muddy slope to the road. He arrived at the road to see her walk toward the open door of another car on the far side of the road, a new Camry with tinted windows. Looking past her, he could see Sani, who raised his hand and moved it in a barely discernable salute. Nancy turned at the open door and stood for a moment to look at Ab, hugging herself tightly, tears streaming down her cheeks. Then she climbed into the car, and it drove away.

Ab leaned against his limousine, the knife pressing between him and the metal, pressing until it hurt. He threw the knife into the back seat and slammed the door shut after himself. The driver did not turn around to look at him as they drove off.

He checked his bags at the airport, then wandered outside and sat on the edge of a planter with orchids in it, drinking gin from a bottle in a paper bag, his feet resting on the leather carry-on case that contained the papers for General Witono. Finally, he thought it must be near the time to leave and went back into the terminal. The passenger lounge was empty and a man was just closing the gate going out to the planes. Ab looked up at the clock on the wall. The plane was not due to leave for half an hour. He ran up to the gate just as the man was turning to leave. "Excuse me, the plane to Yogyakarta? Has it loaded yet?"

The man looked surprised. "Yes. Yes, it has. Are you going there?"

Ab pulled out his boarding pass and ticket as he climbed over the low barrier. The man tore the corner off the boarding pass and Ab ran down the walkway and out onto the tarmac towards the plane. Two airport workers were holding the mobile stairs in place, watching him come. Settling into his seat, he heaved a big sigh and stared out into the bright morning light. Rubber time, they said in this country, but this was the first time he'd seen it stretched to leave early. The engines revved; he took a candy from the tray and leaned back into his seat, closing his eyes as they sped up the runway, and fell into sleep before they were even in the air.

The plane dropped suddenly, and the sun dazzled into his eyes, as if they had been sliding across a thin veneer of ice and snow over a northern Canadian slough and crackled through into the deafening silence beneath. He awoke suddenly out of a deep sleep, and felt himself gasping for breath. His stomach leapt up to meet his tongue. By the time he had sorted out exactly where he was, they were on the ground.

His plane for Jakarta wasn't until later in the day. He took a taxi straight to John Schechter's office, hoping he wasn't out on some mountain-climbing research expedition. John was there, in the little office piled high with papers, the overhead fan turning slowly, his shirt open to his navel, his head down on a pile of newspaper clippings. Ab knocked once on the door frame and stepped in.

"Ha, caught you napping!"

John sat bolt upright, looking bewildered. He rubbed his eyes. "I thought you'd left. Forget something?"

Ab pulled up a chair and straddled it, back to front. "I forgot to find out what you saw the morning George was killed."

The question caught him off guard. "You know what I saw. Claudia must have told you, or didn't you talk about things like that when you were together?" He scowled.

Ab waited, feeling triumphant.

"I didn't see anything. I didn't get as far as the farm."

"You turned around half-way there?"

"That's right. What's it to you?"

"I don't believe you."

Ab stood up, put one foot on the chair, and leaned on it. He spoke in an urgent, firm undertone. "I never did what you think I did with Claudia, John, although in retrospect I wish I had, and I don't even think George did. She's better than you deserve. Waluyo may have killed Susilo and Soesanto, but he wouldn't kill a foreigner. I think you just used that as a cover to get rid of George. I just think you were pissed off at Claudia and her alleged lovers."

Ab felt in control now. Everything was working out. He had to leave Indonesia, but all the threads would be tied up and he could start again, clean. He articulated each phrase slowly, to let it sink in. He could see John tensing up at the mention of Claudia's lovers. When Ab reached the end of his sentence, John exploded into a laugh.

"You are such an asshole. Harold and I talked about the possibility that you might stumble across the truth. But you really are too stupid for words."

Now Ab was off guard. "Harold? Wilkinson?"

Schechter's face broke into a crooked, sarcastic smile. "Oh *him*. A light bulb?"

John ran his fingers back through his hair. He stood up and walked over to the window, silhouetted against the light. He rubbed his chin, as if considering something. "You really want to know who killed your friends?" A smug smile crept across his face.

Ab laughed. "Of course I want to know. Why wouldn't I?"

John turned to face the dust-covered window. "What the hell. No one will believe you anyway." He started drawing smiley-faced circles with his finger in the dust. "Try this story. There are a couple of Communist stooges left over from 1966. Let's call them Susilo and Soesanto, just for simplicity, okay? One of them works on a farm as a manager. It used to *be* his farm in fact. Now it belongs to a General. Let's call him Witono, who lives in Jakarta. He has big plans for it. Lots of foreign money coming in. New cars. Holidays. Susilo looks for ways to get it back. He does stupid things, like steal cow magnets and attach them to strychnine pouches. He plays games with the country butchers. They like this game. They make money on it. Even the Australians are happy. They are encouraging this. They have their own reasons for wanting to make the General and his friends unhappy."

"Findlay," mumbled Ab into his hand. "Peter Findlay."

Schechter clapped his hands. "Such a bright boy! But Witono is unhappy." He draws an unhappy face on the window. "Cows are dying. His project is looking bad. The President himself might start to be unhappy. You don't want the President of Indonesia unhappy. Now let's say one of Witono's agents, who are everywhere, gets the word. Snuff. Susilo is gone." John X-ed out a drawing on the window.

"Agent is promoted to farm manager." He added a new happy face off to the side. "Problem. The body, which has been buried on the farm, is discovered by a bumbling foreigner. Worse yet, the weapon is also found. The agent-cum-manager, not too bright, two ears short of rabbit, has kept the weapon, to which he seems to have a personal attachment. Plus, the weapon was borrowed from a friend who borrowed it from another friend, who is expecting the weapon back, and neither of those friends wants to be connected to any of this. There could be complications. I'll come back to those in a minute."

He moved to a different part of the dirty window.

"Now let's say there's a family. A nice family, well, surviving fragments of a nice family. Let's call them the Sentosa family just for fun, Grandma, Grandpa, and granddaughter Nancy." He drew three smiley-faced stick figures and turned to grin at Ab. "There are more Sentosas in the family. But those are the only ones you need to know about. The Sentosas are the money behind the farm. They have the foreign connections. They are friends with everybody, especially the British, but also the Americans and even the Australians. They are what make the General legitimate. Generals, like drug runners, need a legit connection. This is also good for the Sentosas. Without this connection to the General, they are, let's say, vulnerable. They have these different-looking eyes, you see, and no amount of name-changing can change those special eyes. The General doesn't really like them. But he likes their money. The President likes their money, too, so the General can't really just walk in and kill them and take over the project, even though he has the power to do so. Still, he *could* ruin the Sentosa family with a few well-placed rumours. He doesn't really want to do this either, because it might threaten the deal itself, but never underestimate fear. Especially after 1966, there are no idle threats in this country. So there is a very delicate balancing act going on, and everybody wants stability. Stability is good for the family, good for the economy, and good for the General.

"Remember those complications? Well, you see, not only did this hypothetical Nancy fail to retrieve the knife from Waluyo, but a bumbling foreigner, in trying to check out the souvenir value of the kris he has found, has it shown to Soesanto." He drew a rounded figure at the side with a stick-knife and connected it to the stick man representing Soesanto. "Soesanto has seen this knife before, and is a smart man. Some startling connections jump out at him about the journey this kris has taken from the glass case where he first saw it: Wilkinson to Nancy, who seems to have appeared conveniently from nowhere at a Wilkinson party, and who seems to be over at the Wilkinson house a lot. Nancy to Waluyo. We all know Waluyo is working for the General. Well, he's also working for Sentosa. That's what that anthrax stuff is about. Just to keep the project not too valuable, and the General at arm's length. The General can't manage without the foreign experts, and Sani has the right connections for that. But Nancy-girl, this is a new one for Soesanto.

"So, Nancy has to get the kris back, for her family. And what better way than to get really close to someone who can get it back? She also has to say goodbye to Soesanto. Can't be helped. He knows *way* too much. But she's a big girl. She'll get over it.

"Anyway, getting rid of Soesanto, a dangerous old leftie, that's good. Like dumping ballast. No one, well no one except some loser Canadian veterinarian who will soon go home, will miss him or investigate. The loser Canadian will forget anyway when he gets back to Canada. Distracted by work, girls, life. But damn. The bumbling foreigner who found the weapon actually *saw* Soesanto's killer doing the deed. Just happened to be there to pick up the knife. Geeze, you'll have to get rid of him too. And better do it before he tells his veterinary friend.

That could get *really* messy. A quick stab. Okay, he's gone. Now things are starting to look better. Hmm, might even be able to frame Waluyo. That might come in handy. Now just get the other guy out of the country.

"Now let's get the knife back where it belongs and everybody is happy again. Phew, that was close."

Schechter mock-wiped sweat from his brow and turned around suddenly with a bright smile. "Maybe the veterinarian will even get to marry the bumbler's widow. Hot damn, wouldn't that be a happy ending?"

Ab had been frozen during this monologue, stunned. *In this country knowing too much can be fatal. How many people would you kill for your family? Family is all that matters.* Ab's mind did not want to go there. He did not want to know this. It was a lie. A lie. How could John know all this? Unless. *Think about somebody who goes to all the parties and works odd hours, she had said.* Damn. Double damn. He was so stupid.

Ab stood, frozen in the doorway; his body numb. This was more than he could bear. "No way. That's crazy. Waluyo is the one. He did all the killings. It's the simplest explanation. George saw *him* kill Soesanto. And for all I know, Waluyo is working for *you*, and you're the one who took Wilkinson's kris. Now you'll have to kill Waluyo too, won't you, god-damned Americans?"

John laughed. "Oh yeah, sure. Blame the Americans. I wish I could take the credit. I really would like that. But Nancy's already two steps ahead of us. Waluyo will probably get a kris, but it will be a fake. In any case, if I know the Sentosas, the Wilkinsons will get the real one back, where it will be kept safely under lock and key. Waluyo works for himself. He plays whatever it takes. Like everybody here."

He was watching Ab, a bemused sneer crossing his face.

"You can't believe it was her, can you? Such a nice girl. She really loves you. Only she arranged to have you accidentally killed a few times, didn't she. Remember the fun house? The near accident in the fog at the hash? Probably something in Bali too, if I guess right. My god that girl can bumble things. You'd almost think she cared about you." He put his hand to his chin, as if pondering this as a real possibility.

"Why are you telling me this? How do you know this? Why are you making up these stories?" Ab was backing down the hall.

John raised his voice after Ab. "But don't feel too bad. Findlay thought they were friends too, and he's supposed to be doing intelligence for a living. At least Tri is all right, just a few bruises." He snorted. "It was nothing personal. George just happened to be in the wrong place at the wrong time, with too much of the right information." Ab stood at the outside door, pushed it open. He really, really didn't want to hear this. "And just for the record. Claudia is the perfect cover. We're the perfect team. Like you and Nancy were. Problem is, what could they do with you once the job was over and the General survived his visit to the farm? A dead foreigner is too messy, and they've already got one of those. Besides, once you've had a man's penis inside you, well, it is harder to kill him. Kind of creates a soft spot." He chuckled at his own joke. "Send you home. That's easier. Back home, they'll think you are a paranoid loony."

Ab began talking loudly over-top of John's voice as he walked out the door. "Nice try, John! Good story but it just won't wash! You don't know anything. You're just jealous because all the guys were popping Claudia! You don't know the half of it!" Back out on the street, Ab shook his head from side to side, covering his ears.

Chapter Twenty-three

Ab's heart was pounding. Something still didn't compute. Neither John's nor Sani's story seemed to feel right. Something was missing. There seemed to Ab only one avenue left, one possible source of truth, if knowing the truth were even a possibility at this point. Ab returned to his house. It looked like a whirlwind had been through it. All the contents of the buffet, dishes, placemats, cutlery, were scattered on the floor. In the bedroom the sheets were torn off the bed, and the mattress was pulled half off the frame. He went to the back garden. The knife was still there, buried next to the tree.

His hands were shaking as he banged on the gate at the Wilkinsons'.

Marie emerged from the shadows of the garden, where she had been digging. "Ab! I thought you had left. So wonderful to see you. Don't mind the dirt." She held up her garden gloves. She wore a sun bonnet and had a trowel in one hand. "Orchids. Such a wonderful country, where a person can actually grow orchids." She pulled the inside bar on the gate and pulled it open. "It's okay, Agus! I have it," she called over her shoulder.

Ab stepped into the waiting area, and held the knife toward her. "Nancy asked me to return this. She said that her family is finished with it."

She pressed a dirt-covered glove to her chest, took a breath and bent over. "Just a head rush, dear. Stood up too fast." For a moment, Ab thought her composure would wobble, but she never skipped a beat. "Ah yes, the mysterious missing kris. I wondered if it would come back. Harold assured me that the Sentosas were trustworthy and that there was no question. But here, well, there are always questions, aren't there?" She set down the trowel and pulled off her gloves, setting them on the ground.

She took the kris from his hands.

She took it, pulled the knife partway from the scabbard, and then reinserted it. "It is such a fine specimen, don't you think? Will you come in for tea?" She set the knife down on the low bench just below the glass kris display case.

Abe stepped back towards the door. "No. No thanks. I have a plane to catch. I have to leave the country. I suppose you heard."

She reached out and took his hand and held it tightly. "Ah, yes. That is a pity." He tried to pull away but she held him. What was it with these tough old people? She looked over her shoulder to make sure no one else was around, and then pulled him closer. "Listen. She didn't kill your friend George. Don't believe that for a minute. After Waluyo killed Susilo, he was supposed to return the knife, but your friend George got in the way, and then it went to Soesanto. Soesanto figured out who Nancy was. So she had to…well she didn't have a choice did she? Family and all that. Unfortunately, George saw her that day at Soesanto's. Very confusing for him. But I assure you, she didn't kill George. Why would you kill someone you can just send home? Never for a minute believe it. That was pure, brutal stupidity. It had Waluyo written all over it. If it wasn't for that girl and her family, you would be dead too. Look at me." He stared into her eyes. They were steady, unflinching. "Do you believe me?"

He nodded his head, barely.

"Now give me a kiss and be on your way." She raised her cheek and he grazed the dry, wrinkled skin with his lips.

Just as he turned to leave, she added, "Oh by the way, Gladys said that if I saw you I should tell you that, in case you were wondering, Tri is doing just fine. She said you'd know what she means." There was a pause. "Leaving a couple of girls in port? Tsk tsk." For a second he thought she was going to giggle.

Ab slowed only for a moment, wondering what sorts of bad things he could do to her, then walked out to the main road, and flagged down a taxi.

Ab didn't remember going to the airport, or boarding the flight. Pushing his way through the jostling crowd of taxi-drivers at the new Jakarta airport, he tried to find the courtesy bus for the Sari Pacific Hotel, where Sani had made him reservations. Ab knew that the bus only made periodic trips to the airport, and not always when there were passengers, so when he failed to find it, he finally gave in to one of the drivers tugging at his elbow.

Jakarta was hot and smoggy, and he was sorry that he had not taken the time to select an air-conditioned taxi. By the time they got to the hotel, through the endless, crowded streets, he was bathed in sweat. Inside the hotel was another world, cool and orderly and luxurious; a luxury hotel anywhere in the world. Right now it was all he wanted. His appointment with General Witono was not until the next morning, so Ab spent the afternoon swimming lap after lap at the hotel pool and then wandering the neighbourhood.

The neighbourhood around the hotel was a mixture of open-sewered filth and poverty, hawkers selling fake blowpipes from Kalimantan and fake masks from Bali, small shops and warungs, and middle-class department stores. Ab walked the streets until he found himself, without having planned it, in a pub that served Mexican food, with a live band that played and sang country and western music. He drank beer and nibbled and watched a prostitute trying to hustle a customer at the bar, fighting off the deep gnawing darkness that prowled just at the edges of his thoughts.

Back at the hotel, he flicked between channels offering the movies *Death Wish I* and *Death Wish II*, Charles Bronson dubbed into Bahasa Indonesia. Finally, mercifully, he fell asleep.

The next morning he put a navy sport coat over his cotton batik shirt. He didn't want to take any chances now about maybe not getting out of the country. He ate a big buffet breakfast, three different kinds of rice and a dozen different stir-fried vegetables, chicken and beef saté, stews and fresh pineapple, bananas, hairy-fruits. *Typical Indonesian Breakfast*, said the sign over the table, but he had seen typical Indonesian, and this was not it. Nevertheless, it tasted good and was filling. He checked out and went to catch a cab. If everything went according to plan, he would visit Witono, deliver Sani's documents, pick up his own exit papers, and head right out to the airport. He would be out of the country by nightfall.

When the taxi driver finally pulled up in front of the complex of scummy-green government buildings they had been looking for, Ab was sure they had passed it twice before, but it seemed pointless to say so. He considered asking the driver to wait, but decided that it would be easier to flag a new cab than to explain something to this particular driver.

He signed in at the front table. Then, dragging his two hockey bags, and the leather folder from Sani tucked under one arm, he went down the hall, turned left and up two flights of stairs to Witono's office. The male secretary made a note of his presence, but indicated that General Witono was busy just now and Ab would have to wait. Ab sat in the cramped waiting room, staring absent-mindedly at the mildew in the corner and the portraits of the president and the vice-president. He noted that his name was written on a small chalk board beside Witono's office door. A slow fan circulated the warm, clove-scented smoke-filled air around the room, as nearly everyone who came or went with various bundles of paper and the ubiquitous green file folders was puffing on a kretek.

After about half an hour, the door to Witono's office opened and the General came out to welcome him. Mr. Witono was about Ab's height, which, for an Indonesian, was tall. Although he was not in military uniform, his bearing and manners betrayed his background. He was a muscular man, with short black hair and a clean-shaven, even shiny, square face. His eyes seemed to have a permanent squint to them. He took Ab's hand firmly and without hesitation and asked him in.

Ab gestured towards his bags. "Will they be okay here?"

Witono looked past him to his secretary. "These bags will be guarded," he said to the secretary. Then he flashed a quick, superficial smile at Ab. "Yes, the bags will be fine here."

He carefully pushed the door shut after them. There was no one else in the office. Witono's "busyness" was no doubt intended to serve a social function. It is good to keep your subordinates waiting. He pointed Ab to a chair. "Dr. Abner Dueck. Finally I have the pleasure to meet you." He went around behind his big desk and sat down. "I have heard many things about the good work that you are doing in Java."

Ab sat formally with the leather folder in his lap. "I have only been trying to help the small farmers. I do what I can, that is all. I think perhaps I have learned as much as I have given."

"Ah, yes. It is good to learn from each other."

They were silent a moment, and then Ab partially stood up to hand the folder to him. "I believe that these documents are for you."

Witono, who had begun to lean back in his swivel chair, tilted forward to take the folder. Then he sat back again and opened it. Very carefully, he paged through the documents. A smile played at the corners of his thin dark lips. "Yes, yes. Everything is in order. Order is important, yes?" He flashed his white teeth at Ab. "Especially in so big a country as Indonesia, so many peoples, so many languages, so many difficulties. We are not all so fortunate as Canada, to have order come so easily. Here, we must work at it."

Ab eyed him. So this was the man signing the papers and giving the orders. He felt the bitterness well up within him as he thought of the blood that had been shed, for what? To get a piece of land? To get back at an old Chinaman? He couldn't hold his tongue. "One must not let the Chinese get the better of one, must one?"

But Witono seemed to take the comment at face value, in stride. He laughed. He leaned across his desk as if Ab were a fellow-conspirator. "They eat pigs, you know, and how do you say in America, you are what you eat?" He laughed again, heartily. It was apparently a joke he had told before. Ab felt sick to his stomach.

"I believe you have some papers for me as well?" Ab asked, standing up.

"Oh, yes, I have them right here." He opened a folder in front of him, pulled out two sheets, and handed them to Ab. "I am so sorry about the problems with your visa. That you must go earlier than expected. These decisions are made elsewhere, you know." He gestured with his hand to indicate a non-specific elsewhere. "But we are very pleased that you could come to our country. You speak the language so well. We hope that you can come again, perhaps for a visit."

Ab recalled the visiting Dutchmen. Come back, but don't tell us what to do. He folded the papers and stuck them into the inside pocket of his jacket. They shook hands at the door, and Ab dragged his bags back down the hall to the staircase. Outside, the sky was suddenly overcast, and a few large rain drops splattered against him. He waved down a new-looking taxi and was relieved to discover that it had air conditioning.

They had only gone about a block before the rain hit with full force. It was as if they were in the middle of a thundering waterfall, huge grey sheets of water slapping over the car. Within minutes, the side street they had turned down became a torrent, and the taxi driver, with a shrug of despair, pulled to the side and stopped. Visibility was zero.

"It is not the right time of year for this, is it?" He wondered about the time. His flight wasn't for several hours, but the airport was a long way out.

The taxi driver turned. "It is never the right time of year for this," he said. "And it is always the right time." He laughed, as if this were a joke or a riddle he told often.

Watching the children wade through the filthy water, wondering how many would die from enteric disease, from the effluent washed down from the slaughterhouses and in-city farms—fifteen percent?—Ab suddenly remembered his baptism, the going under and the coming up to new light. And what was lost in that transition? Momentarily, it had all seemed so clear, and yet, he thought, where most of us live it's not quite all under, and not quite all the way up, just wading around in the half-divine half-mortal monsoon thick of it. The rain thinned a little, and he could make out other cars and motorcycles pulled to the side of the street. People were crouched under plastic sheets and storefront awnings. The open sewers at the edge of the street swirled and overflowed, and bits of plastic, plant debris, pieces of wood and feces sloshed along the centre of the street. Three small naked children splashed each other and danced around the taxi. *God, Soesanto, I hope they didn't kill all of you guys. I hope there are a few of you left, the optimists, the quiet activists. I hope the good policemen survive. The good businessmen. The people who ask questions. When Suharto dies, Indonesia will need you more than ever.*

In another fifteen minutes, the rain had stopped and the filthy stream down the road had leaked away, back into the sewer system, into small streams, and into the make-shift shanties along the edges of the larger sewers and streams. The taxi driver started up the taxi, and they moved back out into the flow of people, cars, and motorbikes once more.

They made it to the airport an hour before flight time and Ab waited impatiently in the check-in line. A student in his white shirt and blue trousers and a middle-aged gentleman in a blue batik shirt tried to elbow and push their way past him when he finally got to the head of the line. They held out their tickets into the face of the man behind the counter. Ab very firmly took the arms of both of them and forcefully pulled them back without saying anything, then laid his own ticket on the counter. Ah, the politeness of big city people, he thought. New York, Jakarta. Paris. Wherever. Fuck them.

There were no problems with the papers. In fact, it seemed that things went smoother and faster than normal. Walking out the open-sided breezeways to the departure lounge, looking out at the tropical trees and flowers, he felt an odd combination of light and free, and very sad, and caught. No matter where he went, his whole life, there would be this feeling. What was it? She loved him. *Better get away while you can,* she had said. But Soesanto didn't have that choice. Like old Job, in his afflictions, Ab felt caught in the middle of a bet between God and the devil: *Though she slay me, yet will I love her.*

A caged bird, hanging in the airport gardens, filled the air with its loud, plaintive cry.

Chapter Twenty-four

Mr. John Martin, the desk officer assigned to Ab's project at the Canadian International Development Agency office in Ottawa, was a medium-sized man with pale skin and a face that Ab could never remember the moment he wasn't looking at it. His desk was behind a movable partition in a huge, fluorescent-lit room full of movable partitions. He was carefully going over the financial statements as Ab sat in a chair across the desk from him.

"I'm afraid that the supplies, the needles and syringes and so on, definitely can't be covered. You should have applied six weeks in advance if you wanted special permission to go beyond the contract."

"I didn't know six weeks in advance that there would be an epidemic for which I would need the supplies."

"Yes, well, the government is coming down hard on us now for fiscal responsibility, so, well, that's how it is. If you don't like the rules, talk to the Prime Minister."

"I may do that." It was a lost cause. For what? A few syringes out of pocket.

"And the trip home, well, there are some problems. You see, you were asked to leave the country for becoming involved in local political matters that should not have concerned you. And that could be considered a breach of your contract, in which case we may not be able to cover all your expenses to come home."

"I was investigating the murder of a friend, and a fellow Canadian."

Mr. Martin looked up momentarily from his papers and adjusted his glasses. "Oh, George Grobowski. I believe the official report said it was a case of anthrax. Very sad, that."

"Actually, he was stabbed through the neck directly into his heart. A Balinese-style execution."

"That wasn't in the report."

"Do you mean the autopsy? Was there one? Did anyone see the body even?"

"I'm afraid that was not possible. We can't be sending pathologists on junkets all over the world, and we can't have bodies full of anthrax being shipped around the world, can we?" He smiled up at Ab.

"Yes. Anthrax. A very convenient diagnosis for a coffin full of rocks."

The desk officer pushed his glasses up on his nose. "Yes. Well, we can't choose how we die, can we?"

Ab stared at him. "I shall put the details in my final report, the murders, the attempts on my life, etcetera. Then you'll have it in a written report." He smiled, broadly. "Maybe I can sell it to a magazine too. Shall I mention your name?"

"Yes, well, in the meantime I shall see what I can do to get your travel claim through. But I can't promise anything."

Ab stood up and left the office.

Chapter Twenty-five

Ab brought the rented sports car up to speed on the Winnipeg bypass. He pulled his baseball cap down tightly and opened the window. This was a little side trip to visit his mother, who had retired to a home in Steinbach. He wondered how she would react to his decision to change his name: Abraham Van Dyck. If you were going to reclaim your roots, you might as well go deep. Besides the trip would give him a chance to drive to Altona to pick up some genuine local sunflower seeds. Just once, to save for a special occasion. And then maybe up to Saskatoon, where Sarah was now planning to attend veterinary college. He reached to the seat beside him and picked up the cassette which he'd retrieved from the bottom of his luggage. He opened it and stuck it into the car player, then rolled his window back up. The prairie sun was exploding in red and gold and pink shreds and fragments against the clouds at the horizon. That vast, expansive, freeing prairie horizon.

As the gamelan music came on, his chest heaved involuntarily, jerking, gasping for breath, a deep, sharp, pain. Nancy coming out of the water and the moonlight toward him. He pulled over to the shoulder and stopped the car, swallowed, breathing deeply. The bells and gongs and tinkles of the music surrounded him, moved through him.

He opened the car door and stepped outside, leaving the door open behind him so he could hear the music. A pattern with no pattern. An organic, unpremeditated pattern. Water and moonlight. Chaotic pattern, with the rules so deep you'd need a physicist to find them. But there was something more. It was water and moonlight and *darkness.* Without the background, the light and water were invisible. It was necessary. The music carried within itself, at its base, as its unseen background, a darkness so black it was palpable. The music was all crystal shattering against the hard darkness, a kaleidoscope of moonlit water splashing against a black stone, sprinkling tiny, sharp lights out into the night.

Acknowledgments

I would like to thank Jim and Ruth, in whose red, womb-like shower this story took its shape, and Kathy, for going to China with her mother in 1987 for a few weeks and giving me the time to write the first draft. Also thanks to Stan Litch, for the writing time in his wonderful log cabin on the escarpment overlooking Georgian Bay at South Cape Chin.

Parts of a much earlier version of this book were read at a Conference of Mennonite(s) Writing in Canada at the University of Waterloo, May 10-13, 1990, and subsequently published in *Acts of Concealment: Mennonite/s Writing in Canada*, edited by Hildi Tiessen and Peter Hinchcliffe (University of Waterloo Press, 1992).

Most of the details of Indonesian life come from having worked there for two years, driving the roads, looking at the maps, reading newspapers and talking to farmers, veterinarians and various other Indonesian friends. I am also indebted to information from *The Kris: Mystic Weapon of the Malay World*, by Edward Frey (Oxford University Press, Singapore, Oxford, New York, 1988).

The passage by A.R. Wallace is from *The Malay Archipelago: The Land of the Orang-Utan, and the Bird of Paradise*, (MacMillan, London, 1869, page 273).

The "Blood and Henderson" referred to a couple of times in the book is the standard general text for veterinarians on medical problems of livestock. It is called, simply, *Veterinary Medicine*

(Ballière Tindall, London). Given that he went through vet college in the 1970s, Ab would have been working with the 4th (1974) edition. Later editions have included other authors, especially Otto Radostits.

I'd like to thank Barbara Peters at Poisoned Pen Press for taking a chance on me.

Finally, a very special thanks to George Payerle for helping me to discover what the book knows.

Postscript

Readers who wish to know more about the lives of the Canadian characters in *Fear of Landing*, both before and after the episodes described in this book, should read Waltner-Toews's award winning collection of short stories, *One Foot in Heaven* (Regina: Coteau, 2005).

To receive a free catalog of Poisoned Pen Press titles, please contact us in one of the following ways:

Phone: 1-800-421-3976
Facsimile: 1-480-949-1707
Email: info@poisonedpenpress.com
Website: www.poisonedpenpress.com

Poisoned Pen Press
6962 E. First Ave. Ste. 103
Scottsdale, AZ 85251